CLASSIC IN THE PITS

CLASSIC IN THE PITS

A Case for Jack Colby, the Car Detective

Amy Myers

severn House

This first world edition published 2013
in Great Britain and 2014 in the USA by
SEVERN HOUSE PUBLISHERS LTD of
19 Cedar Road, Sutton, Surrey, England, SM2 5DA.

British Library Cataloguing in Publication Data

Myers, Amy, 1938- author.
  Classic in the pits. – (A Jack Colby mystery; 4)
  1. Colby, Jack (Fictitious character)–Fiction.
  2. Antique and classic cars–Fiction.
  3. Porsche automobiles–Fiction.
  4. Murder–Investigation–Fiction.
  5. Detective and mystery stories.
  I. Title II. Series
  823.9'14-dc23

ISBN-13: 978-0-7278-8355-1 (cased)

All Severn House titles are printed on acid-free paper.

Severn House Publishers support the Forest Stewardship Council™ [FSC™],
the leading international forest certification organisation. All our titles that
are printed on FSC certified paper carry the FSC logo.

MIX
Paper from
responsible sources
FSC
www.fsc.org   FSC® C013056

Typeset by Palimpsest Book Production Ltd.,
Falkirk, Stirlingshire, Scotland.
Printed and bound in Great Britain by
TJ International, Padstow, Cornwall.

To Adrian,
good friend and valued critic

Author's Note

As in Jack's previous cases, my husband James' input on the classic cars featured in *Classic in the Pits* has been the linchpin of this novel, and I'm enormously grateful both for this and for his running the Jack Colby blog (www.jackcolby.co.uk) and website on Jack's behalf.

Most of the action in this novel takes place on or near to the North Downs in Kent. It is there that Jack Colby has his classic car restoration business and carries out his car detection work. Some of the settings are fictitious, notably Old Herne's itself (although there was indeed a First World War landing ground in that neighbourhood), Friars Leas and of course Jack's own Frogs Hill. Most are real, however, although all that can now be seen of West Malling airfield is the preserved control tower. Robin J. Brooks' *From Moths to Merlins* was an invaluable source of information on this former airfield, and Fred Ferrier on the Porsche 356.

My thanks also go to my staunch agent and friend the late Dorothy Lumley of the Dorian Literary Agency and to the wonderful team at Severn House, in particular Rachel Simpson Hutchens and Piers Tilbury, whose enthusiasm for classic cars (especially for the Morgan 4/4) has resulted in such superb cover designs.

ONE

Trouble often comes in disguise, but I didn't expect it to arrive through a friendly chat with Liz Potter, former lover and ongoing friend. True, it was a Friday when the Frogs Hill farmhouse phone rang, but it wasn't the unlucky thirteenth, so I wasn't prepared for the disaster she blithely announced. It began quietly enough.

'Swoosh, Jack! Are you going?'

'Would I ever miss it?' I was amazed at her even asking me. Swoosh was the one event in the Kentish calendar that no car lover would miss.

'You have to be there. Heard the news?'

Even then I didn't get too alarmed. 'Good or bad?'

'Bad. It will be the last Swoosh. Old Herne's is closing down.'

Closing down? Old Herne's – more formally the Old Herne Club for Motoring and Flying Enthusiasts – couldn't close down. No more Swoosh? Not possible.

I had just been given a top priority mission to carry out at Swoosh this year, so this was even weirder. I work freelance for the Kent Police Car Crime Unit, and its head, Dave Jennings, had rung me earlier to tell me I was in on a case, *if* I wanted the job. If? I'd almost have done this one for free when he had explained what it was. (I say almost because I depend on my work for Dave to pay the mortgage on Frogs Hill.) This time, he had told me, the job was to hunt down the missing classic Porsche belonging to Mike Nelson, who ran Old Herne's. Amiable, a former racing driver, and generally beloved, Mike was over retirement age, but I heard he had recently taken on a deputy, which didn't indicate any immediate threat. Nevertheless, Liz isn't in the habit of getting things wrong.

Even so, I double-checked. 'You're sure, Liz?'

'Got it from Jason.'

This was beginning to sound ominous. Jason Pryde was Mike's son – he took his stage name from his famous grandmother Miranda Pryde, who had been a Vera Lynn singalike in the forties and fifties. Jason, even though he was estranged from his father, would surely not be mistaken about this news. I had never met him, but his reputation was worldwide. He was famous for having been the pop star to end all pop stars in the 1990s. Then his star had waned, and he hadn't reappeared on the scene until a few years ago when he'd reinvented himself with a tribute band to his grandmother – and fallen out with his father. Reason unknown, but that's families for you.

'Is he going to be there?' I asked. He'd been conspicuous by his absence at previous Swooshes.

'You bet. He's billed to give a concert.' A pause. 'His singing partner's gone down with a virus and, guess what, I'm standing in for her.'

'That's terrific, Liz.'

Liz has a great singing voice and a great stage presence but she's not a professional singer, so it was indeed a triumph for her to be singing with celeb Jason. Swoosh wasn't just a meeting place for classic car lovers but for devotees and veteran airmen of Second World War aircraft as well – hence the name Swoosh, which covers the thrills of both modes of transport. Swoosh puts on entertainment for veterans, fans and their families. A Jason Pryde concert was going to be an enormous plus.

Swoosh was always held on the first Sunday in June, and this year that was in two days' time. *The last one?* I still could not believe it. After all, I was supposed to be a car detective, and I'd heard nothing of it. I'd been away for a week or so, but surely this crisis could not have flared up in a week? First, that Porsche was stolen, and now this.

Dark clouds were gathering and I was heading right their way.

The theft of the Porsche was a high-profile case because of the car's pedigree. This curvy silver Porsche 356C coupé, with its Carrera 2 four-cam engine and its disc brakes, had been Mike's pride and joy during and since his racing days in the sixties and seventies. It was now kept permanently on display at Old Herne's and had become the club's icon, known to every Porsche lover in the world. For starters, I doubted whether there were even half a dozen 356 Carreras in the UK today. Its disappearance had to be taken very seriously indeed. Mike without his Porsche would be a sad and lonely figure, and if he had to add the possible closure of Swoosh to this blow I couldn't imagine what he must be going through.

First step: discuss it with Len. I was still reeling on the Saturday morning when Len Vickers and then Zoe Grant arrived for an emergency stint in the Pits – our name for the converted barn workshop where they form the crucial part of Frogs Hill Classic Car Restorations Ltd. I, Jack Colby, am merely the owner, although I'm permitted to pay their wages and even occasionally contribute a comment or helping hand. Both of them are welded to their jobs, Len being the engine and Zoe the spark plug. That makes for a great team although there's a forty-year age gap between them. And here was I about to prise them away from their work on a Lea-Francis to discuss the emergency over Swoosh.

I took a deep breath. I was about to ruin their day.

'There's a ridiculous rumour that tomorrow is the last Swoosh,' I ventured casually. 'Old Herne's is closing.'

I expected uproar. There was none. It was Len who for once replied. 'Looks like it.'

Len is taciturn by nature and not inclined to the bright side of life so even then I didn't take the threat too seriously. It was when Zoe put her grinder down and proclaimed: 'That's what Rob says too,' that I really got worried. Rob Lane is the layabout man in her life and comes from a background that gives him a passport into whichever circles he cares to stroll.

'It's just not possible,' I pleaded.

Len glared at me. 'Got the news from Tim Jarvis.'

Then it was serious indeed. Tim was one of the old-school volunteers at Old Herne's, having been on the scene since the year dot – or more precisely the year it opened, which was 1965. Tim oils so much of the everyday machinery that goes into its running that without him it would have ground to a halt long ago.

'I'll nobble Mike Nelson,' I said. 'I've got to have a word with him anyway.'

'About that Porsche?' Zoe enquired.

'*The* Porsche,' I confirmed. 'The Porsche to end all Porsches.' Although Mike had bought his a year or two after it had proudly left its makers in 1963, it still had the original Carrera engine in it. Quite something.

'Not having much luck, what with that and Old Herne's going,' she commented.

'Still seems weird,' I said, trying to make sense of this googly that fate was threatening to bowl at the car community. 'The place could do with a facelift but it's Mike's whole life – he can't seriously be thinking of closing, especially since he's taken on this deputy.'

Len had a face of doom however. 'Arthur Howell's flown over,' he said succinctly.

This was ominous indeed. Arthur Howell, US oil billionaire and former Second World War US Thunderbolt fighter pilot, was a delightful gentleman, but his arrival across the Pond at Old Herne's added weight to the story of its closure. He must be at least ninety now, and makes few appearances in Kent, leaving the running of Old Herne's to Mike. Arthur had founded Old Herne's way back in 1965, handing it over to Miranda Pryde and her husband Ray Nelson to run after their singing careers ended. Their son Mike had taken over when Miranda died in the early nineties and Ray retired. The whole caboodle still belonged to Arthur, however, although I gathered it was tied up in some kind of trust. I'd met him once and taken to him, even though his sharp eyes had summed me up quicker than Len can diagnose faulty engine timing, which is saying something.

Even though he was over here, however, I couldn't believe deep down in my heart that Old Herne's would close. I would surely drive in through those battered wooden gates and find that all was well. Mike would be his usual affable self, ambling around saying hello to everyone and everything. Tim would be fussing around marshalling cars and visitors. All would be well. But then I remembered the Porsche and its disappearance. Coincidence? Or not? Len and Zoe say I have a nose for trouble, and I had an uncomfortable feeling it was not only twitching but building up for an almighty sneeze.

I could hear the cars already as I turned my 1965 Gordon-Keeble off the A20 into the lane that would – eventually – lead me to the hamlet of Old Herne Green on the crest of the North Downs. Hearing the comforting sound of engines growling and purring on a June summer's day – which for once was sunny – put all thoughts of Old Herne's closing into the realms of fantasy. Swoosh was a solid tradition, an unalterable event that was the highlight of the summer season for classic car lovers and their families.

The club was on the site of a former RAF advance landing ground, used for refuelling and for aircraft in trouble returning from missions, and which had served not one but two world wars. The two old runways still existed although now they were linked in a graceful curve at the ends to form a complete track circuit for classic cars. No aeroplanes landed nowadays, but the old control tower was still there, with its ground floor converted into a spectacular reinforced glass-fronted garage for the silver Porsche and for Arthur Howell's 1965 Morgan 4/4 Series IV, which was as dear to him as the Porsche to Mike. Arthur gets to drive it round the track at least once on every visit, and Tim Jarvis ensures it's kept in tip-top condition.

Air veterans from all over the world gather at Old Herne's for reunions, although the Second World War airmen were few in number nowadays – all in their late eighties or nineties, and most of them with carers in the form of friends or family members. But their enthusiasm is infectious, both for aviation fans and for classic car owners, who drop in on track days to drive their beloved cars in company with fellow enthusiasts or hold get-togethers in the bar. This is a lively meeting place for chats of races long ago or dogfights and bomber missions, and at Swoosh the two mingle with the joyous thrill of adrenalin at full power.

I drove through the familiar gateway underneath huge banners proudly announcing that Swoosh was in progress, and then followed the stewards' directions to the area earmarked for classics entered for the 'best of show' competition. I fancied my chances with the Gordon-Keeble, and so I forgot the threat of danger (usually a mistake) and gave myself up to a day of sheer pleasure. I reminded myself that I had a job to do, but as that too involved chatting to classic car devotees, it could hardly be called heavy duty *and* I was getting paid for it. What's to worry about? I wondered.

I tracked Mike down to the clubhouse, where the first hint of unease returned to me. Looking at the paintwork and decor I realized that the facelift was more urgently needed than I had thought, which did not suggest the club was flush with money. Such was the animation all around me, however, that this qualm was quickly dismissed.

I saw Mike sitting by one of the windows in the large bar, wearing his beloved World War II bomber jacket with his cavalry twills. Glued to his side was his formidable wife Boadicea – sorry, I should say Anna Nelson. In classic car circles Boadicea is her generally accepted nickname except in her presence. Boudicca, the form of the name currently in use for the historic British queen of the Iceni tribe, doesn't do justice to the Amazonian fighting image that the name Boadicea conjures up. Today our lady was clad, in true aggressive style, in startling blue – the colour of woad that terrified (or so it is said) would-be invaders. She is Mike's second wife and bears heavily down on anyone she sees as a threat to her wishes. Occasionally, but not often, she can be as amiable as Mike himself, who murmurs defensively that she had a tough childhood as an orphan. Nevertheless, the consensus is that Jason Pryde, who was Mike's son by his long-divorced first wife Lily, made the right decision in his choice of birth mother. Mike usually lets all the hassle flow over him, but today his usual smile was absent and he looked his full age.

'Good to see you, Jack,' he said without conviction.

'Couldn't keep me away from Swoosh,' I said heartily. 'Fixture in the calendar,' I added experimentally.

He did not reply, but Boadicea weighed in on his behalf. 'Not for much longer,' she said grimly.

Time to plunge in. 'I've heard the rumours—'

'All nonsense,' Mike declared feebly.

Boadicea glared at him. 'We'll know soon enough.'

Mike hastily changed the subject. 'How's the Porsche hunt, Jack? The Car Crime Unit said you were looking into it now.'

'Sniffing around. Only got the message on Friday.' It had been missing for three weeks, which was a long time for such a memorable car to have disappeared without a whisper of its possible whereabouts. The news would have spread at top racing speed through the community of Porsche dealers and owners, so my pleasant task today would be to talk to the dozen or so Porsche 356 owners that were booked in and get their take on it. There are hundreds of 356s registered in the country, but as this one was from such a rare breed – only four-hundred-odd ever built – its engine, history and provenance would ensure that if there was any news of it to be gathered it would have reached those here today.

'The place isn't the same without it,' Mike said gloomily. His face without a smile was the nail in the coffin that convinced me that times were indeed bad. I wondered what Boadicea's 'know soon enough' meant. Something to do with Arthur Howell's visit obviously.

'It looks the same old dump to me,' Boadicea barked. 'What are the chances you'll find it, Jack?'

'Can't say,' I replied mildly. 'The police think it's still in the country.' Dave had confirmed that no Porsche 356 had turned up at any exit in the country without being scoured for false identity and so far without any result.

'I've had the insurance people on my back,' Mike grunted. 'Their chaps haven't turned up anything either; it's been three weeks already and after another three they have to fork out, so they're getting anxious.'

You bet they would be anxious, I thought. That Porsche's pedigree and condition would skyrocket its value. Maybe £250,000? More probably, perhaps £300,000. A sum, it occurred to me, that would come in very handy for sprucing Old Herne's up, but I dismissed the idea. It might occur to Boadicea, but not to Mike. That car meant too much to him personally for him to even think of an insurance scam. He had won practically every sports-car trophy going in it, and the car was the best tribute to his past career that he could have.

That sleeping beauty had been in its glass-fronted garage, coming out for occasional excursions round the track, as long as I could remember. That was a long way back, because I used to come as a kid with my father to Swoosh and the silver gleaming curvy car ('Not a straight line on it,' Dad used to say) had hooked me. If it wasn't on the track I would gravitate to its home and press my nose against the glass to admire it. The game I played with my father was to decide which of the two cars – as the Morgan lived side by side with the Porsche – was the finer car. I always got sucked into choosing first, and whichever I picked, Dad would convincingly argue the opposite.

I assured Mike I'd report back to him on anything I discovered during the day about the missing Porsche. I kept coming back to the word 'coincidence'. It could just be chance that the threat to Swoosh had materialized at the same time as the theft. Sorrows, as Hamlet's villainous uncle had pointed out, come not as 'single spies, but in battalions', so he might not have seen a link. But me? I keep my options open.

Before I left the clubhouse, I took one further step. 'I heard Arthur Howell was over from the States, Mike. Is he around?'

Mike's face grew even gloomier. 'We're all lunching together, but he's hopping mad about the Porsche. Sees its disappearance as a threat that his Morgan is next on the list.'

A good point. 'Is there a Thunderbolt flying in the display? That'll keep him happy.'

Second World War Thunderbolts are so rare that it's a pièce de résistance if one joins the fly-past that usually concludes the Swoosh festivities. Nor are there many British World War II fighters still flying, but somehow Swoosh always manages to produce something very special.

'Yes, and it's costing far too much,' put in Mike's personal thunderbolt, Boadicea.

'But a wonderful tribute to Swoosh, especially as it will follow Jason's concert,' I said brightly. Nothing like putting a conversational cat among the pigeons. When I saw the look on Mike's face I felt a twinge of remorse, but if the missing Porsche had any link to the Old Herne's situation then I needed to know every angle. And Mike's son Jason was one of them. In the past he had gone through a much reported personal bankruptcy.

'Arthur's arranged the fly-past,' Mike said abruptly, 'and Jason—'

'It's an insult,' Boadicea trumpeted.

This threw me. A Jason Pryde concert an *insult*?

'That popinjay hasn't been near us for years,' she rampaged onwards, 'and now he comes swanning back *telling* us – not even asking – that he'll be giving a concert at Swoosh. As if anyone wants to listen—'

'Anna!' Mike interrupted, sharply for him. 'It's a tribute to Ray and Miranda.'

On swept her chariot. 'Arranged over your head by Arthur,' she snorted.

'It's good to see Jason again,' Mike said quietly.

By which I gathered that there was still a family upset of serious proportions between Jason and Mike. I wondered whether Jason Pryde felt strongly about Old Herne's and whether the concert was because he'd heard it was likely to close. It could be his bid for a stake in the club by helping its funds. Even a takeover? A somewhat cynical thought on my part – I must be getting as pessimistic as Len.

Swoosh was a wonderland, even if it was under threat. There were classics here that brought tears of emotion to my eyes. Every so often I could see one or two of them take off on a lap of honour, spruced up for the Ascot of the car world. A De Dion Bouton driven side by side with a stately Lanchester and sporty Austin-Healey was a mesmerizing sight, even though strictly speaking my eyes should have been mentally focused on a Porsche 356.

There were so many motor clubs represented here this year that I wondered whether the word that this might be the last Swoosh had spread even further than I had realized. No, I thought, I surely must be imagining the slight air of a wake, socially jolly but with a somewhat forced determination to affirm that the land of the classic car was alive and well, Swoosh or no Swoosh. My fancy, I decided.

Time to do my job, and I threw myself in a general round of information gathering on the missing Porsche. It wasn't very productive. There were about a dozen 356s here and I tracked down most of the owners. They had all heard about the theft and had their own ideas, but none of them took me forwards, save that someone mentioned Sam Fenton, the owner of a local chain of burger takeaways, who might be able to help. I knew him by sight and by his Porsche, a 1972 911S, having seen it around for years. I couldn't find him though, so I made my way back to the general throng.

And then I saw her. It isn't often that the 'across a crowded room' scenario, as immortalized in the song 'Some Enchanted Evening' from *South Pacific*, comes into play – certainly not in my emotional life, as the departure of Louise had left a hole that wasn't healing. I had thought we were on a golden path together, but she had followed her own star. Today, however, swap 'morning' for 'evening' as I looked up and caught the eye of someone chatting in the swirling throng some way away. Just as in the song, I knew this someone was for me. One can ignore such a moment, one can hesitate too long, or one can go for it.

I went for it.

Not that that was quite as cavalier as it sounds. I didn't forge a determined path through the crowds, pushing people aside left, right and centre in pursuit of my goal. I inched my way through to her: smart jeans and blouse, fortyish, dark-brown hair, arguing (from the body language) with a young man (thirtyish). A romantic row? No, a woman like this would never pick a grinning lout for a soulmate – even if he were a good-looking one, I conceded. I could see she needed rescuing as another great exchange of glances with me took place, and I could hear the lout taking advantage of the lull to sneer some more. Until I arrived, automatically checking the lady's ring finger – not that that tells one much now. For what it was worth there were no rings on either hand.

'Jack Colby,' I greeted her enthusiastically as I arrived. 'Good to meet you again.'

She grinned at this unsubtle ruse. 'Peter, meet Jack Colby. Jack, this is Peter Nelson, Ray's other grandson.'

'Who the hell are you?' Peter laughed, less delightfully than the lady. Perhaps the 'other grandson' had riled him.

'Police,' I remarked casually. 'Looking for Mike's Porsche.'

'Really?' he drawled.

Without even looking at him I flicked open my police ID and waved it at him. Strange the effect this can have. Occasionally, it has the opposite effect to that intended and one receives a mental – or physical – punch in the face. More often than not it works, however, as it did this time, and Peter slunk away leaving me with the lady. Excellent.

'You probably know Ray and Miranda were the first managers of Old Herne's,' she explained. 'Peter's the offspring of Mike's younger brother, who lives in New Zealand. Peter used to work here.'

'Used to?'

'Recent parting of the ways.'

That was enough about Peter. 'And you?' I asked.

She looked amused. 'We haven't met before, have we?'

'I'd have remembered.'

'Me too.' A smile, which told me a lot more than the earlier grin. It told me it was genuinely meant, and I had to pull back my imagination fast from the point to which it was racing all too quickly. I changed my mind about her having been in need of rescue, however. This was a lady in full command of herself.

'I really am with the police,' I assured her. 'Civilian recruit on specialist classic car cases. Otherwise plain Jack Colby of Frogs Hill Classic Car Restorations near Pluckley.'

'Jessica Hart. Old Herne's deputy manager under Mike.'

Len had kept quiet about the gender of Mike's deputy, so this was a pleasant surprise and explained the delightful but determined chin before me. 'That's quite recent, I gather.'

'Two months. It's getting too much for Mike to do it alone. He's sixty-eight now.'

I didn't think age had a lot to do with it, because although Mike was the nicest chap around managing was clearly not his forte.

'He told me you were coming to talk to him about the Porsche,' she continued. 'How's it going?'

With that sleek brown hair bobbing around one of the most engaging faces I had seen in a long time, it was hard to think about anything else. I did my best though.

'Every chance we'll get it back,' I said more confidently than I felt. Then I leapt right into it. 'I heard a rumour that Old Herne's was under threat.'

She answered me straight away and frankly. 'It's possible. We just don't know. The place needs a lot of cash spent on it. Mike doesn't have a bean; he's been pouring most of his salary into it, and we don't think Arthur will pay up any more. It's losing money hand over fist.'

It didn't take a great brain to deduce that Old Herne's finances were in a downward spiral, and a genteelly decaying club can only go on so long before the gentlemen, not to mention the ladies, tiptoe out of it. 'How long does it have?'

She hesitated. 'Yesterday it was looking as if it would close as soon as Arthur could sell it, most likely just for the land.'

'And today?'

'It depends on what happens in the next hour or two. Arthur hadn't said anything yet but we know he could well pull the plug on it. Swoosh is obviously its usual success, but he won't let that sway him. I'm due to join Mike and his wife for lunch with Arthur and his family, not to mention Ray, so the news will probably be broken then. Wish me luck. I may be jobless when I see you next.'

I liked that 'when', and it would be as soon as possible. 'Arthur will surely see your potential and give a stay of execution to the club.' I meant it. This lady was impressive. 'Is he here yet?'

'Yes. He'll have lunch and then go out on his usual trip round the track in his Morgan. That and the Thunderbolt fly-past are his big thrills of the day.'

'What brought you to Old Herne's?' I asked curiously. 'Cars or aeroplanes?'

'Neither.'

'You like management?'

'Not sure about liking it. I want to do well here, if Old Herne's survives, but . . .'

When she stopped, I wanted to say: come with me to some place where we can be alone and talk. I wanted to know more about this lady, but being surrounded by several thousand people did not provide the best circumstances for getting to know someone. And I knew I wanted to get to know Jessica – in every way.

'Can we meet later?' I said.

That smile again. 'I'd like that.' Then she gave me a look which suggested I'd passed some kind of test because she continued, 'I'm here because I like saving things. Does that make sense? Saving *good* things, which includes Swoosh, and I'll try my damnedest to do so. Just look at it all.'

She waved a hand and I saw her point because I shared it. I could see people chatting, children racing around, stalls with model cars, miniature and pedal cars for children to drive around, groups of war veterans chatting by the hangars, the bandstand erected ready for Jason Pryde, the usual fairground attractions and, beyond the track, the classics parked for the judges to choose the best car of the show. Which I hoped, of course, would be mine. Of course Swoosh would continue. It had to. And with someone like Jessica in charge there was every chance it would. *If* Arthur Howell saw sense.

'*Can* Arthur close it down?' I asked her. 'I thought Old Herne's was a kind of charity.'

'Not really. It's a family trust. Arthur's still the owner; Mike has been its trustee ever since his mother died in 1991. Miranda and Ray first met Arthur in his World War II days. Arthur has the last word on Old Herne's though.'

'How does Jason Pryde fit in? I didn't get the impression he was close to Mike and Boa— Anna Nelson. So why's he here? Does he have an interest in Old Herne's?'

I noted the hesitation, but then she said, 'Arthur probably persuaded him to come. They get on well so he'll be at the lunch. But who knows what Jason thinks about anything.'

I had the distinct impression she was sorry she had said anything at all about Jason, but just at that moment Liz Potter arrived with a whoosh, as if taking the chequered flag, and threw herself into my arms. She's a small, lively woman to whom fashion is pleasantly unknown, a complete contrast to Jessica's stylish cool.

'Glad to see you too, Liz,' I remarked, highly irritated at this inopportune display of intimacy.

'I'll be off,' Jessica remarked airily. 'Nice to have met you, Jack.'

I detached Liz and just managed to catch Jessica's arm as she strode off in a meaningful way. 'Dinner tonight?' I asked feebly.

'Too much clearing up. Bye now.' And she was off.

'I'll help,' I called after her.

She briefly paused, turned round and shrugged. 'Accepted.'

'Thanks so much, Liz,' I said through gritted teeth, watching Jessica probably walking out of my life forever.

She giggled. 'You can handle it.'

'I bet Colin's not around,' I said. Colin is her nerdish husband who can't stand me – with no reason at all, since I had been out of Liz's life for well over a year before she even met him.

'Minding the shop,' she said happily.

The shop is Liz's garden centre on the outskirts of Piper's Green, the nearest village to Frogs Hill.

I sighed. 'Do you want lunch?'

'Why else would I hug you?'

'My manly attractions?'

'You wish. Let's go eat.'

We non-invitees to the VIP lunch were stuck with the clubhouse café, which proved to be full, and so we headed for the burger stall. This turned out to be much jollier than I expected and I enjoyed the car chat buzz around us. I cheered up, and Swoosh turned into the perfect day again – or would have done if I wasn't still sensing that the situation at Old Herne's was a volcano gently rumbling away waiting to erupt.

TWO

S till harbouring my wistful hope that the Gordon-Keeble would win the best in show award, I made my way back after lunch to where I parked it earlier with its fellow competitors on the far side of the track. Len and I had scrupulously checked each millimetre of my beloved car, polished it up to its Sunday best and cleaned its engine to the nth degree. Nevertheless there must have been a speck of dust left somewhere because it had only been awarded third place. I would have patted it in commiseration if I hadn't been worried about fingerprints on its shiny polish.

I had been wondering what had happened at the management lunch but there was no sign of Jessica or anyone else who could enlighten me. It must have been over because I glimpsed Arthur Howell in his Morgan whizzing round the track. The Morgan was a four-wheeler racing green original and it looked splendid. As I had been used to seeing the Morgan since my youth, only now did I wonder why this 1965 Morgan was so special to him rather than, say, a three-wheeler pre-war model which he might have driven during his wartime career here. That reminded me that I had to talk to Tim Jarvis, who was busy overseeing the laps of honour round the track. And there was still Sam Fenton to nobble.

The latter was the easier, as he had been watching the Morgan too, so I caught him after the crowd dispersed and explained my mission over the Porsche.

'Bad show that. Tried the Porsche Club 356 Register, have you?' he asked.

This was a natural step, but the Driver and Vehicle Licensing Agency in Swansea was more likely. Dave had provided me with a short list of four 356 registrations there in the last month of which two were due to change of owner. That ruled them out of my reckoning because if they were stolen cars the Agency's records of previous owners wouldn't tally.

The other two were first registrations, which for a classic Porsche would imply that a car acquired overseas had now entered the UK and needed UK registration – all perfectly legal. Unless, of course, the foreign documentation required for registration and an old-style logbook, dating back to the year of manufacture, were forged, along with the number plates. So the DVLA line didn't look hopeful either, unless the engine and chassis numbers on Mike's car had been left unaltered, in which case they *would* show up in the Swansea records and set the alarm bells going. With today's class of criminal, however, that was unlikely, although changing figures with a number punch is not an easy matter.

Unlike the DVLA, with the Porsche Club 356 Register there was a chance that even if the numbers had been changed something would smell fishy to them, as, dealing with such a specific subject as the 356, every single number ever issued would be known to them. The drawback to this line of enquiry though was that the new keeper of Mike's Porsche would not stick his neck out by registering it with the club, or possibly not even with the obligatory DVLA, depending on what his intentions were for his new acquisition.

'Might turn up something,' Sam said. 'Good luck. I did hear a rumour that someone in the area was asking if there were any 356s in good condition for sale. Happens all the time, so probably nothing for you there, but you never know.'

It sounded vague but indeed one never knew. 'Any idea *where* he or she was asking?'

'Huptons. Know it?'

I did. It was one of the chain of garages that belonged to Harry Prince, local mandarin and millionaire who had his beady eyes on buying Frogs Hill and the Pits. I stored Sam's information in my mind for later evaluation, but it didn't look good. Harry Prince sails close to the wind and when it blows he is adept at heading instantly for harbour, leaving others to weather the storm.

Tackle Harry or Huptons? The latter, I decided. It was too indefinite a line to justify using up what little goodwill Harry had towards me. Meanwhile, there was work to do here today. I had to consider whether the car had been stolen for its monetary value or because it was Mike's car or because of its iconic status at Old Herne's, so the more I knew about those involved the better.

Top of the list was Tim Jarvis, Len's chum. I went in search of him – not easy in these crowds – and eventually I spotted him lovingly taking charge of the Morgan again after Arthur had finished his tour. I knew him through Len, so apart from a slight defensiveness he was willing enough to chat to me. He was about the same age as Len, in his sixties, but even more weather-beaten in the face, and they shared the same general air of the fanatic plus one of overall gloom and doom.

'I looked after that car as if it were my own,' he told me truculently the moment I mentioned the Porsche.

'And it showed,' I said to smooth him down. He had the kind of rugged independence that made me worry about him. What could he do to replace Old Herne's in his life if it closed? I asked him to fill me in on the details of the theft. It must have been well planned, even though I doubted whether security here was exactly state of the art. I'd heard the story before from Dave but there's no substitute for the horse's mouth.

'What do you want to know?' He was still guarded.

'Let's start with the outside gates. Locked?'

'Eleven thirty, after the bar's closed. Found them open in the morning.'

'CCTV?' I asked without much hope. I'd seen the said lock – which was merely a padlock, although a hefty one.

'No need.' He glared at me defiantly. 'The gates were always locked.'

'Was the padlock forced?'

'Gone. Had it replaced,' Tim added proudly.

All this told me was that it wasn't a chance theft – and I'd been sure of that anyway – but the clincher would be the access to the control tower garage. 'Did you notice anyone odd hanging around?' I asked him. A daft question, but daft questions have to be asked and answered if one's to get the general feel of the situation.

'Not odder than usual.' Tim was highly pleased with this witticism and readily agreed to accompany me to the Porsche's former garage.

The control tower was between the two remaining hangars from its earlier RAF days, and several hundred yards from the clubhouse. The hangars had been converted into archives or museums – however one terms such glorious collections of memorabilia, ranging from bits and bobs from old cars too precious to throw away to letters, photos, car and plane models – anything that spoke of Old Herne's past.

On the far side of the control tower, Thunderbolts Hangar (or Thunderbolts for short), so called in honour of Arthur, was devoted to aircraft, and the other hangar, predictably called Morgans, housed classic car memorabilia from 1896 onwards, and I loved both of them. Pride of place in Thunderbolts Hangar was given to the Crossley fire tender that meant a lot to Arthur Howell. Crossleys had served the RAF nobly during the Second World War, and the driver of this one had saved Arthur's life when his Thunderbolt crash-landed at Old Herne's in 1943.

'What about the door keys to this garage?' I asked Tim. The garage's double doors were at the far end of the building and set into the control tower's sturdy walls.

'Like the main gates, the padlock disappeared. I've replaced this one too.'

Why should the thief take the padlocks with him if he'd forced them? I wondered. Fingerprints? DNA? Possible, but there was another explanation. That the thief had had a key – with the help of inside knowledge. I had to ask him. 'Where are the keys kept, Tim?'

His eyes looked like those of wounded spaniel. 'I have them.'

'There must be spares.'

'In the clubhouse. Mike's office.'

'That's on the ground floor. Is it locked?'

'No.'

I didn't ask any more questions on that subject – no need. Dave's team would have covered that, although hope of fingerprints and suchlike was nil. Anyone with knowledge of Old Herne's could have pinched them. Instead I just commented, 'The Porsche was an odd choice to steal. It's too well known, if only because of its rarity and condition. Even if the number plates, engine and chassis numbers were falsified, it would still be recognizable.'

Tim gave me a scathing glance. 'Of course it's *recognizable*. Mike raced it.'

One up to Tim and I had mud on my face. He was right. It
would have been modified with a roll bar welded to the body
channels to give it more strength for racing. This undoubtedly
had been a professional job, whether with inside help or not, but
I ruled out the idea of the theft being on behalf of a nutty collector
to keep under lock and key. This wasn't like a valuable art
masterpiece; classic car lovers want to show off by driving their
prize possession and to chat about it to envious chums, not hide
it away just for private consumption. There was something very
strange going on – and I couldn't rule out the fact that Old
Herne's future looked very precarious.

Realizing that Tim was getting itchy about the Morgan still
being at the track and away from his all-caring eye, I suggested
we made our way back to it. 'Difficult time for you,' I said. 'I've
heard rumours that Old Herne's might have to close. I find that
hard to believe.'

'That's what they're saying, all right. Not doing well. That's
why this Miss Hart's been brought in, going to take over from
Mike. Good thing all round, or the old place would have to
close. Mike's like me. His heart's in these cars, not in running
the place. Not like in the old days when his mother was
running it. No, Mr Arthur won't close it, you'll see.'

He looked up at me as we reached the Morgan he'd looked
after for so long and I could see his eyes were full of tears. I
only hoped he was right.

The afternoon seemed to whizz by. Having done all I could on
the Porsche front, I was free to revel in the glories of Swoosh but
I could spot no one to revel with. There was no sign of Len or
Zoe, nor of Liz, who was doubtless busy preparing for the concert.
The bandstand was looking increasingly in business, with electri-
cians dashing here, there and everywhere with cables and sound
equipment. The cacophony of their tests mingled with the roar of
classic cars on the track was intoxicating, and the children's screams
of delight at the old-fashioned dodgems, trampolines and other
delights only added to the heady mix.

The concert was due to begin at five, and the fly-past was at
six. That was always timed to be overhead as the Crossley fire
tender was driven round the track by Mike as a tribute to Arthur.

By four thirty, however, crowds were already gathered at the bandstand and I hurried to join them, knowing that Liz would never speak to me again if I was not visible at the very front. At least Colin wouldn't be there so the daggers from his eyes wouldn't be piercing me like pins in a witch's waxen image. The concert of Miranda Pryde songs would add an extra dimension to Swoosh and I was looking forward to it. After all, if it was going to be the last one, Old Herne's would be going out in style.

Frogs Hill's personnel assembled in force, but as the front row was reserved I found myself a spot on the grass between the seating and the stage. Len and Zoe with their respective partners opted for seats elsewhere, but I had my camera poised to take pictures of Liz at her moment of glory.

I was so intent on not missing any opening appearance by her that I wasn't keeping an eye on the seats filling up behind me. A minute or two before the show was due to begin, however, I turned round to see Arthur Howell just arriving to sit in the front row with Boadicea, now in glorious pink technicolor, and Peter. Next to Peter at the end of the row was a wheelchair occupied by another aged gentleman – Ray Nelson, I presumed. During his reign as manager of Old Herne's with Miranda, I had mostly been working abroad in the oil business so I didn't know him, except by sight from my youth. On Arthur's other side was a stoutish man in his sixties and a slender supercilious young woman in her late twenties or a year or two older.

Boadicea looked as though she might be about to brandish her spear ready to hurl at Jason, and the rest of the family weren't looking too jolly either. I could see no sign of Mike, who might still be at the track or in the hangar preparing the Crossley for its star appearance. Somewhat odd, given that Jason was his son, but there was no sign of Jessica either, so perhaps they were together at the back.

I was still cherishing my mental image of Boadicea on the warpath when Jason Pryde came on to the stage. Everyone remembers his stormy presence on the pop scene of the early nineties with songs such as 'I'm a bad, bad, lad', but then came his headline grabbing disappearance from the charts after he vanished into detoxing clinics and bankruptcy. Silence had then followed until he reappeared with a female singing partner in Pryde of the Past, his tribute band to his grandmother Miranda Pryde, for whose famous songs they were now known. In the last year alone 'Yesterday is Tomorrow' and 'Sail Away with Love' had hit the charts.

Jason came on alone, no band members, no Liz. He bore little resemblance to Mike, being slight and not very tall, and at first sight lacking Mike's commanding presence. When he began to sing unaccompanied that dramatically changed. The slightness became strength, so that his tiniest movement had a magnetic quality that together with his voice made one forget that Miranda had been female and he was male. No doubt about the latter, I thought, and indeed whether he was gay or not was immaterial as he sang. I could listen to that voice for a very long time. I was almost sorry when the band and Liz came on to join him. I was proud of my Liz (well, she hadn't been *my* Liz for a couple of years) as she sang. There was not a trace of nervousness after she'd got going and I cheered her enthusiastically. By the time Jason finished with his solo, 'It's time, that time again, that time to part', I had a lump in my throat. It had indeed been a tribute to remember, a tribute to Miranda Pryde and to Old Herne's too.

Perfectly timed came the roar of the fly-past aircraft – the Thunderbolt, a Hurricane and a Tempest – and I have to confess I didn't recognize the Tempest until my neighbour of the grass breathed its name in awe. Nor, as we all peered upwards at this majestic display, did I take in that there was something missing from it. Not until after the aircraft had disappeared and the applause died down. I hadn't been aware of Len's approach until he nudged me.

'No Crossley,' he hissed.

'What?' I'd forgotten about that element of the fly-past, while I was so wrapped up in the concert and the overhead performance.

'The fire tender. I was watching for it. It's not on the track.'

A jolt of unease, but then I saw sense. 'Mike probably couldn't start it. Or maybe he has a surprise ending planned.'

Nevertheless we were both worried enough to go over to Thunderbolts Hangar. I had some idea that between us we might be able to get the old crock going before everyone gave up waiting for it. The crowds were beginning to move towards the car park now, especially those with families. Even so, there were still a lot of people around and I could see a crowd round the closed visitor entrance to Thunderbolts.

And then I picked up that the screams I could hear weren't coming from the dodgems or the Haunted House. Without a word both Len and I ran for the double doors on the far side of Thunderbolts. As we entered I could see the Crossley's rear and a dozen or so people shouting, screaming, choking. As I reached them, I could see there was something on the ground in front of the Crossley. I pushed my way through and then I could see all too clearly what it was.

A body, very bloody, very mangled. The bomber jacket alone told me who it was. It was Mike.

THREE

Not the swoosh of classic cars and aeroplanes now but that of police cars, incident vans and purposeful major-crime-scene operatives moving about their business. The business was murder. The police seemed to be assuming it was no accident, and so was I. Mike had been run down by the Crossley fire tender. That much was obvious, but the tender couldn't have revved up sufficient speed in that confined space, either with or without a driver, to cause such horrific injuries, and if it had been driven at him from outside the hangar it would surely have attracted attention. The fireman's axe lying not far away had so much blood on it that it must have been the decisive factor, whether Mike had been run down by the Crossley before or after the axe attack.

Even now though, an hour and half after the discovery of Mike's body, I couldn't fully take it in. Swoosh? Murder? The two words didn't fit and yet it had happened. The crowds were thinning out fast, with police monitoring the exits, but there had been plenty of time for Mike's killer to disappear from the hangar before the body was discovered. Out of the thousands here today how on earth could his murderer be traced? Sometimes I'm glad I don't have Detective Chief Inspector Brandon's job. Sometimes I'm sorry I have mine in situations such as this. Brandon likes being hands-on for some cases and was currently the senior Investigating Officer at this crime scene.

I liked Mike – everyone did, or so I had thought. Who could have hated him to this extent? Did his killer want to remove Mike the person or was it because of his connection with Old Herne's? If the latter, the outcome of today's lunch meeting could have something to do with it. Or – another dark thought – was his death connected with the theft of the Porsche? I couldn't focus on any reason that it could be, but the timing of the two events made it a possibility. Had Mike, for instance, known who was behind the theft and confronted him?

'You again,' DCI Brandon had remarked dispassionately, when

it became my turn to be called to the clubhouse room chosen for a temporary incident room.

Those in the Thunderbolts Hangar when the police arrived had been herded into one of the other clubhouse rooms, save for Peter Nelson and Boadicea who had been unfortunate enough to find Mike's body, having become concerned, as had Len and I, over his absence from the fly-past. Their cries had brought others running, and by the time Len and I had reached the scene the emergency services had already been summoned. Mike's family and staff, including poor Boadicea, were now in the bar area. The police cordon now surrounded Thunderbolts and all approaches to it, and scene-suited personnel were carrying out their gruesome tasks within.

At least Brandon tolerates my presence now without giving in to his natural instinct to first throw cuffs on me and then throw away the key, so my grilling this time was more a light charring rather than heavy barbecuing.

'Job for Dave,' I explained, when asked why I was here. 'Anyway, no one would miss Swoosh.' I was still on autopilot, I realized, while part of me grappled with the enormity of what had happened.

He conceded this point. 'I know about the Porsche, but what brought you to that hangar so quickly, Jack?'

'The Crossley fire tender hadn't appeared on the track as scheduled, I assumed there'd been a breakdown and Len and I went to see if we could help. We thought the head volunteer Tim Jarvis would be there.'

'He wasn't when we arrived,' Brandon commented. 'And I've been told Mike Nelson had a deputy. I haven't met him either.'

'Jessica Hart. No motive there,' I whipped back more quickly than I should have done. 'She's only just arrived in the job.'

'So you think it's murder?' Brandon said mildly. 'I need to talk to her too.'

I'd fallen for that one and perhaps done Jessica no service. 'Surely it has to be,' I replied. 'That axe followed by the Crossley to make sure he was dead.' I began to feel distinctly sick at the thought. The Crossley had been somewhat forward of its usual position in the centre of the hangar, ready to back out of the double doors for the drive to the track.

'Seems that way,' Brandon agreed. 'The axe must have preceded the Crossley attack. It looks as if he was right in front of the Crossley then, maybe even looking under the bonnet. The blood spatter pattern fits that, and if the Crossley attack had come first there would be no certainty of killing him.'

Perhaps he saw my involuntary shudder because he became chummy – for him. My star must be rising. 'Would you stick around, Jack? Find Jarvis and Jessica Hart for me. They may be with the Nelsons downstairs in the bar; Dave Jennings says you know them.'

'Only Mike and his wife, and I wasn't a close mate.'

'Even better. Keep a friendly eye on them. They're with one of ours.'

'Now?' I was dubious about this, but with the police already sitting in with them it might help to have a friendly face around, even if Jessica and Tim weren't there.

'Why not?' Brandon gave me one of his glances, which always make me think my brain is being X-rayed for its innermost thoughts.

'Could be plenty of reasons.'

'All overruled.'

I braced myself, but unnecessarily. The constable at the clubhouse main door told me most of the family had gone with the policewoman to High House as Mrs Nelson was in a state of collapse. One or two people were still in the bar, he said, but the remaining visitors and staff were in Morgans Hangar, which had seating in the video room, as well as at several other points. Jessica wouldn't be at High House and nor would Tim, so I checked the bar area first.

The bar itself was untended and looked as if the staff had left their posts in a hurry, as in legends of the *Marie Celeste*. Empty glasses and coffee cups stood on the counter, a tea towel lay tossed beside them, and a half eaten cup cake waited for attention on a plate. The entry door to the staff side of the counter was wide open.

Then I noticed two people sitting by the window. With the dying sun streaming through the glass I did not immediately realize who they were, until I saw one of them in a wheelchair. The other one was sitting in a wing armchair so large and high that it seemed

almost to be making a statement of solidarity with the elderly man
it sheltered. Both men must be around ninety; one I knew, and it
didn't take much to work out who the other one was. The silence
between them and the angle of their chairs confirmed it. I recognized one as Arthur Howell and the other, frailer in body, must be
Mike's father Ray. They spoke not a word, neither to each other
nor to me, and the atmosphere was stuffier than a 1930s Austin
on a cold day. Natural enough with the shock of such a tragedy,
but I wondered what Ray was doing here rather than being at High
House with the rest of his family, mourning his son's death. Grief
isn't always rational.

I forced myself to say, 'Mr Nelson? I'm Jack Colby, a friend
of your son's.' I offered my sympathy to both men, but there
was still silence, and my hasty withdrawal was clearly called for.
Then I remembered that Brandon had wanted me to 'stick around'
and he said nothing without reason.

It was Arthur Howell who finally replied, although as I drew
nearer to them I could see he too was in shock. 'You're Jack
Colby,' he said. 'The man Mike told us had been put on the
Porsche case. We've met before. Goodwood Revival 2007. Right?'

'Right,' I agreed. He had a keen memory, because I never
flatter myself that I make an unforgettable impression on those
I fleetingly meet. This was a man who had got where he was in
the world by remembering. At Goodwood I had met a buoyant,
happy Arthur Howell but he was hardly recognizable in the Arthur
before me now. He was watching me though, and I had little
doubt he was as shrewd as ever.

'Were you there when Mike was found?' he shot at me.

'Shortly afterwards.'

'He was murdered?'

No point in pretending otherwise. 'It does look like it.'

'His killer has to be found. Quickly. That right, Ray?'

The other man raised himself in the wheelchair to glare at
Arthur with such venom that I physically shrank back. 'Not far
to look,' he growled.

He was a thin-faced, suspicious-looking man and hard to recon-
cile with the suave, good-looking singing partner of Miranda Pryde
that I had seen in so many photos of the 1940s. He had been very
much the junior partner, and it was Miranda's voice that lingered

in the memory. I hadn't seen him since my childhood because I'd
been abroad in the oil business for many years.

I had to ask him, because sometimes people say things in the
heat of extreme emotion that they *do* mean, as well as those they
don't. 'Does that mean you know who murdered your son, Mr
Nelson?'

Silence was his only reply. He stared at me, expressionless,
and so I left the two old men to their private grief. Whether
Brandon wanted me here or not, this was no place for me. I
could be of more use tracking down Jessica and Tim.

Morgans Hangar was crowded and I couldn't face it at first.
There were two police constables logging in all arrivals and
departures, so I checked with them whether Jessica and Tim were
present. Neither was. Perhaps I'd been wrong and Jessica was at
High House with the family, but Tim wouldn't be there. Then I
realized where he must be.

I found him there. Sobbing his heart out. Sitting on the ramp
into the garage that currently housed the Morgan but not the
Porsche. The Morgan looked lonely without its mate. I said
nothing to Tim, just sat by him for a while. There was no need
of words.

Eventually, I had to speak. 'The police need to talk to you,
Tim. I'll walk back there with you.'

He didn't demur, just blew his nose into a large cotton hand-
kerchief, carefully replaced it in his pocket and stood up.

'When did you find out, Tim?' I asked him.

'I was down at the track. Mike . . .' His voice faltered then
he tried again. 'He said he'd bring the Crossley down. Didn't
come. Should have been there at quarter to five so I thought he'd
changed his mind and gone to the concert first, but he wasn't
there by twenty to six either. So I went to Thunderbolts – and
there he was.'

I went very cold. 'You saw him *before* Peter and Anna Nelson
got there?'

'Must have,' he muttered. 'Ran straight out. Couldn't face it.'

'You'll have to do that now, Tim. We all will,' I said gently.
This wasn't going to look good in Brandon's eyes.

I escorted him to the clubhouse to wait for Brandon then
returned to Morgans Hangar, where the remaining crowds were

still looking bemused at this terrible end to Swoosh. On the way I spotted Jessica and fulfilled the second part of my immediate mission for Brandon with a quick, 'See you later,' to her.

To my pleasure, I found Len and Zoe patiently waiting for me when I reached Morgans. I could see Mrs Len talking to a friend, but Zoe's partner Rob had vanished – his forte at times of trouble. It was a happy surprise to see Len and Zoe, though, and I told them I appreciated it.

'You're free to go, Jack?' Zoe asked anxiously.

'Not yet.' I'd have to get clearance from Brandon, although the planned clear-up that Jessica had foreseen would no longer be on the cards with a crime scene in operation. 'Brandon wants me to stick around.'

'Careful who you stick with,' Len grunted. 'Funny people, these Nelsons, so Tim says.'

I took this seriously. I knew Tim rated loyalty highly and wouldn't have passed on his opinion of his employers without foundation. 'Tim's with the police now.'

'He'll take it badly,' Len said. 'This is going to be the last straw for Old Herne's. No saving it now.'

'I was told Howell's decision was going to be announced at lunchtime.'

Len snorted. 'Maybe it was. The Nelsons are skint and so is the club. Mike wasn't too good with cash. Swoosh may be first class, but a good paint job doesn't mean there isn't rust underneath.'

With these words of wisdom, Len decided to take Mrs Len home, but Zoe lingered.

'Bad day for you, Jack,' she said sympathetically. 'Shall we talk about something else?'

'Let's do that.' It might take my mind off Mike, though I doubted it.

'I saw you chatting Jessica Hart up earlier,' she said airily.

'All in a day's work.' Taken by surprise, I managed to be equally airy.

'Good. But so's a steamroller in its right place.'

'Very droll,' I commented.

'Take care, Jack,' Zoe said seriously. 'You don't want another follow-my-own-star woman in your life.'

I froze. Zoe might be right on the ball but she had stepped too far into my private territory. Louise is a celeb and had chosen her career on stage and in films in preference to a life at Frogs Hill – and as I could not leave Frogs Hill to be a trailing spouse that spelt goodbye to happiness. Louise's departure from my life was *my* problem, however. Luckily, Zoe realized it.

'Sorry,' she added, 'but next time you need a sticker, not a runner.'

I alternately fumed and was grateful for her concern, and was glad when she left to find Rob. Rob was a first-class sticker – otherwise known as a leech – but did I envy her that? No way. I'd follow my own star, and currently I could see it coming right towards me.

Correction: although it was indeed Jessica, albeit some way away, it was Liz who reached me first. *Again.* I received another embarrassing hug, and over her shoulder I saw Jessica retreating. Almost worse, I saw Liz's nerd husband Colin approaching – not that in the scale of things after Mike's death I was over-concerned for Colin's feelings. Liz was looking shell-shocked, however, and was clearly in need of reassurance.

'You did a great job this afternoon, Liz,' I told her. 'Didn't she, Colin?'

'I got here too late,' he announced stony-faced, glaring at me with his sharp microscopic eyes, as though I were a hitherto unknown species of slug.

'It was a terrific concert, for all its aftermath,' I told him. 'You'd have been proud of Liz. She sang like a real pro.' Perhaps an unfortunate word to choose with Colin's suspicious nature.

'Jason seemed pleased,' Liz contributed with some effort. 'Until afterwards, that is. Terrible for him. Terrible for us all.'

'Where is he?' I asked. 'At High House?'

'I've no idea. I haven't seen him since the concert ended. He's in an odd mood today anyway. We didn't think he was even going to turn up for the concert. We were waiting and waiting until the very last minute.'

'He sang well.' I stored the information away in my mind.

'That's what he does,' Colin said heavily. 'What's all this about a murder, anyway? I'm not having Liz involved.' Another glare at me, as though I was about to take her into custody on behalf of the police.

'I've told you, Colin,' Liz said patiently. 'It's Mike Nelson who's been killed. It's nothing to do with Jason's band, only with Jason himself.'

'Nevertheless, it's high time we went,' Colin said, then glanced at me and added a meaningful *'darling'* to his command.

'OK, Colin,' Liz agreed, then darted over to give me a quick farewell hug. 'Thanks, Jack, for being there for me.'

Unfortunately, Colin darted back too, put a possessive arm round her and yanked her away from me – just as Jessica once more appeared at the wrong moment. She had other things on her mind this, however, and didn't even comment as they left. She looked very white. 'I've been looking for you, Jack. I've just been grilled by the police and grilled by the family and I'm . . .'

She began to sway and I grabbed her just in time. 'I need to see the police again,' I told her, 'so let's go over to the clubhouse. Maybe we can get a drink or something to eat from the kitchen. The bar's pretty empty so we can find a quiet corner.'

'I *daren't* relax. And anyway, your girlfriend—'

'Is just an old friend. She's not my wife or my girlfriend and that's her husband with her.' I then linked her arm in mine for physical as well as moral support. What to say now? No avoiding the subject of Mike, that was for sure, but I tried not to make it sound like another grilling. 'You said the family had been questioning you, Jessica. Did you mean Mike's?'

'Arthur Howell's too. His son is a beefy chap called Glenn, and Glenn's daughter Fenella is here as well, an all-American stunner. They're both gearing up to – as they put it – protect Arthur's interests, once it's seemly to do so.'

'Arthur seems well able to protect them himself.'

'He doesn't get on with Ray Nelson too well and not with Peter either. Arthur thinks he's Ray's number one spy, which he is. And then of course there's—'

'Boadicea,' I finished for her. 'Doesn't Arthur see eye to eye with her?'

'Did the Romans get on chummy terms with Boadicea?'

I managed a laugh. 'What about Jason Pryde? He's a Nelson and is Ray's grandson too.'

A pause. 'Jason? Arthur gets on with him well. I haven't seen him since it all happened, but he certainly won't be comforting Boadicea. They're at daggers drawn and have been, so I was told, since Mike married her fifteen years ago.'

'Is he still at odds with his father too?'

She didn't answer this except with a non-committal, 'Well, he was here today,' as we reached the clubhouse. I was longing to know what had happened at the lunch but I was forestalled before I thought it seemly to do so.

'Jessica!' Sweeping out of the main door was Boadicea herself, by now clad in subdued grey. She still looked distraught and little wonder, but the fighting spirit was to the fore again.

I began to express my sympathy but she swept it aside. 'Have they found out yet who did this monstrous thing to my husband, Jessica?' Then her eyes narrowed as she saw me. 'What are *you* doing here?'

'The police asked me to stay. As I explained, I came to discuss the Porsche with Mike.'

'Then discuss it with me,' she snapped. 'It's mine now, although it's only three weeks until the insurance is paid out. What are you going to do about it?'

Even for Boadicea this was quite something, and there was no way I was going to discuss car business now. 'I'll keep in touch,' I said shortly.

That appeared to be that, and even making allowances for shock and distress I was stunned at this bizarre conversation so hard upon the heels of her husband's murder. Of Mike she said not a word, but as she stalked past us out of the clubhouse I saw her face collapse with a complete loss of control. Grief takes people in strange ways.

The bar was deserted now, but Jessica knew her way round the kitchen and at my urging found something for us to eat. I wasn't concerned on my account but on hers. She needed to get back to some base of normality, and this was a good way of doing it for us both. I felt I'd been catapulted by an enormous swoosh into a kaleidoscope of whirling images of Mike's destroyed body. Someone had been very determined to see him dead.

Jessica and I had half an hour together before Brandon descended and spotted us, but it had been a relatively silent one. I wrestled

with my conscience since I still did not know what had happened
at the lunch meeting, but I could not question Jessica further.
Beyond saying she had been at the concert, she wasn't interested
in talking. I could understand that and said I'd call her. She
couldn't have heard me because she murmured that she would
call me. Brandon came over to us and asked us to call in at
Charing HQ on the morrow to sign statements, but surprisingly
lingered after Jessica left.

'Thanks for rooting out Jarvis and Jessica Hart for me,' he
said. I thought he might elaborate, but he didn't. Instead: 'Tell
me what you know about Old Herne's.'

Interesting, I thought, that this was his choice of line to follow,
and for me it was much easier than talking about Mike. I did
my best, ending up with: 'Great institution running downhill
faster than a Ferrari out of control.'

'What if this Arthur Howell takes it over for himself? I'm told
he's the owner.'

'That doesn't seem likely unless he ran it in conjunction with
someone. His decision was going to be announced at a lunch
today. Was it?'

Brandon is a practical man. He knew I'd find out anyway, so
he told me.

'Reprieve for Old Herne's, according to this new broom you're
sweeping along with, Jessica Hart.'

Only this morning that would have been great news. Now the
picture had dramatically changed. For instance, could someone
who wanted the club to be closed have taken decisive action?

'Will it work out? How do you rate her?' Brandon continued.

I forced myself to be objective. 'She's only on the starting
grid, but it looks promising. This sort of place runs on trust and
familiarity so it's early days to tell.'

'Who's your informant?' he shot at me.

'Tim Jarvis, Jessica herself and my own impressions.'

'An obsessive volunteer, a new broom and a prejudiced
outsider,' Brandon summed up.

'That doesn't mean it's wrong,' I pointed out, nettled. 'And
delete the prejudiced.'

Brandon switched tack. 'Have you met the widow?'

'Several times. A formidable lady.'

'They're all formidable. Old man Nelson saying he'd been expecting something like this; one arrogant twerp of a grandson claiming he'd have done it himself if he'd thought of it, only he hadn't; and the other grandson, Jason Pryde, not saying anything. Singer, isn't he? Met him, have you?'

'No.'

'Ah. Now . . .' Brandon became formal again. 'About this Porsche. Any line on it yet?'

My antennae shot up. 'One or two leads that might be helpful: the Porsche Club 356 Register and one other. And there's the DVLA, of course.'

Brandon frowned. 'Swansea won't help, will it? The car couldn't be re-registered.'

'It could if it was fixed to look like a first registration from abroad. Why are you interested in the Porsche though? Because its owner's been murdered?'

'Quite,' was Brandon's reply. 'It's a good reason for you to stick around for a while. Get to know the politics of this place. Could be useful.'

Which meant that he thought the murder could indeed link up with the car theft. Had Mike confronted the thief? But if it wasn't linked, whom would Mike's death benefit? One thing was clear. Brandon didn't think this was a random killing.

'There was blood all over the place,' I called after him as he left. 'Could help?' Brandon stopped in his tracks.

'Yes,' he said. 'Jarvis told me the axe belonged to the Crossley – and so did an RAF uniform greatcoat. That's missing.'

Dusk was falling fast as at last I returned to the exhibitors' car park by the track. I'd gone over to the main car park before I left, with Brandon's permission. I'd been hoping to catch Liz again but her car was gone. There were still police cars and vans there, as well as several civilian cars – amongst the latter might be some early bird journalists who had caught a whiff of what was going on. Tonight the visitors to what would probably be the last Swoosh had already driven along the lanes of Kent to the highways that returned them to their known world: home. Soon, thankfully, I would be one of them.

I walked over to my Gordon-Keeble, which was standing in

lonely state by the track, but did a double take as I reached it. What I had assumed was part of a tree trunk in the shadows bordering this area of Old Herne's suddenly walked towards me. Forties, thin brown hair, a slight build and nondescript – or would have been except for the fact that I knew who he was.

Mike's son, Jason Pryde.

'I like cars,' he told me conversationally, looking at mine. 'This one – it's good.'

'Thanks,' I said warily. 'I liked your concert too.' I expressed my sympathy for his father's death but he merely stared at me. Not in surprise or in obvious grief or shock, but as if I had said nothing and he was summing me up.

Then he remarked, 'My grandmama had a Gordon-Keeble. When I was a kid, I got a kick out of the tortoise – still do.'

The tortoise is the emblem of the Gordon-Keeble, said to have been chosen because a pet tortoise unexpectedly crawled across the path of the prototype.

'Miranda Pryde was a great singer,' I said awkwardly, as his father's murder was clearly off the subject list and Jason was still staring intently at me.

He nodded. 'Yes, she was. You're Jack Colby, aren't you? Liz told me about you. You're a car detective, here about my father's Porsche.'

'Correct.'

Unexpectedly, he smiled. It lit up his face and changed him briefly from a mystery man to a human being. 'I loved that car. Did you know Steve McQueen drove with a broken foot when he came second in the 1970 twelve-hour race at Sebring? He was in a Porsche 908.'

'No, I didn't,' I replied, somewhat thrown. 'I hope I find the missing Porsche for your family.' One part of me was aware this was a crazy conversation with his father's death hanging over us, but I told myself again that grief has strange ways of showing itself – and also it reminded me that Jason Pryde was no ordinary individual.

'Do you?' Another of those amazing stares. 'Good. My father said he'd leave it to me in his will. Don't know whether he has or not. I've already got a 1972 Porsche 911S. But I'll try to help you find my father's car.'

I wasn't sure whether I'd welcome his input, but I made suitably gratified noises, adding, 'It would be a wonderful inheritance for you.' The pound signs flashed up in my mind. A quarter of a million and rising. As an inheritance, whether it was sold, or retained, it was a major asset – and if it was never found, so was the insurance.

'My stepmother won't think so,' he replied with great seriousness. 'She expects it to be hers.'

From the way she had been talking, she might still do so. How would she take it if Jason was right about his inheritance? Not well, I was sure of that.

'Have you met Arthur?' Jason continued.

'Briefly. He was sitting with your grandfather in the clubhouse.'

'Was he? That's odd. Arthur's a nice man, isn't he? I like him very much.'

There was a childlike simplicity about Jason Pryde which was engaging, but I warned myself not to underrate him. Children, after all, are a lot more intelligent than we often assume. Jason's own family life had been and still was dysfunctional to say the least. With Mike, Boadicea, Ray and Peter possibly lined up against him, it was hardly surprising that an outsider like Arthur Howell, who had Old Herne's interests at stake, should be a good ally for Jason. It had been Jason who'd told Liz that Old Herne's was closing – was he glad or sorry that it'd had a reprieve? That, however, had been before Mike's death.

'Arthur wants to meet you again,' Jason added.

This was a surprise. 'I'll look forward to it.'

Jason stood aside as I got into the Gordon-Keeble. 'I'm glad I met you,' he said.

'Do you want my mobile number in case you want to get in touch?' I asked politely.

He confounded me yet again. 'I already have it.'

FOUR

Frogs Hill was a welcome haven after the events of the day. It was dark as I drove the Gordon-Keeble home. The winding lanes from Piper's Green have no street lighting and I felt an idiotic splurge of gratitude as my security lights blazed out in their friendly way as I arrived. My farmhouse and the Pits seemed a refuge. Frogs Hill had been my childhood home until my university days, my oil career and my early (brief) marriage took me away. When my father's illness had brought me home some years back, living at Frogs Hill had cured any remaining wanderlust for ever. I was here to stay (hefty mortgage or not), which meant that Frogs Hill Classic Car Restorations, begun by my father and Len, was a permanent fixture. I doubt if Len or Zoe would even notice if I said it was closing. They'd just carry on working. Correction: they might feel differently if Harry Prince took it over. His eyes are permanently fixed on acquiring Frogs Hill not only for the business but for the Glory Boot, housed in an annex to the farmhouse, and it was there that I decided to take a belated snack when I returned.

My father's priceless collection of automobilia varies from the nut bolt that fell off a Liège–Rome–Liège winner to a collection of paintings by the now world-famous Giovanni, who still blows in once in a while to re-examine his surreal works of glory. This task usually reduces him to tears of admiration at his prowess, which are only dried by a bottle or two of the finest Chianti.

I don't exactly chat to Dad in the Glory Boot but I undoubtedly feel his calming (or reproving) presence there. I certainly did tonight as I perched on an old leather rally seat, still punch-drunk from the combination of Swoosh's magic and Mike's murder. The two just did not fit. I'd be the last person to say that the classic car world doesn't know the seamier side of life but events such as Swoosh are their showcases, when everyday life is put aside for a while. The fact that it had intruded with such violence took some readjustment on my part – especially as I'd liked Mike and felt his death personally.

Dad would have felt the same way, which is probably why I could sense so clearly what he would have had to say about my problem. I had been at Swoosh on a straight car job for the Kent Car Crime Unit to find a stolen Porsche and I still had to carry on with it. Brandon, moreover, had suggested that I hang around Old Herne's, implying the theft was connected to Mike's death. Was I comfortable with that? Not entirely. I'd liked Mike, I loved Old Herne's and I fancied Jessica Hart. Did these ingredients glue together? I wasn't sure, even though they could give me an entrée into the Old Herne's world behind the scenes. On the other hand, there could be a possible conflict of interest, as Jessica would be at least the temporary successor to Mike. There was also the question of the Porsche's ownership if it was found again, and if not there was the insurance issue. Quicksand ahead. A foot wrong and I was sunk. Would that stop me? No.

As I closed the Glory Boot door behind me, I sensed a waft of approval from its founder. OK, I told him, I'll sleep on it, and if you really think it's a good idea for me to stick my nose in, come back to me tomorrow.

My landline promptly rang at eight a.m. the next morning. I detached myself from my coffee mug, padded over to answer it and received a boom in my ear.

'Jack Colby? Glenn Howell, Arthur's son. Can you get over here right away? Dad wants to talk.'

Phew, that was quick! I mentally congratulated my own dad. Whatever Arthur Howell wanted to see me about, it showed a degree of interest beyond the stolen car. Glenn made it sound as though he was conferring a favour, which remained to be proven. Arthur would hardly be consulting me on the future of Old Herne's, but the stolen Porsche alone seemed an unlikely topic in the current circumstances.

'Can't make it before eleven, I'm afraid.' There was a delightful six-cylinder 1935 Wolseley Hornet Special with engine trouble booked into the Pits at nine thirty and Len wanted me to share the excitement of the diagnosis.

A brief silence at the other end of the line. Then a slightly incredulous: 'Sure about that? He's real keen.'

I said I was sure so, sounding somewhat disgruntled, Glenn said he would meet me in the Cricketers Hotel lobby. Another family on the horizon, then, which might have its own agenda. I could see Jessica's position might become that of battering ram between two families. Which end would be wielding the power?

Len spent so long discussing the Wolseley with its owner and then – the real fun – reaching his own diagnosis with me as an admiring stooge that I feared I wasn't going to make it on time, but at last I managed to prise myself out of the Pits and into my Alfa. The trouble, he had informed me with pride, was faulty ignition timing advance. All this excitement took me away from the tragedy at Old Herne's and why Arthur Howell wanted to see me. Whatever it was, it could be a valuable contribution to my job and judging by the speed of his summons it must be urgent.

The Cricketers is a great place. It's on the outskirts of Harrietsham, a village on the A20, and the hotel had acquired its name from the fact that the famous nineteenth-century cricketer Alfred 'the Mighty' Mynn lived locally and played for the Harrietsham Cricket Club. The hotel doesn't possess a private cricket pitch but it does have plenty of old prints and paintings to celebrate the sport.

I found not Glenn Howell but his daughter Fenella the Stunner awaiting me; she was the supercilious lady I'd noted at the concert. She did not look particularly pleased to see me and she was indeed a stunner. Slim as a beanpole, stylishly and expensively clad, and cool as a cucumber – the latter being a traditional remedy for sore eyes, as she was. The message she was putting over, however, was that whatever plans she had for her life they would not include Jack Colby. Fine by me, because inscrutable felines – and her mask-like face did give her this resemblance – aren't my speciality. My welcoming smile relaxed the mask, albeit only by a millimetre or two.

'I saw you yesterday at the show,' she informed me almost accusingly.

'It was a tough time for you as well as the Nelsons.'

'Especially my grandfather. He's in one of his moods today, so we've no idea why he asked you to come here.' She made it sound as though this were my fault. She took me up in the lift to a suite on the top floor, from which there was a glorious view of the Downs. I expected to find Glenn installed with his father but there was only Arthur Howell sitting by the window. Fenella too departed, presumably at Arthur's wish. I was intrigued, not knowing whether to be glad or sorry that I wasn't to get the full family experience. On the whole I was glad, I decided. One to one is usually more productive.

Arthur looked his full age this morning, and I wondered what on earth was coming my way. Just a request for an update on the Porsche? Coffee and croissants were on a table before him, but no sign of his having touched them himself.

'Sit down, Mr Colby,' he said quietly and I took the armchair facing him. 'Coffee?' He poured it with a steady hand and then there was a silence for a few minutes as I drank it and he made a token attempt at doing the same. 'See those hills?' he eventually asked.

He was looking out at them and a fine sight they were in their early summer green, but Arthur didn't wait for any comment from me. Instead he continued, 'I'm going to tell you why I set up Old Herne's. OK by you?'

It was, but I became even more intrigued as to the reason for this visit.

'My father was British-born,' he told me. 'Saw war the first time round and went to the States later. He fought on the ground and had a bad time at Messines in 1917. That's what made me choose the air. Thunderbolts, Jack. That's what I flew in World War II. Stationed at Debden in Essex, Fifty-Sixth Group. Been to the American Air Museum at Duxford, have you?'

I had, which impressed him.

'Great building, isn't it?' he continued. 'Thunderbolts are rare beasts nowadays, but they house one there for a private owner. I go and look at it once in a while, and go back to Debden too, but my heart's buried deep at Old Herne's.'

'I heard you crash-landed there.'

'Right. Summer of 'forty-three that was, mid August. Flying the new model P-47D. Ever been in a Thunderbolt?'

A rhetorical question because he swept on: 'Monsters they were, not like your Spitfires. Joke was you could get lost finding your way round the cockpit. We were day fighters, escorting the heavy bombers – Fortresses, Liberators – and under arrangement with West Malling airfield here in Kent we could refuel there. Old Herne's was its auxiliary advance landing ground. Black Wednesday – heard of that? Bad day for the Eighth Air Force bombers over Regensburg and Schweinfurt. We fighters mostly fared better – not me though. Thunderbolts had belly tanks then which meant problems. I caught some strikes from some Focke-Wulfs – engine trouble, and I only just made it to Old Herne's. The Thunderbolts were noble beasts and I got away with only minor burns and cuts, thanks to the Crossley guys. I was taken to West Malling, and they checked me over and sorted out the Thunderbolt wreckage. I was a lieutenant, so I stayed at the Manor House – know about that?'

'A new one on me,' I told him.

'It was the West Malling officers' mess. Great place, flowers, lake, lawns. When you were there, you could pretend there wasn't a war on. Till the next mission, that is. It was there I met Miranda Pryde. Her voice,' he continued, 'you'll have heard on records and film, but that was nothing to the real experience. You think Jason can sing? He can, but not like that. Miranda and her partner Ray toured, so I got them to come up to Debden once or twice and the next year I was back in Kent at the same time as they were. D-Day time, when we were trying to persuade the Luftwaffe that we were planning to attack Calais, not Normandy. Heard of the Twitch Inn?'

'No pub of that name round here now,' I told him. I'd have remembered a name like that.

He grinned. 'It was a nickname for the cellar at the Manor House, used for entertainment in the evenings, music, drinks – quite a place. A substitute night club. Only problem was there were no women allowed there – except for the barmaid and sometimes the singer. That's where Miranda sang. In the weeks following D-Day, I made a vow. If I got through this I'd make enough dough to do something as a memorial to Old Herne's – that's if we won the war. None too sure of that then. I wanted Old Herne's to be remembered. Over here you have your castles and churches and all that history around you. When twenty years later I heard Old Herne's was for sale, I thought I'd add to this heritage of yours by making sure the old place didn't disappear. Miranda and Ray had given up touring by that time and Mike was already addicted to racing, and so it seemed to me we could combine the two to the satisfaction of all. Mike had his Porsche and I bought that Morgan.'

'So yesterday's tragedy must have been a personal blow, having known Mike so long.'

All this time he had been gazing out of that window but now he turned his face to me. 'Yes. A long time, Mr Colby.'

'Jack,' I murmured.

He nodded. 'They all call me Arthur. Reckon that's a good name to have around these parts. Your King Arthur's supposed to have fought a battle or two in Kent.'

'That's the legend.'

'Where do legends spring from? Guess no one sits down and says I'll dream up a great legend today. Somewhere there's a truth hiding inside. That's why I called you here.'

I was thrown for a moment. 'About King Arthur?'

He didn't even notice this idiocy. 'About Mike. I'm told you're some kind of private eye.'

Tread cautiously, I thought. 'Yes, to find stolen cars. I work with the Kent Police Car Crime Unit.'

'The folks in the hotel say more than that. There's a story about an Auburn and a murder round these parts.'*

'That's true but I'm not employed in that capacity.'

'*I'm* employing you, Jack. Any objection?'

A mental sledgehammer hit my face. 'For Mike's murder?'

'Your police are good, I'm told, but it's my guess you can do what I want quicker. You can tell me what's going on. I don't care if the police get there first with the chains and cuffs. I want the background story all the way along and I want results.'

'Hold on,' I interrupted. 'Sorry, but this is not possible.' I had a vision of Brandon's face if he ever found out. True, he wanted me to 'stick around' but I knew full well that was limited in scope.

'It would clash with your police job?' he shot back at me.

'Yes, but there's another angle that worries me more. Mike

---

* See *Classic Calls the Shots*

Nelson was one of the most likeable chaps I've ever met and I can't see who would want to kill him unless it's to do with Old Herne's and possibly the Porsche too.'

'Agreed. But your Porsche job gives you a free pass to nose around Old Herne's.'

'If,' I continued doggedly, 'Mike's murder *is* linked to Old Herne's, that means people *you* know being involved – his family, his employees, even you as owner.' The more I thought about it, the more likely the Old Herne's angle seemed. Mike would not have been happy about a casual stranger messing around on the Crossley, nor, if he had been checking under the Crossley's bonnet, would he have asked a stranger to start her up.

'I see where you're going, Jack,' he said quietly. 'Go on.'

'And therefore *your* family could be involved too.'

He looked at me. 'Why do you think we're on our own here, Jack? And I made sure the room isn't bugged. Always do that anyway. You're a straight man, that's what I'm told, and I reckon that's what I see. I don't know who killed Mike, but I'm going to find out and I want you to help me *whatever* the result. OK by you?'

I quickly thought this through. Could I depend on him still to think this way if push came to shove? 'With reservations,' I told him.

'Name them.'

'First, whether the results do or don't please you, I have to report to the police.'

'Goes without saying,' he grunted.

'Second, I have to tell them of any material discoveries even if they don't seem to be leading anywhere.'

'Understood.'

'Third—' I hesitated over this one, but I had no choice. 'I heard you've given Old Herne's a reprieve, but I need to know more about the situation before I begin. Are you still considering closing it down, what's the legal position now, and does Mike's death affect what you're planning to do?'

I thought I'd wrapped it up well enough but he still took the point.

'You mean am I a target?' Arthur shrugged. 'Jack, I'm ninety years old. There's Someone up there who deals out death more efficiently than Mike's murderer and at ninety years old He already has His eye on me. Sure, I could be a target for this killer but finding him is top of the agenda, not a bulletproof vest for me. That clear?'

'It is.'

'So now I'll tell you about Arthur P. Howell and his ownership of Old Herne's. For your ears only, Jack.'

'They're a safe house.'

'We never did get on, Ray and I, right from the time we met at the Twitch Inn, and that grandson of his, Peter, takes after him. Nevertheless, as I said, when I bought the old place it seemed to me that he and Miranda would do a good job running it. Miranda did most of the work, I reckon, and when she died in 1991 Ray retired and Mike took over. His racing days were in the fifties and sixties and since then he'd had some kind of admin job in the motor racing world, but he wasn't good at business. I found that out soon enough. Too likeable, Jack.' His voice shook slightly and I quickly intervened.

'I heard there is a trust of some sort.'

'Yeah. There was and is. I remain owner of Old Herne's. Miranda was my trustee, looking after the management and finances, and after her death Mike took the role over. Any profits got divided up between me – as long as I was alive and kicking – and Mike.' A pause. 'You've met his son Jason?'

'Briefly,' I said diplomatically.

'He's a good lad. Takes some knowing though.'

'This must be a hard time for him. I was told he didn't get on with his father.' I had added this tentatively, as I wasn't sure how it would go down.

Arthur fixed me with a look. 'Right, but it would have sorted itself out.'

I didn't comment. If no holds were to be barred in this investigation I needed the truth, but it was too soon to make rash judgements on how far I might have to go to find it.

'After my death,' Arthur continued, 'Mike would have inherited the whole lot, with the profits shared with Jason.'

'Only, there have been no profits.' He had made no mention of his own family being included in the trust and I wondered how they regarded that. Probably, there was enough money to satisfy them without Old Herne's, but on the other hand I've noticed that the richer some people are the keener their urge to improve their lot still more.

'Too right. Only losses,' Arthur replied. 'So I came to a decision that the old Thunderbolt days have passed and Old Herne's couldn't go on. Glenn and Fenella have been pressing me for a long time to pull the plug and I reluctantly had come to the same conclusion. There aren't many of us veterans left now and most of the revenue comes from the classic car side. I'd see Mike was compensated and anyone else affected, but basically it was finished.'

'But if it's a trust and Mike was in total charge, *could* you just close it down? Doesn't it work like a charity?'

'No way,' Arthur said. 'It's a *Revocable* Living Trust. As long as I'm alive I can change it, cancel it, sack the trustee any time I choose.'

Now I was beginning to understand, and it raised all sorts of questions. 'You had been planning to revoke it at the lunch yesterday?'

'That's what I came over to do, Jack.'

'It seems to have been generally believed that it was going to close.'

'In family and close circles, yes.'

'So how does Mike's death change the situation?'

'It depends on what you find out about his murder.'

The enormity of this statement left me gasping. 'That's a big responsibility you're laying on me.'

'I've had ninety years to discover that sometimes things don't work out. I can live with that. Can you? You'll go ahead?'

Call me crazy, but my instinctive reaction was to say yes – and so I did.

'Then there's one more factor I have to explain. I woke up yesterday morning, looked out of the window and saw those classic cars making their way up the hill. Hundreds of them.'

This was more like it, and on Swoosh's behalf I waited hopefully.

'The day before Swoosh, after I'd settled in at the Cricketers, I met Jessica Hart and asked her for a frank run-down on the finances. It didn't look good, and when the whole gang came over to the dinner that night I told them all that. Said I was going to sleep on it. Next morning, when I saw the cars and we drove into Old Herne's itself I knew I couldn't do it. So at lunchtime I told everyone that Old Herne's was going on. Mike would stay at least for a while and the trust would continue for the foreseeable future.'

And that, I thought, must have set a lot of emotions running riot.

'Less than four hours later,' Arthur finished, 'Mike was dead. Want to change your mind, Jack?'

I wanted to say yes, I wanted to say no. The no won the battle but it was a hard fought decision. Looked at in the light of this family-led situation it seemed a minefield for any outsider to enter. That must be exactly why Arthur had wanted my input – the outsider's view. I told him I'd reconsider and give him my answer tomorrow.

'Good. After that we can talk money,' Arthur said approvingly. 'And another thing. That Porsche. I feel as strongly about that as the Morgan. Get it back.'

Talking money is something I usually like, but today I seemed to have been hit by a sandbag. Find the Porsche? Find Mike's killer? Related search? The warning signs were flashing in earnest now. Drive on or stop right now?

I went back to Frogs Hill and stared into space for a while. Unfortunately, space provided no immediate answers. What I had learned from Arthur needed to be digested for a few hours, given that the motivation for Mike's death could well lie right there. Instead, I began the Porsche search in earnest. Hunting down a man's beloved car when he had just been murdered seemed a tasteless task, but if it was linked to his death delaying it was worse.

Dave had not given me details of the two outstanding Swansea registrations, so I contacted the Porsche Club 356 Register, which as I expected had all the information on Mike's car – not just on the technical side but even on my involvement – but there had been no attempt to register it either under foreign or UK plates. They would be on the alert at any such attempt because of the rarity of Mike's Porsche; the engine and chassis numbers, whether the correct ones or altered, would be a crucial element, because alterations meant the car would not tally with their series numbering records.

On the thesis that the trail to the Porsche could hardly be bleaker, I decided to tackle Harry Prince on the slim chance that since Huptons was part of his empire he might have heard a whisper about it and an even slimmer chance that he would convey this news to me if I presented myself on his doorstep.

Harry seems a great guy until you cross him. He and his wife live in a plush mansion in the village of Charden on the way to Ashford. I like his wife very much, which suggests that Harry must have a tender side, the existence of which has eluded me. I do have to admit that Harry is sometimes willing to do me a good turn even though a bad one is equally attractive to him.

The garages he owns are all reasonably honest – or if they aren't he turns a blind eye until the truth comes out and kicks him in the face. I went to see him on Tuesday morning – unannounced, as that way Harry is more likely to be available, because he is always hopeful I've come crawling to beg him to buy Frogs Hill. Not in a million years. My luck was out, because so was Harry. I tried again in the afternoon and this time Harry was actually in his forecourt when I pulled up at the electric gates. Even Harry didn't go so far as to refuse to open them.

'Bad day on Sunday,' I said as I parked the Alfa.

'That why you're here, Jack? Come to sell up?' Harry shook with guffaws of laughter.

'Yes, but not to sell up. It's about Mike Nelson's Porsche.'

'Poor old Mike,' he said reflectively. 'I heard it had been nicked.'

'Any line on it? Someone told me that Huptons had a customer asking about a Porsche 356 for sale.'

A pause. 'Is this official, Jack?'

'Yes.'

'No.'

'Then make it unofficial, Harry.'

An agonized look. 'You know me, Jack. Always willing to help when I can. Yes, someone did ask about a 356. Why not?'

'And could Huptons give this customer any help?'

'As it happens, they could.'

My day was brighter already. 'Huptons had one for sale?'

'Well, yes, they did.'

'What makes me think this particular customer wasn't interested in that one?'

'Which customer?' he asked carefully.

'The one who was asking about a particular Porsche,' I said trying to hang on to patience. 'What did they sell him?'

'They didn't. It wasn't Mike's. They'd know that one. Mike was a customer of theirs.' He blew out his cheeks defiantly.

'*Tell* me, Harry.' I flashed my ID ominously.

He licked his lips and then burst out with, 'Someone at Huptons referred him to someone.'

'Who?'

Explosion of laughter from Harry. 'Doubler!'

Dark clouds immediately rolled in again. I could understand why Harry found it so funny.

Doubler's real name is lost in the mists of the underworld. Everyone knows him as Doubler. Some say he gets his nickname from his eagerness to double-cross both foes and friends although he objects strongly to being double-crossed himself. Others say that it comes from his boast that he can double your money for you – but that he'd rather kill you than hand it over.

Whichever, he was bad news. If the theft was indeed linked to Mike's murder – and after my talk with Arthur this seemed likely – the name of Doubler made it much, much worse, and something that no one who valued his tenure on this earth would pursue.

So what did I do? I drove back to Frogs Hill, rang Arthur and took the job. I always like a challenge.

FIVE

'd never met Doubler, but I'd heard about him. Who hadn't in the car trade? Doubler works to his own rules, and Rule Number One is: you don't find him – he finds you. Address? Office? Phone number? No way. Like T.S. Eliot's Macavity the Mystery Cat, whenever there's trouble around, Doubler's not there, and the furore over Mike's murder is just the kind of situation he avoids at all costs. The mere idea of murder hurts Doubler; it hurts him so much that he sends his hit men round rather than knifing you himself. Letting Doubler know that one is on his track is a risky business at the best of times and at the worst downright stupid.

I had thanked Harry, of course, and after he had recovered from his paroxysm of mirth, I had belatedly tried to shut the stable door after the horse had undoubtedly galloped off to inform Doubler.

'That customer at Huptons can't have been after Mike's Porsche then,' I'd said in the vain hope that my name wouldn't reach him.

Finding the car through other routes was therefore a priority before the winds of fate blew him my way. If it had been one of Doubler's men who killed Mike the less I involved his boss at this stage the better. But would Mike ever have let one of Doubler's men near the Crossley? This faint ray of hope vanished when I realized that there were at least a dozen volunteers around, each one of whom Mike would have trusted and any one of whom could have been a Doubler hit man.

On the Wednesday morning I turned my attention back to the two first-time registrations at Swansea, one of which had been a 356 coming in from Ireland, the other from Spain. Dave's team had initially passed these as genuine and for one of them I agreed. I wasn't so sure about the other one, though. Now duly registered with British plates, it belonged to a Jennifer Ansty, who lived not a million miles away in Sussex. It all sounded above board but it was worth rechecking. If that failed then the Porsche must have left the country despite Dave Jennings' vigilance, or was under heavy wraps until the fuss had died down and the insurance paid up. The latter might be a distinctly unsavoury possibility, and with Mike's death and probate to sort out, it could take some time. Jennifer Ansty, I therefore decided, was first port of call.

The best laid plans are sometimes rewarded by a touch of serendipity along the way. An hour later I had a call from the Porsche Club 356 Register to tell me that Mike's car could be the one that had just been registered with them. The number plates did not match, of course, being newly allotted, nor did the engine and chassis numbers, but with the Carrera engine this was a rare car, and the engine number supplied did not match any ever built. The car was now owned by – guess who? – Mrs Jennifer Ansty.

I put the receiver down to find a message from Dave Jennings ordering me to call him back pronto.

'We're fairly sure we've found the Porsche,' he told me with great satisfaction. 'Spotted in Sussex.'

'Mrs Jennifer Ansty,' I said. 'She blithely signed up with the Porsche Club 356 Register, and the numbers don't check out.' I received no congratulations.

'Good. I'm picking you up at nine tomorrow. Not my idea,' he told me again with great satisfaction. 'Brandon wants you along with me in case there's a link with his murder case – he doesn't want to scare the birds by coming himself.'

'Is Mrs Ansty a possible killer bird?'

'Hard to see how. But that's Brandon's job. Tomorrow, ours is the Porsche.'

And a dream of a job it was too, save that this poor women was going to be in for a rude awakening if, as was probable, she was entirely innocent. No one would clock in with the 356 Register if they knew the slightest thing about stolen cars. Nevertheless, I automatically distrusted anything in which Doubler was involved, even if (or because) the Mystery Cat wasn't present himself. Any fish that cat had been pawing over stank.

And then there was the Porsche itself, assuming that this wasn't a fishy red herring. Great to know it was safe at least. Would I get the job of returning the car to its rightful owner? If so, who was that going to be? Boadicea? Jason? Or the insurance firm, if I'd been misled and it had already paid out? And how did that fit with my job for Arthur? I had run my arrangement with Arthur past Brandon yesterday and he hadn't been pleased. Far from it.

He had been within an inch of forbidding me anywhere near his case when he reconsidered, read me my rights and his rights, and then informed me he couldn't stop me, but if I crossed his path on the way, I'd be obstructing justice.

He drew breath, and then added, 'And incidentally we found the greatcoat. Stuffed up in a bundle in the hangar storeroom, covered in blood.'

A date with Dave on Thursday would leave me the rest of Wednesday to take Arthur's challenge forward. No contest as to where to begin. Old Herne's. I had to juggle as many aspects of this situation as I could, and if the theft was involved in the murder there could well be quite a lot to juggle there. As soon as I reached its car park it was obvious there was still a police presence, but when I walked over towards Thunderbolts Hangar I saw that the crime scene was now clear of cordon tape. Old Herne's had a general air of desolation though, as if it were in mourning for the loss of its leader.

As the clubhouse looked closed, I made for Morgans Hangar, where as I entered I could see Tim. He was engrossed in repositioning a splendid print of a *Saturday Evening Post* advertisement for a 1930 then-revolutionary airplane-type-engined Franklin for which – to quote their claim – riding is gliding. He straightened up as I approached, eyeing me (I thought) warily.

We exchanged a few words and I asked if the police were still active in Thunderbolts.

'Off and on,' he grunted. 'Haven't been there myself. Couldn't face it, though the police said I can go in if I want to.'

I was sympathetic. 'You'll have to face it sooner or later. Want to come over right now with me?'

He hesitated, but agreed that my support would be a plus. When we reached Thunderbolts, I could see all too clearly that although the crime scene had been lifted, reminders of it were everywhere, including the chalk marks on the flooring where the body had lain. Somehow the whole place had lost its atmosphere of history; it spoke only of the aftermath of murder.

'Where's the Crossley?' I asked him, seeing no sign of it. The question was more for the sake of hearing a human voice in this depressing place than for information.

Tim must have felt as I did, because he clutched at this opening. 'Still with the Old Bill. What they expect to find I don't know.'

'DNA of whoever was in that driving seat and wearing that greatcoat,' I replied. 'There might be trace evidence on the killer's clothes or the seat.'

Tim sniffed. 'Plastic seat covers,' he pointed out. 'The coat was lying behind the seats, and the axe was around if you knew where it was.'

If you knew where it was . . . I caught Tim's eye and he looked away.

'We all did,' he muttered.

'No casual day visitors then,' I said as lightly as I could. Doubler's hit man was still on my mind – if not, then the killer was a lot closer to home. 'Do many people drive it?'

'Not drive. But sit there, yes. Even Arthur. After the Morgan it's his pride and joy. It's the tender that saved his life when he crashed, so that's natural enough. It's the devil of a job to look after though. Kids clamber in and out all the time, putting their sticky hands everywhere, leaving me –' a belligerent glance – 'to clean up.'

I knew he had a team of volunteer supporters so I kept a diplomatic silence on this point. There'd be an impractical amount of elimination prints for Brandon to gather. 'It had to be someone whom Mike wouldn't be surprised to see at the wheel.'

Tim's face quivered. 'He'd have been about to back it out of the double doors for its track run. I've been thinking – someone could have offered to do it for him.'

At least Tim was talking about it now, which was a good sign. 'Or more likely,' I said, 'someone sitting there cranking while Mike was looking at the engine.' The whole terrible picture began to form. 'No,' I corrected myself. 'He was hit first with the axe, and if he was still conscious after that he wouldn't be in any position to stop his killer if he saw him climb up again into the Crossley driving seat.' That meant it wasn't necessarily a spur of the moment crime; it could have been at least partly premeditated.

Tim swallowed. 'Police asked me I ever drove it. I said yes, but not at the chap I'd worked with for forty years.'

He sounded truculent but it was obvious how heavy a toll this was taking on him. Nevertheless, I had to carry on. 'Would there have been people around?' The concert began at five and most people were already seated by four thirty, but surely not everyone would go to the concert. 'Was Mike killed during the concert or before, do you think?'

'Before,' Tim barked at me. 'Told the police that. He wanted to see the concert himself so he was going to bring the Crossley to the track before that and leave it with me. I was down there with Arthur.'

'In which case, how could his murderer be sure that people weren't milling around here?'

'Visitor door was bolted at four o'clock,' Tim said briefly. 'Mike wouldn't have people around when he took the Crossley out. Health and safety, Mike said, so he always closed the doors and cleared Thunderbolts at least half an hour before he intended to set off. If staff came in, we used the double doors.'

Once again it looked as if the killer knew Old Herne's, though that might apply to Doubler's men too.

Tim was looking round despairingly. 'I'll not feel the same about this place again, Jack.'

My reply was inadequate but the best I could produce. 'It will still mean a lot to Arthur and other veterans and aviation lovers.'

'It'll close now, that's for sure.' His gruff voice did its best to hide emotion.

'That depends on Arthur,' I pointed out. 'He'd decided to reprieve it, but even if Mike's death changes the situation, Old Herne's might still stay open.'

'Reprieve it?' Tim's face was a study in shock.

I belatedly realized that the news had not percolated through to him. That made me uneasy because theoretically Tim would have had some kind of motive, in that with Mike still running the place Old Herne's would go bust. I rejected it outright even as a theory.

'It wouldn't be the same place without Mike,' Tim continued gloomily, 'even though he wasn't good at organizing things. Let things slip, he did, but he gave the old place its magic.'

'That could still happen with your help,' I urged. 'If Jessica Hart takes over, she will make a go of it from the business point of view but it will be up to you to keep the magic going.'

I'd had enough of this place, and Tim must have felt the same because he hastily followed me out. 'Not yet,' he muttered. 'Can't stay here yet.'

The clubhouse door was now open, so I hoped I might find Jessica for a private chat both on the personal level and for my job. I didn't envy her own position at Old Herne's; she was an outsider caught between two families.

The bar was deserted and so were the other downstairs rooms, so I went upstairs – only to hear the sound of raised voices. I stood where I was, undecided whether to breeze in. Although I'd hoped to find Jessica alone, this was the sort of situation where I might pick up crumbs that both Brandon and Arthur would like to hear. So I breezed in.

Poor Jessica. It wasn't just one family engaged in the row but both of them, with her looking lost in the middle. Peter Nelson and Boadicea (in regal purple) represented the Nelsons, while Fenella and, presumably, her father Glenn were waving the Howell flag. Glenn, portly even for his sixty-odd years, looked like an affable W.C. Fields, an image that didn't quite fit with Fenella who still resembled an inscrutable if beautiful Egyptian cat. I wasn't sure which side I would back if push came to shove, and from the atmosphere that hit me that seemed likely.

Boadicea did not look well for all her regal pomp. She seemed heavier, greyer in the face, which was natural enough after the shock of Mike's death. It hadn't affected her fighting spirit, however, because it was she doing most of the shouting as I barged in.

'The whole idea is nonsense. You've no experience. There is only one person who has the experience to run this place and that is myself. I need money and I am Mike's successor!'

Run Old Herne's? *Her*? I must surely have misunderstood.

'It's Arthur's decision and he has made it,' Fenella contributed coolly.

Boadicea shot back a poisonous arrow. 'Under pressure.'

Jessica looked too stunned to reply but Glenn wasn't. 'It's Arthur's decision, Anna.'

'Not without help.' Boadicea's chariot then swiftly changed direction as she took in my presence. 'What are *you* doing here?'

'I'm here to see Jessica.'

'What about that car?' Peter Nelson threw at me. He'd been keeping a low profile, albeit with the supercilious grin on his face that I now associated with him. 'Are we going to get that insurance money or not?'

'We've a positive lead on it,' I replied with great pleasure, noting his 'we' in connection with insurance money.

'What is it?' Boadicea barked.

'I'll tell you more when there's any news.'

Boadicea seemed about to shoot her next arrow but decided she had more important victims than me, and turned back to Glenn. 'You know nothing about Old Herne's, Mr Howell,' she declared.

'I know a lot about my dad. That's enough.'

I was floundering. This sounded as if Glenn might be in charge, either temporarily or even permanently. Whichever, why hadn't Arthur mentioned this to me when we met? Or had it happened afterwards? Why on earth would Arthur have made such a controversial decision when he seemed to want to calm the situation down?

Jessica rallied. 'You may know Arthur, Glenn, but I know Old Herne's.'

'Right, Jess,' Glenn said smartly. 'That's why we're keeping you on.'

Not exactly diplomatic, I thought, but it certainly suggested that Glenn was accustomed to getting his own way by *affably* steamrolling over any opposition.

'I am Mike's successor and she's nothing to do with the family,' Boadicea pontificated.

Followed by Peter. 'Right, *Aunt* Anna. But Jessica won't be running Old Herne's and nor will you. You're the wrong generation and Jessica's an outsider. I'm the right person to take over, and Miranda Pryde was my grandmother just as well as Jason's.'

An interesting swerve of focus, I thought. With Old Herne's power struggle between the Nelsons and Howells, where had Mike fitted in? Was he the victim of somebody's ambition?

'And incidentally,' Peter continued, 'Jason is *so* concerned about Old Herne's that he isn't even here.'

'Perhaps he has more taste,' Jessica snapped back.

'Not clever, Jessica,' Fenella observed. She sounded bored, as perhaps an inscrutable cat would.

'I'm sorry.' Jessica climbed down immediately. 'We're all overwrought. It's too soon after Mike's death for any of us to discuss this properly.'

'No discussion needed,' Glenn put in calmly. 'My father has decided what he wants. But I guess you're right, Jess. We'll get no further today. What with strangers poking their butts in,' he added with a jolly laugh.

'Merely here to offer my help,' I said airily.

'Yeah,' Glenn said – a trifle sourly, I thought. 'Dad told me he'd hired you as some kind of consultant on cars.'

So that was my official role. 'Anything I can do for you, Jessica?' I asked. Like rescue her from the lions' den?

'Thanks, Jack,' Jessica picked up quickly. 'I'll join you in the bar in a few minutes. OK?'

I nodded and made my way back downstairs, perturbed as to what on earth was going on. Arthur, was giving Glenn some kind of job at Old Herne's, while keeping my role quiet from him; Boadicea was assuming she would be next in line for running the place; and Peter also seemed to be making a claim. So where did that leave Jessica – and who might have wanted the job so much that Mike had to be removed from the picture? Another theory I dismissed.

When I reached the bar, I saw to my surprise that instead of the usual barman there was a girl of about twenty in charge. And what a sparky looking girl she was. Curls piled on top of her head, huge earrings, short frilly crimson skirt over high black boots and tights, all topped with a generous smile of welcome.

'Looks like I'm your only customer for the day,' I said cheerfully.

'We've had to close the place to the public. There were trillions of ghouls yesterday, and we couldn't cope.'

We chatted for a few minutes as she produced me a cappuccino with a car marked out on the white foam – her speciality, she told me. I learned her name was Hedda, she lived nearby in Harrietsham, at first with a part-time partner to whom she'd given the boot, and now on her own. She loved it.

'Nice name, Hedda. Norwegian parents?' Ibsen's play *Hedda Gabler* was the only connection with the name that I'd ever come across, so it was worth a shot, even though the young Hedda here didn't seem much like her namesake.

'Parent, not parents. Mum's Norwegian. I'm Jason's daughter.'

'Jason Pryde?' This was a day of surprised indeed. I blinked.

I had not associated Jason with marriage and children; nor, indeed, had I given much thought to whether he was heterosexual or gay. He was just – well – Jason. 'Were you and your mother here on Sunday for the concert?' I asked curiously. 'It must have been tough for you.'

'Yeah, it was. Mike was a great bloke, but Mum wasn't here. She split with Jason centuries ago. I see the old guy a lot though.'

I interpreted the 'old guy' as being her father, who was hardly in this category to me or his fans.

'He's got a house here though, out on the Downs,' she continued, 'so he drops in here when he feels like it. And yeah, it was tough on Sunday.'

'Were you at the bar all day?' Brandon would no doubt be following up who was where during Sunday afternoon but Hedda could be useful too. 'Who was around?'

A sharp look. 'Me – till just before the concert. Got my kicks in the last fifteen minutes or so before I ran over to the bandstand. Ray arrived with Peter, groaning on about Mike letting the place run down, then there was a panic about where Arthur was when Glenn and Fenella marched in five minutes later, then Mike's wife Anna blew in too looking for him – always time to leave, so I handed over to the relief to go and listen to Dad.' Hedda looked faintly amused. 'So, Mr Detective, what brings you here?'

'Cars,' I said promptly.

She looked me up and down. 'You're the one Dad told me about.'

'Possibly.'

'Right.' She eyed me thoughtfully and I wondered what else 'Dad' had said. I still couldn't think of Jason as a father.

I tossed out another feeler. 'Wonder what will happen to Old Herne's now?'

'Dunno. Perhaps Dad'll buy it.'

That rocked me, remembering that it was Jason who told Liz it was going to close. 'Seriously? What about the band?'

'Oh, Dad wouldn't run it. But he's kind of fond of the old place.'

At this interesting moment, Jessica arrived, looking stressed out to say the least. Hedda produced a coffee for her but Jessica left it untouched.

'Can we walk?' she asked. 'I need air not coffee.'

'Sure.' I paid up and we duly walked. She meant it – this was no mere stroll round the block just for a breath of fresh air. She walked so quickly it seemed as if she was trying to put as much space between Old Herne's and herself as she could, even if her smart trousers, light jacket and flimsy shoes made her an incongruous figure once we were outside Old Herne's gates. She turned off down a trodden but still fairly muddy footpath and it was only when we were in the middle of a huge cultivated field that she halted and took several deep breaths.

'Sorry,' she said at last. 'It's all getting to me.'

'Tell me.' I was uncomfortably aware that I was here in dual roles, and that at any moment they might clash.

'Tense situation?' I prompted her when she stayed silent.

Then she began. 'Not one I expected. After what happened to Mike, I thought Arthur would close the place down as soon as he could, having been presented with the perfect opportunity.'

'And?' I prompted her again.

'There were a few conditions and changes. He had told me on Saturday afternoon when I showed him the figures that it was unlikely that Old Herne's would be going on but if it did I would probably take over as CEO when Mike retired from active management. So I didn't hold out much hope for it, because even if Mike did continue I could see it going bankrupt before I got my hands on it. Nevertheless, it was great when Arthur announced the reprieve. It gave me time.'

'But all that changed with Mike's death.'

'Yes.' A pause. 'When Arthur told us at the lunch, I saw everyone's reactions and not all of them looked happy, so I thought there might be repercussions when the lunch ended. And there were – Mike's death.'

'If connected,' I said. 'Not proven but possible. Arthur must have been fond of Mike for he's determined to find out what happened.'

'They got on well. Anyway, Arthur doesn't like his plans being upset.'

'Was there any chance he would have put more money in?'

'No. That's what he told us at the lunch, anyway.'

'How did Mike take that?'

'As Mike would. Thrilled to bits about the reprieve and ignoring the finances. Said he'd pay for the refurbishments himself out of the insurance money on the Porsche if it wasn't found. I knew nothing would work though because, the way he ran it, Old Herne's could still be bankrupt within a year. Whereas if *I* could have taken it over right away there was a chance it could survive.'

That was frank enough. 'How's Peter taking it? Does he see himself as Mr Successor?'

'You bet. He never got on with Mike during the time he worked with him. Told him outright he could do better. Mike took umbrage, got rid of him and brought me in to replace him.' Jessica set off at a brisk pace again, although her eyes were fixed on some distant point of her own – unless the food processing plant in the far distance was of great interest to her. Sheep were peacefully grazing, birds chirping, and there was little but fields to be seen for miles. Murder and company politics made a stark contrast.

'At least out here I can breathe,' she continued at last. 'At present Old Herne's is a nightmare. I just can't believe this is all happening.'

'Define *this*.'

'It's not settled yet, but it looks as if Arthur's plan is for Glenn to be manager, perhaps even the trustee, with me as deputy until the place gets back on its feet. Then he'll rethink. So the jackals are out. Glenn thinks his moment of glory has come but recognizes he needs me as a deputy who knows something about the place, Fenella wants me edged out and herself in. Full stop.'

So Glenn *was* to be manager. It was obvious from the row that he was being given some authority but to be overall manager right away was mind-boggling. No wonder Jessica had looked so stricken. She and everyone else, including me, must have thought she would be number one. Glenn hadn't even been a contender. Affable though he might appear, there was a toughness there that meant I wouldn't care to cross him. Nor the inscrutable Fenella either.

'Is Peter in too?'

'If Peter has anything to do with it, yes, but Arthur's said nothing and Fenella plays her cards close to her skinny chest.'

'What do you think of the Glenn plan?' Unwillingly, I noted that Mike's murder didn't seem to be the focus for those most affected by it – although they might all be suppressing it because it was too much to cope with. Arguing about the politics of Old Herne's could be an escape valve. On the other hand, the murder could have been a fuse to set off this political bomb. I braced myself, because that was why Brandon wanted me to 'stick around'.

'Glenn's better than Boadicea as manager, but not much,' Jessica replied.

'What does Boadicea think about it? Did she calm down after I left?'

'No. She got even more vocal and so did Peter. She's hopping mad, rabbiting on about how she'd been deprived of a childhood through being an orphan and wasn't going to miss out on her rights as an adult. She really sees herself as number one, believe it or not. And me her deputy? No thanks.'

'That wouldn't have lasted five minutes.'

'Nor would Old Herne's, so at least that's spared us.'

'But Glenn lives in the States, so how is it going to work?'

'That was the next sock in my face. Dear Glenn has retired early, likes the look of England and has decided to stay on.'

'With or without the inscrutable Fenella?'

'With.' Her tone indicated that discussion was closed.

Too bad. 'Has the Cat declared her position?'

She managed a brief laugh. 'No, but do you see me being best mates with Fenella? Dark-haired temptresses make me nervous.'

My turn to laugh. 'You've nothing to worry about.'

'Thank you.'

She said it so humbly that I was flummoxed. 'I can see two Jessicas,' I told her quietly. 'The public I'm-the-winner and the private I'm-not-so-sure.'

She stared straight ahead. 'Which one attracts you?'

'No-brainer. The private Jessica.'

'Are there two Jack Colbys?'

'Of course. Everyone has two such faces. Mostly they dovetail but sometimes they don't. Yours don't, though.'

I was very aware of her at my side. She was clearly struggling with the events of the past few days, and the anguish showed on her face. Being in the countryside can strip away defences as the fresh air blows through. Sounds pretentious? Maybe, but it still remains true, although it isn't always for the good. One needs defences.

I took her in my arms, her trembling body against mine, and felt her relax. I found myself kissing her automatically, took command of the situation and then lost it again – as one does. It was Jessica who broke away.

'Later,' she murmured, but I knew she meant it.

'Not much later, please.'

I supposed she was right even though I'd been thinking along different lines. Impractical even for a sunny June day I supposed. Sex in a secluded glade dappled with sunlight, sex in a meadow, sex amongst the sandy dunes or deserted beaches, but in the middle of a cultivated field, somewhat muddy from recent rain, it isn't quite the same. I tried to convince myself it wasn't, anyway.

'So tell me,' I said firmly – anything to get my mind off its current preoccupation. 'What are you going to do in the battle between the Nelsons and Howells? Accept what Arthur offers?'

'Probably, if only to give me thinking time.'

'That seems an indecisive role for you.'

'Only because of Mike, Jack.'

I understood and liked – loved? – her for it. The *real* Jessica, I thought.

'His death has changed everything,' she continued. 'I can't understand who would want to kill him.'

'The answer starts with why,' I said soberly.

'Because of Old Herne's?'

'It could well be. It seems likely it was someone he knew.'

'Why?' she asked. 'Because it wasn't a planned murder? The use of the fire tender and that axe and all that blood—'

'You saw it?' I interrupted. She hadn't been there when I arrived.

'I was at the back of the concert crowd, so not far from Thunderbolts Hangar when the first cries went up. I rushed in – and saw him. I knew I was going to be sick, so I ran outside again. I couldn't take it . . . I told the police all this,' she added, perhaps reading my expression correctly.

One part of me stowed the information away together with the fact that *theoretically* she had reason to want Mike out of the way. Conscience-stricken at even thinking of this, the other part away of me won and I gave her a cuddle of sympathy.

Nevertheless, it had to be said. 'From the Old Herne's viewpoint there are several people who might have wanted Mike out of the way.'

'Me?' she asked sharply.

'Theoretically yes, but dismissed.' Another quick cuddle – partly of relief that she herself had broached the matter.

'Then dismiss Arthur too, even though Mike was busy ruining Old Herne's.'

'Considering he's ninety I feel we can do that,' I said gravely. 'Also Ray Nelson for the same reason.' I felt we were skating on delicate ice, though, bearing in mind that Ray, Peter, Boadicea, Glenn and Fenella only seemed to have been in the bar for part of the interval between Mike shutting the doors to the public and the time his body was discovered.

'There's Glenn,' Jessica said firmly. 'He resented the fact that Mike was losing his father money and saw himself as number one. Which he now is.'

'Early days, but yes.'

'And Fenella.'

'Again, early days, but in theory yes. Improbable but possible. And what about Peter? He sees himself as Mike's natural successor.'

'Of course.'

'And Boadicea?'

Jessica made a face. 'She would be losing her meal ticket. That's why she must have made that stupid claim to take over.'

'Jason?'

'*Jason*?' Jessica stopped in her tracks. 'You can't be serious. Look at him. Anyway, he says he was at the track with Arthur before the concert. Do you see him murdering anyone, let alone his father?'

'I don't *see* him at all. He's an imponderable. That's why I can't ignore him. He's close to Arthur, and there was a rift between him and Mike.'

She still wouldn't have it, and perhaps she was right. But even so there would be crowds at the track, and how does one define 'with' in such crowds?

We both fell silent as we turned back towards Old Herne's and what had been a theoretical exercise became all too real again.

'There's another theoretical possibility,' I said unwillingly. 'People who weren't at the lunch and might have thought Arthur would change his mind about closing it down if Mike were out of the way.'

I didn't have to name names. Jessica had a clear mind. 'You mean volunteers and staff.'

Unwilling though I was to think in such terms, I did indeed mean people like Tim – and theoretically Jessica. Tim said he'd been at the track with Arthur. But for how long?

It was early evening before I reached Frogs Hill. Our discussion had brought murder back to the forefront of our minds, and Jessica's 'later' was, by mutual unspoken assent, gently laid aside as regards ratification. Nevertheless, I had discovered she lived in Bearsted, a village on the outskirts of Maidstone, and that she had an ex-husband somewhere and a daughter at university. She in turn had discovered about my Spanish werewolf ex-wife Eva, now safely living in Spain, I hoped, and also (rather reluctantly) I told her about Louise. I also explained I had a daughter Cara, living in Suffolk with her farming partner Harry, who divided her time between freelance journalism and running a farm shop for Harry. My past, I told her, was a locked door, except that Cara had a permanent key.

Frogs Hill was deserted. The Pits' doors were long shut and Len and Zoe gone for the day. There was a message on the landline from Dave changing the pick-up time to nine thirty on the morrow. Even the pleasure of possibly being able to drive Mike's Porsche home didn't cheer me this evening though as I went into the front drawing-room to open the windows for some fresh air before night closed in.

And then I heard it. It was coming up Frogs Hill Lane, just the faintest sound. Someone whistling. So what, I told myself uneasily. Even in these days men sometimes whistled at work.

But who would be *walking* along the lane at this time of night? Country walkers do so by day, but this was early evening, and besides, country walkers don't usually send a shiver up my spine – and this whistling did. I could hear it getting nearer. Dog roses bloomed in the banks each side of the lane and the air was full of the sweet smells of June evenings, but the whistling still came on, nearer and nearer.

I identified the tune – it was 'Mack the Knife', the creepiest sound of all in the still evening silence, and then I knew who the whistler must be. You don't find him, he finds you.

It was Doubler.

SIX

I summoned up what sangfroid I had left and walked out to meet my foe, feeling as if I were in Hollywood's version of the Wild West. This was real, however, and this was now; it was not the OK Corral, though it might seem like it. Overstating the case? Not where Doubler was concerned.

The gates were still open and I stood by them, waiting. The whistling had stopped at the final bend in the lane before the entrance to Frogs Hill and so at any moment he would be marching through the gates. He'd have heard my footsteps crunching on the gravel forecourt, so he would know I was here.

And then in the fading light I saw him.

First impression: what was I worried about? He was slight, shortish and thin-faced. I was over six foot, solidly built and definitely looked pugnacious (I hoped).

Second impression: I should run like hell. This was one creepy guy and not just by reputation. He looked it. The face was reptilian, and so was the way he walked. He didn't exactly slither, it was more of an inexorable glide; he turned slightly from side to side as he did so, as though distributing his venom from an invisible spray can. This was a man who walked with a purpose and he was coming my way.

By superhuman effort, I stayed where I was. 'I thought I heard someone out here.' I tried to make it sound offhand but I could hear the croak in my voice.

He came through the gates – and I took an involuntary step backwards. He was invading my space – and then I realized he wasn't. It had only felt like it. He was three feet or so away, although it seemed a whole lot closer.

'Doubler's the name,' he told me, sounding so matter of fact that I was almost fooled.

I nodded. 'Jack Colby.' My voice sounded almost normal.

'Heard about your place here.' His eyes roved over the Pits, whose security lights were now flashing again like crazy. I didn't blame them. So were my internal signals.

'And I've heard about you.' I tried to sound nonchalant.

'Have you now. You surprise me. I could do with a drink.'

'Pub?' Images flashed through my mind of what might happen if I allowed him inside the farmhouse: dagger in the back; a sharp snap of the neck; those hands round my neck . . . car detective found murdered in his own kitchen . . . found hung from a tree in his own garden . . .

'A nice mug of tea is what I fancy.'

'OK.' I tried to take comfort from this and from his reputation of not carrying weapons. Unless he'd made an exception . . . Mike had died and possibly at the hands of the Porsche thief, who could well have been Doubler. Should it be the Pits or the farmhouse? The Pits has a small cordoned-off kitchen area for Len and Zoe's use, but then he would see what was inside the Pits, putting our cars at risk. I took the gamble. 'Come into the farmhouse – more comfortable there.'

A nod and I could see he knew exactly what my reasoning was. He followed me in like any normal visitor. He sat at my kitchen table just as if he were one of my chums; and yet somehow his presence turned the usual friendly warmth of my kitchen to something quite different. The atmosphere was heavy and almost menacing, as though I were the alien here, not Doubler.

'I heard you'd been asking about me, Mr Colby,' Doubler began conversationally.

'Not spot on, Mr Doubler.' Two could play at politeness. 'I was asking around about Mike Nelson's Porsche on behalf of the Car Crime Unit and your name came up.'

'Good blokes at the Unit,' he said approvingly. 'I'd be sorry to put any of them down.'

Swift move called for. After the split second it took me to take in what he'd said, I played my queen on this open chessboard. 'For your own sake that would surely be a bad move.'

Doubler considered this and let it pass. 'Heard you've found the article in question.'

'That was quick,' I said with genuine admiration. 'It's only just been located, but it's not verified yet. That being so, what I

can do for you?' Or would he do for me? I dismissed this
unwelcome thought.

'Not bad tea, this.' A pause, then he looked most serious.
'Sometimes in life, Jack, you takes a wrong turning, as you might
say. One sees a thing of beauty, breathtaking beauty, and thinks
to yourself: no, that thing is far too beautiful to be lost to the
world.'

I blenched, hoping I didn't come under his category of
breathtaking beauty.

He noticed, but continued: 'So I relents. I, as you may have
heard, Jack, have a soft heart. There aren't too many beautiful
things out there in this mucky old world of ours and I like them
to be preserved.'

Time to make another stand. 'I haven't a clue what you're
talking about.'

'And that, Jack my friend, is how it's going to remain.
Get it?'

I did. Gone was soft-hearted Doubler. Here were the cold
hooded eyes, the calculating look. Just for an instant he deliberately let me see the killer in him. If I was at risk, he would strike
now, and I watched his hand on the mug like a hawk. It didn't
move. The moment passed, but I'd lock my windows very tightly
tonight.

'*Very* nice tea this,' he added approvingly.

I informed him it came from Pluckley, not far from Frogs Hill
and the village considered to host more ghosts than any other in
Kent.

He listened carefully before commenting. 'So, Jack, it's like
this. I'm like one of them ghosts. You haven't seen me and
I've never been to this place. Not a whisper, not a word or
you'll be one of them. Got it?'

'Wrong. The police are following the Porsche story up and
I'm involved. So might you be. I might stop, but the police won't.'
All my fingers were mentally crossed – or would be when they
had stopped trembling.

'Just leave them to me, Jack.'

I couldn't let it go at that. '*If* I can.'

A vision of Brandon and Dave's faces if they thought I was
trading with Doubler floated before me, and momentarily I forgot

the more immediate threat. 'There's Mike Nelson's murder to consider,' I continued. 'The car might be connected to that. Somebody wanted that car so badly they hired you to pinch it.'

He actually grinned. 'You disappoint me, Jack, you really do. I don't go pinching anything. I arrange things for people – weddings, funerals. I'm what you'd call a consultant.'

'Including Mike Nelson's death?'

The cold eye treatment again. 'That's what I came here for. To remind you I don't touch murder.' A long pause. 'Unless I've no choice.'

He stood up. Any minute now . . . I could feel my heart pounding as he put his mug down, carefully placing it on the coaster, and put his hand into his pocket. 'I'll just use your toilet, Jack, and then I'll be going. It's a long walk back.'

'Can't afford a car?' I quipped, weak with relief when all he produced from the pocket was a torch.

'You will have your little joke, Jack. Just remember I don't do jokes. I do like walking. I can think better that way. The car's at Piper's Green.'

What, I wondered, was I going to find when Doubler had gone? A Medici-like contraption on the lavatory to plunge a dagger into me? Electrified wash taps? Poison in the soap?

He left Frogs Hill quietly enough, and I heard him whistling all the way down Frogs Hill Lane until the sound faded. Only it wasn't 'Mack the Knife' any more. It was 'John Brown's Body'. Oh great! I found no poisoned soap left behind however, nor daggers, only an artificial poppy probably left over from last Remembrance Sunday. Odd, because Doubler did nothing by chance.

'You what, Jack? This a joke?'

I've never seen Len look scared before, but at my mentioning – for my own safety as much as anything – that Doubler had been at Frogs Hill the evening before he went white with shock.

'Didn't let him into the Pits, did you?' he threw at me.

'No way.' Thank heavens I hadn't. Len would have spent several months checking every nut and bolt in the place for sabotage.

Even Zoe looked perturbed. 'I hope you know what you're doing, Jack.'

'I'm not *doing* anything with Doubler. He came here uninvited.'

'What for?' they demanded in unison.

'I wish I knew. He was undoubtedly involved in the Porsche theft, but that doesn't automatically make him an active participant in Mike's murder.'

'I don't follow,' Zoe said aggressively.

I tried to reason it out. 'Involvement in the murder as well as the theft would imply some kind of insurance scam but then the car wouldn't have been found again. It would have been out of the country quicker than a Sunbeam Tiger on the loose. Instead it turns up in Sussex, probably bought in the marketplace.'

'That's not like Doubler,' Len commented.

'That seems to be his line too.'

Silence. 'Well, at least the Porsche is safe,' Zoe said practically.

It was, so why *had* Doubler come to see me, as he must have heard that the car had been found? Was it to dissociate himself from the Porsche – or to warn me off? I couldn't see why he would have materialized in person for a mere stolen car, even that Porsche, but nor would he have done so if it *was* involved in Mike's murder. His talk of not destroying a beautiful object didn't make sense if it was Mike's car he was talking about, because there was no way Doubler would have returned it to its rightful owner, even if he had gone dewy-eyed over its beauty. Nor would anyone in their right senses, let alone Mike, destroy that Porsche for an insurance scam when it could have been sold for its full insurance value.

'Doubler's trouble, Jack,' Len warned.

'I know that. I'm not planning on doing business with him.'

I got my comeuppance for sarcasm. Two backs were turned to me as they bent over the Wolseley Hornet twin carburettors that had to be synchronized during their tuning of this beguiling car. I left them to it, having heard the toot of Dave's horn, and I went outside to join him. He duly drove in with a flourish in his police BMW and wound down the window to yell greetings at me. Time to meet Mrs Ansty – and the Porsche.

'Good to have a day out now and then,' he added as I joined him in the car.

'Great. Especially as you're paying me for the honour.'

'Delighted,' he replied wryly. 'We're meeting the Sussex lads HQ at Burwash Forstal, where the unlucky owner lives.'

'How did she take the news?'

'Badly, I'm told.'

'How old's this Mrs Ansty? Youngish blonde, trendy? It has to be someone with a real eye for Porsches.'

'Oldish blonde. Mid sixties.'

'Buying that Porsche?' I was flabbergasted. 'Who is she? A relative of Bill Gates?'

'School dinner lady, just retired.'

'You *are* joking, Dave?'

'I take my work seriously.' He grinned at me. 'It's true.'

'Then how, when, why and where?'

'That,' Dave said, as we negotiated a difficult turn at Biddenden, 'we shall discover.'

Burwash and its satellite hamlets Burwash Common, Burwash Weald and Burwash Forstal are not far inside the Sussex border if one is travelling from Kent and so I knew the area well. Even so, when Dave turned off into Appleoak Lane I was in new territory. Ahead of us were the rolling hills that had so attracted Kipling at the turn of last century. I mention him because he lived at Bateman's on the far side of Burwash in a similar lane to this one. It now belongs to the National Trust and I know it well. I've a great affection for Bateman's – especially for the honour awarded to Kipling's splendid Rolls-Royce Phantom I displayed in its own garage in the gardens, glass-fronted like the one at Old Herne's. I drool over that car quite frequently.

The hamlet of Burwash Forstal was not far from Burwash village, and Broome Cottage was one of a small nest of houses. It was an attractive white-painted stone detached house with a garden at the front and no doubt at the rear as well, giving the picturesque impression, as so many cottages do, that it was sheltered from the storms of life. Its garage was independent of the house but our quarry was not in it. The Porsche was parked outside the front door, looking out of place but magnificent 'eye candy', as they say.

It was Mike's. No doubt about that, and with its stylish headlights pointing towards us as we approached it looked almost indignant at its current residence. There it was, its silver paint gleaming, looking as spic and span as the day it left the Stuttgart factory in 1963.

Further along the lane I could see not only the Sussex police car but also a parked low-loader, so any hopes that I would be driving the Porsche back to its Kentish home myself receded. By the side of the Porsche stood a truculent-looking lady, arms folded aggressively across her chest and ready, it seemed, to defend her rights against all comers. She had her eye on the driver of the low-loader, who was walking along to join us together with the Sussex reinforcements. These consisted of a rather nice looking chap in his thirties, who introduced himself as DI Maine, and a constable, PC Middlemas. They told us they had arrived fifteen minutes earlier, had been routed by the dinner lady and were regrouping for another assault. The low-loader driver took a closer look at the opposition and wisely returned to his cab to rejoin his companion and admire the distant hills.

'Leave this to me,' Dave said grandly. Being a family man, he reckons he has a way with elderly ladies.

Not that this one looked elderly. Medium height, medium build, but there was nothing else medium about her. She had blonde hair, was neatly clad in the kind of clothes magazines deem suitable for 'country living', and had eyes flashing fury at us like warning lights at a level crossing. Hers were going to take longer to clear, I reckoned.

She stood her ground as Dave and I approached.

'Detective Superintendent Jennings,' I introduced the party. 'Kent Car Crime Unit. Detective Inspector Maine, Police Constable Middlemas, Sussex Police. I'm Jack Colby, working with them on this case.'

'*This case*,' Mrs Ansty repeated with scorn. 'I've been informed you all believe that this car has been stolen and that you insist it still belongs to the previous owner. Well, have I got news for you. It's mine.'

Constable Middlemas was already checking the plates and inside of the car, so I tackled the chassis number and engine, which of course didn't tally with Mike's. A number punch had been at work, falsifying enough numbers to ensure it went through the registration process safely. Why, it occurred to me, had the 'dealer' – presumably from Doubler's set-up – not shipped it abroad where the registration process could be simpler? However, this was certainly Mike's car. Naturally enough there was no service book in the door pouch to prove provenance, but the engine and the roll bar welded to the body channels put it beyond doubt. All we needed now was the fake documents that Mrs Ansty must be holding. I nodded to Dave to say I was satisfied and she interpreted this correctly.

'Come inside,' she said wearily. 'I've got all the paperwork laid out for you including the bill of sale to prove I bought it from a dealer and therefore that means the car belongs to me. Nevertheless –' the hint of a smile – 'I suppose I could run to some coffee for you.' She might be calmer now but she showed every sign of being a hurricane when roused.

Three of us went in, leaving the constable to watch for any last minute rescue attempts by persons unknown hiding in the undergrowth. A sense of fair play made me think we were somewhat crowding her inside this small house, but I need not have worried. Three hulking policemen were nothing to her. She dominated the small room to which she led us. Coffee preparations accounted for one table, a desk was laid out with the papers, and chairs were dotted around for convenience. She had been fully prepared.

'There it all is,' she indicated. 'Take your pick.'

She busied herself with coffee while we did just that. Dave and DI Maine began to go through them but I was more interested in the lady herself. Why had she chosen this car to buy? For a retired school dinner lady it seemed a mismatch, to say the least.

'I'm told the person you think owns the car has died, and so I'm doubly sorry for his family,' Mrs Ansty told me, and she was clearly sincere. 'But I do have rights, I'm sure of that. I bought it in good faith from a dealer and it's an expensive car, so you can't expect me to hand it over just like that. I tried to ring the dealer to tell him I was having trouble but there was no reply.'

Dave looked up at this and cleared his throat. 'The problem is, Mrs Ansty, that this dealer of yours, Samuel Palmer, he doesn't exist.'

'Nonsense,' she said happily. 'Of course he does. I bought it from him – well, from his partner, which is the same thing. The partner is Samuel Palmer, but it was Simon Marsh who made all the arrangements. He assured me the car was a bargain.' For the first time a note of doubt flashed across her face as she looked from one to the other of us.

'Did you go to the office to see the car?' Simon Marsh's 'office', Dave had told me, was said to be in south London, and, guess what, that didn't exist either.

'No. It was such a way to go that Simon said he'd drive it over here for me to see.' More doubt on her face. 'I'd not long moved here, so I was all too glad to accept. I'm retired now and it was a new life, so I wanted a new car.'

'The firm of Palmer and Marsh truly does not exist,' DI Maine assured her. 'We've checked it out.'

'But Simon Marsh does because I've met him,' she said obstinately. 'He had all the paperwork from the last owner – a gentleman in Spain, I believe. Anyway, as you see, it's now been registered with Swansea and they didn't find anything wrong with the documentation.'

'They wouldn't.' I tried to break this to her gently. 'For them it was a first registration, so if the foreign paperwork all added up and the engine and chassis numbers had been altered so that they didn't show up on their records, no alarm bells would go off. But the Porsche Club 356 Register whom you contacted is a different matter,' I explained. 'They know the engine and chassis numbers of every 356 ever built and every series. Yours didn't fit in the engine sequence numbers so it was an instant giveaway. Did you register it yourself with Swansea?'

'Well no, Simon said he'd do it for me, because he had all the previous owner's paperwork, but the registration document came straight to me from the DVLA. All in order,' she said crossly. 'I spent a lot of money on this car.'

My heart bled for her. Simon Marsh had done the registration? How generous of him. 'How much did he charge you for the car?'

'Twenty thousand pounds.' She looked at our astounded faces, slightly puzzled. 'That's a lot, isn't it?'

She must have been thinking that our astonishment was because she had paid too much, poor woman. Considering the insurance on this car must be for at least a quarter of a million pounds and probably much more, she had a bargain – or would have done if it had been a legitimate sale. Even without Mike's car's provenance, any Porsche 356, with that Carrera engine, would be insured for way over the twenty thousand she'd paid.

The formalities took some time to sort out, and Jennifer Ansty grew quieter and quieter, answering questions briefly and not volunteering any more information. When DCI Maine told her they'd have to take the car back with them, she seemed past raising any objection, which suggested she was licking her wounds with a vengeance. If this car had anything to do with Mike's death, now was the time to find out, by stepping in both as counsellor and investigator.

So I made a start. 'If you're going back to Heathfield, Dave, could you pick me up later from the Bear pub in Burwash village? I'll get a bite to eat there.'

A nudge is all Dave needs, luckily – he guessed what my plan was. Burwash village was easily within walking distance and the Bear is a favourite pub of mine. Kindly Dave might be, as well as understanding Mrs Ansty's devastation, he would also realize I might get nuggets of information on my own that wouldn't be revealed to a threesome. It was midday when they left so the timing was perfect for me to invite her to lunch.

'We'll be off then,' Dave said in an artificially jolly way that should not have deceived a mouse chasing a lump of cheese, but Jennifer Ansty was past noticing. She was too busy watching her beloved car vanish on to the low-loader.

'I don't understand,' she said forlornly. 'I paid for it, it's mine and it's registered.'

'Talk about it over lunch?' I suggested. 'Come to the Bear with me.'

'I haven't got a car,' she whipped back smartly. Then she relented. 'I suppose the walk will do me good.'

It took fifteen minutes or so to reach the Bear, and as she stepped out smartly beside me chatting generally about life in Burwash, I wondered again why on earth she had chosen this Porsche. Generalizations are notoriously dangerous, but the Porsche never seemed to me a very feminine car and Jenny, as she had asked me to call her, was a very feminine lady.

'The police told me you worked at a school before you retired,' I said.

'Yes. The Sandborne Academy for Girls, near Sherborne in Dorset.'

I'd heard of it and was impressed. 'You were the chef?' I asked politely.

'Dinner Lady Supreme,' she rejoined, more cheerfully now we were on safer ground. 'Choose it, cook it, serve it. With help,' she added, actually managing a laugh.

'Most people retire *to* Sherborne,' I pointed out. 'You seem to be doing things the other way round.'

She didn't answer and it wasn't until we arrived at the pub that she relaxed a little. Indeed, she walked into it with the air of knowing it well, greeting all the staff by name before we went into the rear garden to choose a table with a view. 'Are you a regular here?' I asked.

'They know me quite well. I used to stay here before I moved to Burwash, when my uncle was alive. When he died I inherited the cottage, but I rented it out until this year.'

'So that's why you moved east. Unusual though.'

'Ah,' she said. 'That was the point.'

'Point of what?'

'Buying the Porsche. I expect you've been wondering.'

'I was. It's an outstanding car but not one I'd have thought would be your first choice.'

'Because it's old?'

'No. There are plenty of classics around that would suit you if that were the reason. An Austin-Healey for example. You have to really know cars to love Porsche 356s and know them even better to pick one with a Carrera engine. Most people admire them from afar, but to love them enough to buy them? That's really something. Would it surprise you to know that the car you've briefly possessed could be worth over three hundred thousand pounds?'

She blinked. 'I don't believe you.'

'It's true, but then you're not a car enthusiast or you'd know that.'

She was highly indignant. 'How can you possibly judge?'

I sighed. 'The price and set-up alone should have been decidedly suspicious to anyone, not just a car buff.'

'They weren't to me,' she said obstinately. 'Simon did all the business side. I'd been introduced to him, after all.'

Well, of course, I thought. To a woman like this an introduction would make all the difference between trustworthiness and mistrust.

'Where did all the negotiations take place?' I asked.

'At a hotel where I met him – at a Women's Institute meeting.'

'He belonged to the WI?'

This earned me a scathing look. 'He was another member's brother, so he said. We talked about cars – I needed one and he told me about the Porsche. A real bargain he told me. He didn't live far from me and the office was miles away so he said he would drive it over for me to have a look. No obligation.'

'And you bought it on the spot?'

More indignation. 'I'm not that daft. Of course I didn't. I had to arrange the money.'

Even so, a Porsche? I thought. Something didn't fit. This was a lady who knew her own mind. She might have fallen for a confidence trickster but she wouldn't pass over what to her was a small fortune for a car she didn't fall for hook line and sinker, with or without the careful checks on the car and its seller. And I could not imagine this woman as part of a master gang under Doubler's rule.

'Anyway, why shouldn't I?' she finished, avoiding my eye. 'Don't you make instant judgements sometimes?'

'No.'

'Why not?'

'Experience.'

'Of what? Women or cars?'

There was a definite flirty note in her voice, but not, I thought thankfully, personal, given the age gap, so it was safe for me to reply, 'Both.'

She considered this. 'You're right and you're wrong. I did want the Porsche. Loved it at first sight, but if I'd been ten years older – even five – I wouldn't have bought it.'

'Too powerful?'

She swept this aside. 'Wrong image.'

'Image of what?' I asked curiously.

'It's quite simple, Jack. I've been a widow for five years.

Sherborne is not the world. I wasn't ready for retiring from the world, only from the school. I wanted a new life, as I told those policemen.'

'And you thought you would find it in Burwash?'

'Yes. I moved three months ago. I've now unpacked all the boxes and I'm ready for the new world. By which,' she added, 'I mean men.'

I reeled at this matter of fact statement. 'Another husband?'

'No. I'd prefer to phrase it as "choice of male companionship".'

'The merry widow?' I was still absorbing this angle.

'Exactly, and what better for that role than that Porsche – which, as you said, is a man's car, rather than a woman's. But,' she said darkly, 'now that's been stolen from me. Do I get compensation?'

'Not unless the owners are generous.'

'Who are they?'

'I can't tell you that.'

'No need to be stuffy. It was Mike Nelson's, wasn't it? That poor man who's just been murdered.'

I said nothing, which gave her my answer.

'It's obvious, I suppose,' she continued, 'but I really thought I'd bought it legally. And,' she added warningly, 'you can tell the family and their solicitors that I'll be in touch.'

'Quite a lady,' I told Dave when he eventually arrived. Jenny had returned to Broome Cottage and left me contemplating the Downs. Her 'merry widow' explanation of the car added up, I conceded, and this Simon Marsh sounded just right for a Doubler associate. And yet it was still an odd story and did not tie in with Mike's death.

'Bought it from a man she'd met in a hotel bar,' Dave said in disgust. 'Wouldn't believe women could be so daft, would you?'

'Not just women,' I pointed out. 'And it's not always straightforward.'

He looked at me with interest. 'In this case?'

'Probably OK. She's seems bright enough.'

'Did she tell you she paid cash?'

I groaned. I don't often miss a trick but he'd caught me on

this one. At least it pleased Dave, and he'd milk this one for all it was worth. He was grinning like a Cheshire Cat that had no intention of disappearing.

'Did she, or rather Mr Non-Upright Citizen – who doubtless is not called Simon Marsh – give a reason for wanting cash?' I asked.

'Two. He and his partners were apparently sole traders and had been rooked too many times by accepting dodgy cheques and, as she admittedly rather shamefacedly, he had told her they would have to add VAT to the bill if it wasn't cash.'

Unlike magpies, one reason is OK, but it's two that usually bring sorrow. There *is* no VAT on second-hand goods. So that was it. Jenny had indeed been hoodwinked.

'Cheer up,' Dave said. 'I'm taking you to Heathfield.'

'For what?' I asked suspiciously.

'That's where the police pound is. You can drive the Porsche back to its home when they've finished with it. Won't be long.'

The day looked a whole lot brighter 'Thanks, Dave.'

'Not at all. Saves us money. Anyway, I bet you packed your Frogs Hill plates in that bag of yours.'

'As it happens, I did. Only reason I came,' I joked. I should have known better.

He had the last laugh. 'No need to put it on your bill then.'

SEVEN

Oh what a beautiful morning. Or so it seemed as the Porsche and I sang a sort of duet as I drove it along the A20 on its way back to its rightful home. What could possibly go wrong while Porsche 356s remained to cheer the darkest hour and the sun shone approvingly down on us as the Carrera engine purred? Answer: I was well aware that quite a lot could go wrong, beginning with the fact that the 'rightful home' had a question mark attached to it, now that Mike had died. For this brief interval, however, I decided to put the gruesome horror of his murder out of my mind while I and this magical car were the cynosure of all eyes this Saturday morning as we sped along.

As I turned off the A20 to drive up Stede Hill on the way to Old Herne's, uncomfortable reality began to kick in once more. I plunged into the familiar maze of lanes, wishing I could see my way forward over my mission for Arthur Howell as clearly as I knew this route – and aware that I was driving a possible key element in it. Work out why, and I would be well on my way. But the key remained elusive. The trees overhanging the lanes seemed as though they were gloating over me, delighted that they could remove the sunlight from my path.

Already, it was ceasing to be such a beautiful morning. I knew Jessica was working this weekend and the prospect of seeing her was a big incentive, but there were a lot of minuses to face. Once Dave had officially notified the insurance people and the solicitors, I had rung to tell her I was coming, as there had been a snag. I'd expected to be told to deliver the Porsche either to Boadicea at High House or to Jason, but far from it. The instructions were to take to its garage at Old Herne's, where someone would be waiting. Regardless of who this someone was, I knew I'd be treading on eggshells. Only six days had passed since Mike's death, but *something* must surely have emerged about who had inherited the car if it was found.

When I rang to ask if there had been any developments on Mike's case that I should know about, Brandon had been non-committal, save on one point. 'Nothing on the prints on the Crossley – too many of them,' he told me. 'Nor on the floor. But the greatcoat has Jarvis's DNA on it. We're waiting for the lab on everything else.'

After the initial shock I realized that the greatcoat would almost certainly have had Tim's DNA on it – and no doubt that of other volunteers too. As for the Porsche, Dave had told me that no prints of interest had shown up on it – only mine and Jenny Ansty's.

'The dealer wore gloves in summertime?' I had asked smartly.

Smart answer back. 'If he's one of Doubler's crew, he's a pro.'

I had told Dave most of my conversation with Doubler and endured the inevitable grilling that followed. I'd be marked down as a double agent from now on – a difficult situation to be in, though I had pointed out that it could be useful too. Grudging assent from Dave, but I was a marked man.

'No damage to the car though,' I had pointed out. 'That's interesting too.'

'Could be,' Dave had replied, as if indulging a small child.

It was interesting to me at least. The Porsche wasn't Chitty Chitty Bang Bang. It couldn't have flown from Old Herne's to Burwash, and clean though Doubler liked to maintain his hands it must have gone through at least two pairs of mucky ones before Mrs Ansty obliged with her cash. One pair to nick it, probably one to fix the plates and another to sweet-talk Jenny Ansty under the name of Simon Marsh.

On the latter front I had had a minor breakthrough. One of my contacts had rung me with a name. This contact believes in codes at all times and so when he mentioned Bernard it immediately rang up the name Alex Shaw in my mental data bank. Shaw was one of the suavest villains around, and thought to be one of Doubler's closest allies – 'thought' because with Doubler nothing is known for certain. But Shaw was just the type to appeal to Burwash's merry widow; apparently, he so subtly indicates he is from the upper echelons of society that Jenny would have trusted his patter – at first, anyway. The cash element should have made her blink. Anyway, this was a good lead.

Only, nothing looked exactly good as I drove up to Old Herne's gates. Old Herne's itself has some bushes but hardly any trees around its perimeter except on the northern side where High House stands. There woodland looks forbiddingly over to the club as though given the right circumstances those massive oaks would advance in an unstoppable phalanx to repel invaders.

There's a legend about a ghost called Herne the Hunter who haunts Windsor Great Park and who brings trouble in his wake when he decides to walk. He's said to have been a hunter who hung himself in the park centuries ago, but it's more likely he dates back for many more centuries when he was not a hunter but a Celtic god. Old Herne's Club derives its name from an old word for corner, but I did wonder if Herne the Hunter's ghost occasionally travelled to Kent for a trip, having packed a whole load of trouble in his backpack. He might be here now. The sun had gone in, the clouds were gathering and those trees looked distinctly menacing. There were a lot of cars in the car park although I knew Old Herne's was still officially closed.

Whether the hunter's ghost was here or not, I ran into trouble right away. The 'someone' whom I'd been told would be meeting me at the control tower garage turned out to be a formidable line-up of 'someones' outside the clubhouse. The word had clearly got around quickly to produce this reception committee. No way could I drive past with a mere cheery wave. As I approached I could see Boadicea, Glenn, someone I didn't recognize, Tim – and Jason. His biker jacket hung on him, his shoulders were hunched, and yet as he moved to welcome me he turned from a nondescript figure into a man of grace and charm.

Maybe Herne's ghost was indeed here, because none of them looked happy, which set me back, as the discovery of the Porsche, albeit in these circumstances, was surely to be welcomed. Thrown off my stride, all I could say as I leapt out of the Porsche was a weak: 'Here she is. Not a scratch on her.'

The only person to whom that brought cheer was Tim, who hurried over to touch the car with a loving hand as if to make sure it was real. He then prowled round it twice and dropped to the ground to check its underparts.

'It really is Mike's,' I assured him. 'The Frogs Hill garage plates are on it now, but you'll need new ones of course, Tim.' Not knowing who now owned it, Tim seemed the safest to address.

The stranger, a man in his fifties and formally dressed, cleared his throat. 'Mr Pryde –' he turned to Jason – 'you can take the car if you wish. It is legally yours.' By which I assumed he was the solicitor for Mike's estate.

'*That* is not yet certain.' Boadicea, clad today in regal purple, shook with indignation. 'My husband no longer possessed the Porsche – if this *is* the same car – when he died, so there was nothing to bequeath to Jason. Now it's returned it's mine, just as the insurance money would have been my husband's and now mine.'

I'm no lawyer but this sounded dubious. I was right, for the solicitor prepared for battle. 'The will and the law are quite clear, I'm afraid, Mrs Nelson. As I've explained to you, the car was merely stolen but legally still belonged to Mr Nelson when he died, and therefore now belongs to Mr Pryde.'

He glanced at Jason, who nodded, and then he continued with what sounded a well-rehearsed speech. 'Mr Nelson wanted Mr Pryde to have the car because it was with his mother, Mr Nelson's first wife, that he shared his early years of ownership of the car.'

Looking at the assembled faces, I could see the car was already a bone of contention because no one reacted – except Boadicea.

'Nonsense,' she said firmly. 'That car was my husband's only asset and, as I said, I need money. He would never have left me penniless. He was a man of honour. There must be another will somewhere. He was estranged from Jason and would have retracted the will you claim is valid.'

This was obviously not a new line because the solicitor merely replied wearily, 'Then you must find it, Mrs Nelson. I do not have it, and nor did your late husband ever mention it to me. You're free to drive the car away, Mr Pryde.'

Drive it away? The shock on Tim's face was pitiful as Jason promptly came round to the driver's door and opened it. 'You're not going to take it away from Old Herne's, are you?'

'Not far, Tim,' Jason told him. 'We don't want it disappearing again, do we?'

The agony on Tim's face was unbearable. 'But it belongs here, at old Herne's.'

'Leave it with me,' Jason replied ambiguously.

Boadicea had not given up on the solicitor, however. 'I shall contest this. My husband could not bequeath the car to anyone once it had been stolen. So it is mine, but I shall look for that second will which undoubtedly exists.'

I thought she sounded less sure of herself now. No one replied and Jason started up the Porsche with that familiar confident roar of its engine. My part in its story was over. I had some sympathy for Terminator Boadicea. Mike had been broke, and if the house belonged not to him but to Ray Nelson the car would indeed be important to her without his salary coming in. The fact that Mike had bequeathed the Porsche to Jason in memory of his first wife must also be hard for Boadicea to take.

I'd arranged with Len and Zoe to pick me up when I was ready to leave, but I delayed calling them until I'd had a chance to talk to Jessica, who had already returned to the clubhouse. So I strolled over to the track to wait a while. The bandstand was still waiting to be dismantled and it was hard to remember last Sunday's concert, with the air full of music and songs. Just their names – 'Forever England', 'Yesterday is Tomorrow' – conjured up the familiar rich soaring voice of first Miranda Pryde and then Jason.

The track, too, held memories of past Swooshes, not only for me, of course, but for all the veterans of the last world war who recalled the sound of the Spitfire Merlin engines. For Arthur Howell this track would always bring back memories of the day his Thunderbolt crash-landed. It was little wonder that he cherished his ride round it in the Morgan and Mike's ceremonial drive in the Crossley.

What would happen to Old Herne's under Glenn's rule? He might be full of confidence about its future himself, but no one else seemed to be. I paid a reluctant farewell to the track and returned to the clubhouse. There was no sign of anyone outside so I went in cautiously, not wanting to precipitate myself into a lions' den without prior warning.

No one seemed to be around – except for the lovely Hedda, who giggled when she saw me. 'Looking for the gang? They're getting ready for the next round.'

'Upstairs?' I asked.

'Dunno. Retired to their corners, anyway.'

'Jessica too?'

'Last time I saw her she was calming my step-granny down.'

I pitied her that job. Boadicea didn't look in any state to listen to reason.

I decided to wait awhile and track Tim down in the meantime. As I reached the control tower I could see the Morgan in solitary state through the glass and it looked even lonelier now that its companion had been found and driven away again. I was puzzled as to why Jason had taken it, but he obviously didn't trust its being left here and perhaps he had good reason for that. I could see no sign of Tim in Thunderbolts, but as I turned back I saw him emerging from Morgans with Glenn. Tim still looked far from happy but gave me a nod as he scuttled past me as if to imply he had urgent business elsewhere.

Glenn, however, greeted me with benevolent affability, as though I were his favourite drinking chum. It was hard not to warm to him although I wouldn't want to work with him and I pitied Jessica. J. Edgar Hoover probably presented a similar jolly face while he constantly denied the existence of organized crime in the US.

'You stalking me?' Glenn joked. 'Dad said you'd be around a lot. You've sure made a good start with that Porsche.'

Like for like. 'Thanks. Good to hear you'll be around for a while too.'

'Till we've sorted something out for this old heap of a business.'

Ominous. 'Don't sort it too much,' I told him. 'A heap of relics is what Old Herne's is about.'

'Old relics don't bring in the dollars, Jack. Footfall does.'

'Footfall needs carrots to tempt it.'

'Good food. Good drink. Smarten the place up.'

I could hear alarm bells loud and clear. 'Make sure you don't throw the baby out with the bathwater.'

'Baby? What baby?'

Language breakdown. 'Don't throw the car away because the number plate's rusty.'

He eyed me narrowly – as in all the best thrillers – but that didn't mean I wasn't going to take Glenn very seriously indeed. 'Nice way of putting it, Jack. Nope, just need to tidy the place up.'

In my view, non-tidiness was what gave Old Herne's its special appeal, but I decided I had taken the battle far enough. It would be Tim's and Jessica's job to gallop up to the front line. My role had to be appeasement.

'You're taking over in tough circumstances,' I said.

'And how.'

They might be tough, but that might also be in his favour. Mike's family, including Jason, would be focused on other matters than running Old Herne's, so if Glenn's aim was to ease out the old guard the timing would be good. Except for Jessica – and Peter Nelson. Peter had not made an appearance today, but that didn't mean he was abandoning a claim on Old Herne's. Biding his time? Jessica too, perhaps. She had only been here for two months and so with luck she might count as new not old guard in Glenn's eyes. Whether she could be persuaded to adapt to any great new designs that Glenn (or Fenella) might come up with was another matter. I wondered if Glenn's plan might be to run Old Herne's for a year or so, getting Arthur to put money into it, then return to the States and persuade Arthur, who looked good for a long time yet, to break the trust and put Old Herne's on the market with him as chief legatee under Arthur's will.

'What do you reckon, Jack? Does this place have a future?' Glenn continued. His tone was casual, but the eyes were as sharp as a kestrel's. There were several birds of prey that frequently visited Old Herne's, but this one looked as if it could be dangerous when hungry. I thought of all Old Herne's had to offer. I thought of all the magical places in the world that, like Old Herne's, had become political battlegrounds, bringing so much destruction that the original attraction had been reduced to ruins. I couldn't bear to see that happen to Old Herne's, but I knew better than to ride my charger into battle before requested.

So all I remarked was: 'I hope so.'

He pounced. 'So what are *you* really here for?' Luckily, before I could answer he continued, 'Dad said you're some kind of consultant on the classic car side, but what with the Porsche being back and Tim to advise me I guess you'll be off pretty soon.'

And wouldn't that be good, was the unspoken message. I put

on a look of astonishment. 'Not for a while. I'll be liaising with your father on the car side of the business.'

He wasn't going to fall for it. 'And that's all you're here for?'

'No.'

'What else?' A distinct edge in the amiable voice now.

'Jessica Hart.'

The kestrel's eyes relaxed. 'Good-looking lady, that.'

I'd batted the ball back successfully but another one zinged along.

'Give her a tip from me,' he added. 'Tell her to take it easy with Fenella.'

'Not in my remit.'

'Then here's something that is.' The kestrel circled for another attack. 'Reckon the Porsche has anything to do with Mike's death?'

Careful how you take this corner, I thought. 'Hard to see how.'

'Stuck for cash was Mike. Always wanting more.'

'For the club or himself?'

'Both. He did OK out of this place, drew a decent salary. Dad saw to that. Know how much that car was insured for?'

'About three hundred thousand pounds?' I'd upped my earlier estimate.

'Not a bad guess. Three hundred and *twenty* thousand. I should know, because Dad paid the premiums although the loot was in Mike's name.'

'*What*?' This one caught me off guard.

'Dad reckoned the Porsche was an asset for the club, so he coughed up. I reckoned that that meant any insurance cash would come to Dad, but he said no. To Mike. So when Mike found himself short in the cash department, what better way to reap the rewards?'

I tried to restrain myself. 'You're suggesting Mike *arranged* to have the car stolen?' I remembered that the same thought had occurred to me, but to have it aired as a distinct possibility was something I had to deal with.

'Sure am. Reckon that wife of his pushed him to the edge. She's a real piece of work.'

'But the car's now safe,' I pointed out. 'There *is* no insurance money.'

Then I remembered Doubler talking about the loss of a beautiful thing. Could Glenn conceivably be right? Had Mike asked Doubler to pinch the Porsche and ensure it wasn't seen again? Thankfully, reason came to the rescue of my addled thinking. 'You're wrong,' I said. 'Mike could have sold the Porsche for just as much as the insurance money any day.'

'Oh yeah?' Hearty laugh from my amiable friend. 'And how do you think Dad would react to that? It would have been tantamount to saying that he didn't look after his staff too well, plus that Old Herne's was going bust because its manager had no faith in it.'

He could be right – save in one respect. 'Perhaps you didn't know Mike very well,' I said. 'He would never, *never* have sold that Porsche.'

'You think Mike was some hero-type, you and Dad both,' Glenn replied dispassionately. 'All Mike wanted was money. Why do you reckon he hung on here with the place falling down all around him – for his wages, that's all. In the words of *Peanuts*, Jack, Glenn couldn't run a lemonade stand in a drought despite all the money Dad threw into it. Mike chucked money down the drain with his wonderful schemes that never came to anything. That's why he wanted the insurance money – to chuck some more away. Dad had refused to pay out.'

I clung on to reason. 'I still say he would never have deliberately had that car stolen.'

Glenn shrugged. 'Think what you like. It's my problem to make Old Herne's tick. And Jason's got the car.'

'His stepmother doesn't accept that.'

'Too bad. I'd have said Anna Nelson was right in line for batting Mike to death herself if it hadn't been for that will leaving it to Jason. Otherwise the Porsche would have been a nice little nest egg to comfort her.'

The gloves were off, and Mr Nice Guy seemed to have vanished. 'But,' I pointed out, 'she didn't *know* the car was going to Jason.'

Glenn laughed. 'She knew all right.'

That changed the picture. 'She *knew*? Are you sure? And what about this new will she thinks exists—?'

'All baloney. Sure, she knew about Jason getting the car, but she *didn't* know Mike was going to die on her. All that lovely insurance on the car would have been theirs, if Mike was still alive and you hadn't found the car. Look at it this way, Jack. She was as mad as hell when Mike died. Wanted to take over the club herself so she could help herself to Mike's salary. Now he's dead she's trying to make out the car belongs to her because it was stolen before Mike died. She wants it all ways. No chance, Anna baby.'

'Does she have *any* kind of a case?'

'Leave that to the attorneys.'

'What's Jason making of all this?' I asked curiously.

'No idea. He's busy setting up house with Dad.'

'Jason's going to live with Arthur?' I asked incredulously.

'Other way round. Dad's moving for a few weeks into Jason's house – Friars Leas, way over on these hills somewhere. It has first-class security, Jason sees to that.'

'Are you staying there too?'

'Fenella and I, we got ourselves a rental home outside Faversham. Nice little place. Reckon we'd best lock our cars up safely, now we know what goes on round here.' Another guffaw ensued as we parted.

On my way to find Jessica, I distilled my impressions of Glenn. If Mike's murder had been motivated by Old Herne's then Glenn stood right in line for motive, and so did Fenella if they had the protection of the family fortune in mind. To have the club continue under Mike would be the surest way to tie up yet more of it, with the likelihood of losing the lot. If Arthur dissolved the trust and sold the place, there would be a great deal more cash coming Glenn's way and in the meantime Glenn could ensure that Old Herne's continued existence would be in accordance with his and Fenella's interests.

'Jack! I thought you'd left.' A look of sheer pleasure crossed Jessica's face as I reached the clubhouse – which put one on mine as well.

'With you around? No way.' I kissed her – with the promise of a real kiss later. 'How are things?'

'Dire,' she pronounced. 'Let's go walkies.'

'In the fields again?'

'No time. Just outside. Once round the track will do.'

So over we went and even this short walk helped. 'Is the aftermath of the murder getting too much for you or is Glenn winding you up?' I asked.

'I try to separate the two. Leaving Mike aside, it's not Glenn – try Fenella. She's the self-appointed re-designer. I've seen some of her stuff – door knobs carefully hidden, toilet signs so discreet you crawl along the corridors pushing every door in sight. Water taps cunningly designed not to provide water if they can possible hide it from you. Everything so tastefully decorated it looks like nondescript porridge.'

'Does Glenn go along with her ideas?'

'And more. The bar refurnished with neat little tables and spindly chairs.'

I was horrified. 'He's leaving the leather sofas, I hope?'

'To the scrap heap they go. Too shabby.'

'The plush curtains?' I asked hollowly.

'Nice oatmeal coloured blinds.'

'I don't want to hear any more.'

'Wish I could say the same. She's going after the hangars next, although Glenn's more involved there. Complete redesign. Display cases, neat little walkways and labels . . .'

I groaned. 'Does Tim know?'

'Yes. And worse – only, Tim doesn't know this, or I hope he doesn't. The volunteers are to be edged out. The old guard will be changing.'

This was even more appalling. 'Surely Arthur can't know about this? Old Herne's isn't a lap-dancing club – it's a testament to the past, so it has to *live* that way.'

'Arthur's in shock, Jack. That's why Glenn and Fenella are moving so fast. Do the damage first and it can't be repaired. That's the strategy.'

'Talking of which, there's no sign of Peter today. Has he abandoned the ship of politics?'

'I wish,' she said fervently. 'We're not exactly pals, so my guess is that he's waiting to see my next move. If I left, then Glenn couldn't cope alone. Full stop. Which leaves a clear path for Peter. With Arthur so set on this new plan, he'll get nowhere, though, so he'll cosy up to Arthur but not take part in the infighting. Well, not obviously, anyway. Behind the scenes is a different matter.'

'Is that Fenella's strategy too?'

She was impressed. 'You're right, Jack. Answer: I don't know. Her eggs are firmly in Glenn's basket at present, but if he and Arthur fall out I wouldn't like to predict what would happen next. I suspect Fenella has her eyes on becoming a London celeb designer and needs a power position to work from. I wouldn't like to be in her father's shoes.'

'Or yours,' I pointed out.

'I'm needed, Jack. For the moment, anyway.'

'Does that suit you?'

'*Only* for the moment.'

'But the first victim would be you.'

'I can already feel the dagger scratching at my back,' she said ruefully.

'Where do you stand on Glenn, Jessica?' I had to ask, mindful of the fact that she had a stake in Old Herne's future.

She didn't answer immediately, but then said carefully, 'I'm still stunned. I need to see how it will work. If it's the only way— I need to talk to Arthur, though, and I can't get to him yet. You've heard about the move?'

'Yes. Did Arthur want to go there or was he pushed?'

She looked surprised. 'He wanted to go, probably because of the fuss over the club. He doesn't want to be closely involved. Glenn suspects foul play, though. He thinks Jason is up to mischief.'

'And is he?'

'What kind of mischief could that be?' she countered.

I shot off an arrow into the blue. 'Could he have plans for running the club himself?'

'Why would he? He does well with Pryde of the Past, and he inherited all the copyrights in his grandmother's music, which still brings in a pile of cash, and anyway can you see Jason running anything, let alone Old Herne's?'

'He might want to try, though. Perhaps with you as manager?'

I wondered if this had already occurred to her, but she replied, 'You're way off, Jack. He's a musician first and last.'

'Does Pryde of the Past have a manager?'

'Yes, but,' she admitted, 'Jason does most of it himself.'

She made a face as she realized she had scored an own goal.

'Don't worry,' I said comfortingly, 'he can't both be on tour and run Old Herne's.'

'I'm not planning to spend my entire life as a number two, Jack,' she said forcefully.

'You're always number one with me.' But even as I said this, Louise tiptoed into my mind. I told her to get out of it again. She had abandoned my life, and so she should have the decency to leave my mind alone.

But what I said pleased Jessica anyway, so I tucked her arm into mine, felt her relax and made hopeful plans for the evening. I'd be glad to get away from Old Herne's. Its politics were beginning to cloud the central picture, even though they could be germane to my case. Mike had been savagely murdered, and yet the wolves were howling on their own behalves. Jessica could be excused on that front as a newcomer to the scene, but with the others in whose hands Old Herne's might lie, I could see its magic fading, gone, along with Mike. Was that inevitable with his death? No, but I could see no sign of a miracle on the horizon. What I *could* see was that Mike's death and Old Herne's were almost certainly connected. There were more vested interests here than in Grand Prix Formula I.

EIGHT

Another beautiful morning – after a beautiful night. I'm not sure beautiful is spot on as a description. Exciting, memorable and definitely soon-to-be-repeatable would be preferable. Beautiful is too transitory as an adjective. Jessica was a multifaceted lover, confident, warm, generous – all of those. Oh yes, I was hooked. No doubt about that. I'd woken up with a curious feeling that I had only rarely had before – that love was hovering not too far away and that I had only to reach out a hand and it would join me. Almost literally, as I was alone in the bed. I thought she had departed for work without a word to me – but then I remembered it was Sunday. When I ran downstairs, she was in the kitchen with breakfast laid for two.

'Tea? Coffee?' were her first mundane words to me, but the accompanying warm smile and lift of the face made it clear that these items, important though they were, weren't at the top of her agenda. A shared night of pleasure is a joy that communicates itself without words.

I murmured something about needing to kiss her without coming to difficult decisions about tea and coffee, and she obediently folded herself into my arms.

'Coffee,' I eventually answered.

'I'm a tea person.'

'Then we complement each other admirably.'

'I remember,' she told me solemnly, which led to another kiss, and that meant it was some time before we actually tucked into breakfast and then – reluctantly – the matter of Old Herne's.

The more I sifted away, the more golden nuggets I might pick up. My conscience told me it was unfair to cross-question her further but I calmed it down on the grounds that Jessica seemed eager to discuss it. Talking can help. She agreed with me that the club was more likely to have motivated Mike's murder than the car, with the caveat that Old Herne's couldn't be divorced from family issues.

'Are you sure Arthur doesn't know about Glenn's makeover plans?' I asked.

'Pretty sure. Or if Glenn has told him, it hasn't sunk in.'

'Shouldn't you push for a talk with him then?'

She hesitated. 'Not politic at present.'

Was being politic the point? I wondered. 'Have you told Glenn how you feel?'

'No.' She must have seen my look of surprise and struggled to explain. 'I suppose I must still be dealing with Mike's death, Jack. I didn't know him very long but to me he *was* Old Herne's. I can't believe he's not still at the helm. Glenn's plans are too much to cope with even though I know I should try. There are the Nelsons to be taken into account too.'

Any doubts I might have had about Jessica were thankfully laid to rest. Her heart was in Old Herne's. 'Who owns High House?' I asked.

'Pass. I hope Boadicea does or she'll be left with nothing.'

I should pay the Nelsons a visit, I realized. Arthur had assured me that his own family was not above suspicion where Mike's murder was concerned, and therefore nor should the Nelsons be. They were all strong characters with their own plans and convictions, and Mike's killer was more likely than not to be amongst those closest to him.

Sunday and the night that followed were just as glorious as Saturday night, but Monday morning reared its depressing head all too quickly. On the pretext of needing help over the V5 registration document required for the change of ownership of the Porsche, I arranged to call in later that morning at High House. I do sometimes get landed with helping out over such matters when stolen cars are returned to their owners. Before High House, however, I drove Jessica back to Old Herne's where her own car was still parked.

'Thanks for this,' she said as we drew up. 'You've no idea what a difference it makes, arriving here *with* someone. In the last week I've had to summon up courage to come at all and every time I've done it I seem to be driving through the gates of hell. You make it seem normal, Jack.'

It wasn't the greatest compliment I've ever been paid in the circumstances but I took it as one. Before leaving, I had introduced her to the Pits where she had been suitably impressed even though she claimed she wasn't a 'car person' at heart. I'd also shown her the Glory Boot, which had greatly pleased her, 'car person' or not. She must have seen a fellow 'saver' behind it, and I hoped that as the Glory Boot and Morgans Hangar have a lot in common over their approach to collections, the visit might have helped in a small way towards explaining where the true value of Old Herne's lay.

As I left the club I began to think that her 'normal' was more of a compliment than I had thought. From a platform of 'normal' one could feel able to tackle anything the day had to offer. Such as the Nelsons.

When I arrived at High House I thanked my lucky stars that Ray answered the door, not Boadicea. 'Come in,' he said from his wheelchair, in a tone so unwelcoming it surprised me. True, he must still be in shock over his son's death, but I reckoned I should count as one of the good guys because I had returned the Porsche to his grandson.

High House was an anomaly, situated as it was on the crest of the Downs. Red-brick, mid-Victorian, staid and smug, it was guarded by evergreen trees, which were designed as shelter from the winds but seemed vaguely repellent to more sociable visitors. Inside, the house looked comfortable rather than smart and was surprisingly large.

I followed Ray along to the end of the original building and through a door into a modern extension, obviously his domain. The living room to which he escorted me was curiously impersonal. The few photos that were on display were all of himself and Miranda, not of their children, and included one of their wedding. No flowing white dresses then, as it was wartime, but a severe looking suit for Miranda and an army uniform for Ray, as they must come under the auspices of the forces' entertainment arm, ENSA. Two eager faces looked out towards a future that would not include war or foreign dominance, and indeed the Second World War's end must then have been in sight.

As at our earlier meeting, he seemed less on the ball than Arthur, although sharp enough to watch me with great suspicion. When I again expressed sympathy for Mike's loss, he just stared at me. 'You must find the police investigation exhausting as well as painful,' I added.

'In and out, in and out. Treat the place like a hotel,' he muttered. This I doubted, as I had seen Brandon's team at work many times. 'Accident, I told them that,' he ranted on. '*Accident*.'

'It's hard to see how that could have happened,' I murmured.

'Nonsense. That Crossley – handbrake wasn't on – rolled forwards, knocked him over and he fell on the axe. I told them that. *Murder*,' he snorted. 'Too many of those TV thrillers around if you ask me. No one goes round murdering folks just like that.'

There was no answer to this, as it was not just improbable but impossible, given the medical evidence. Instead I said, 'I'm told your younger son lives in New Zealand.'

'Said he'd fly over when we're allowed to have a funeral. What he thinks he can do, I've no idea. Damn stupid. What about this Porsche then?'

'I wondered whether Mrs Nelson or you would have Mike's registration document and service book for the Porsche. The new owner,' I added diplomatically, 'will need them.'

'She's dead.'

'I beg your pardon?' Such was the sombreness of this house I wondered if Boadicea was indeed lying lifeless upstairs.

'My wife. She died in 1991.'

'I meant your son's widow.'

'Oh her. She's still here, worse luck. Means more people traipsing in and out. Never know who they are. Now, if Miranda were here, she'd know where the stuff you're after was,' he assured me. 'My Miranda. That's her.' He looked over at the wedding photo.

'I heard her sing once at a local charity show, probably after she gave up singing professionally.'

'After *we* gave up singing,' he corrected me. 'All this pop rubbish, Rolling Stones, Beatles, Beach Boys – Ray, she said, it's time we faced facts. We're the old brigade. They don't want us no more. They will, I told her.'

I could see tears in Ray's eyes. He was indeed living in the past.

'They will,' he repeated. 'And now she's not here no more and that pipsqueak Jason thinks he can sing her songs better than her.'

'Your grandson's very good,' I told him. 'Aren't you proud of him for bringing Miranda's songs back to life?'

His face came alive. '*Proud*? After he swindled me out of the copyright?'

'Who?' I was thrown for a moment.

'Young Jason. Worked on my Miranda and got her to leave her copyrights in the songs to him. What about me, eh? All I got was the recordings to live on. Fat pension that is.'

I decided to ignore this and change tack. 'It's good news that the Porsche has been found, considering how much it meant to Mike. Will Jason agree to its being shown at Old Herne's again, do you think? It doesn't seem the same place without it.' I stopped, aware that again Ray was staring at me with a blank face. Was he 'with' me, or in some place of his own?

'Mike raced it,' he said at last.

'It must have meant a lot to him, especially as he left it to Jason in memory of his first wife.'

I'd hoped this might draw him out, but received another blank look.

'His good luck symbol, he called it, and look where it got him,' he continued. 'Bought it in 1965. Had it since he was twenty.'

'A generous gift from you both.'

'Both?'

'You and your late wife.' Silence, so I continued, 'And a very valuable car now. The theft was rough on the lady who bought it, but I expect Jason will compensate her.' Nothing like a provocative statement for breaking silences.

Ray still made no comment, so my less than subtle hint on Jenny's behalf fell on deaf ears.

And then the door opened. 'I thought I heard voices in here.'

It was Boadicea, but not in warpaint. Indeed, she looked haggard with grief and her voice lacked its usual vigour. I leapt up and gave her my armchair, pulling forward a dining chair for myself. 'I'm here about the Porsche,' I told her.

She glared at me. 'Isn't that Jason's affair?'

'Probably, but if so he'll need the former registration document under Mike's ownership.' True enough. 'I think it was two years old when Mike first had it in 1965. I hate to trouble you at a time like this, Mrs Nelson, but might the original logbook, the current registration document and service book be amongst Mike's papers?'

'I doubt it. All the insurance papers were dealt with by Arthur. Mike made that quite clear. It would all have gone to Arthur.' She didn't sound too antagonistic.

'Are you sure they're not here? Could you look? The service book at least might be around.'

'Have you any idea what you're asking?'

Even now she wasn't over-aggressive. The opposite, in fact, as she was giving every sign of surrender.

'Yes,' I said gently. 'And I'm not expecting miracles, but if you could find anything it would be invaluable for the paperwork.'

'I'll try.' She said this with a finality that left me no room to manoeuvre, so I had nothing to lose by overstepping the mark.

'They might turn up if and when you decide to move from here, Mrs Nelson.'

A return to the Warrior Queen. 'Move? Why should I?'

'This seems a large house for you to run.'

'*Run*?' Definitely hostile.

An unexpected chuckle from Ray Nelson, who came to my rescue, probably unintentionally. 'What this fellow means, Anna, is that now you're broke you might have to sell up. He doesn't know this place belongs to me. It's me who'll do the turfing out.'

Warrior queen she might be, but this was taking matters to extremes, and I was relieved when he continued, 'Don't worry, Anna, I won't do it. I need a bloody carer at my time of life and better the devil you know and all that.' He cackled again, although I doubted if this was meant as a joke, and Boadicea sat there stony-faced. I could hardly blame her.

I wasn't laughing either.

I found Jessica in the clubhouse, where a brightly clad Hedda lit up the bar area, singing happily to herself, while piped music of completely different melodies emerged from the loudspeakers. Jessica was not alone, however, for which I was personally, if not professionally, sorry. She was with Peter Nelson, who had obviously emerged from the shadows where we had thought he was lurking as regards Old Herne's. Having greeted Hedda and obtained a much needed coffee from her, I went over to join them. They seemed on much more amicable terms today, and lounging in jeans and a sweater, Peter looked a less truculent figure than he had on that fateful Sunday, although the superior grin was still prominent.

'Jess tells me you've been to see Grandpops and darling Aunt Anna,' he said as I sat down with them.

'I have,' I agreed.

'Bet that made a cheery morning for you.'

'Understandably, no.'

'Typical for High House,' he commented.

'Your grandfather seems to consider your aunt is his carer,' I said casually. 'Is that the case?'

Peter laughed. 'That's only to rile her up. She cooks most of the meals, that's all. For everything else, there's someone comes in every night and morning plus a cleaner or two. Now the nasty stuff has hit the proverbial fan though, they might have to cut down on this life of luxury.'

'Jason would support them, wouldn't he?'

'Jason only looks after one person's welfare and that's Jason's,' Peter whipped back smartly. 'After he fell out with Mike, that was that for the family as far as he was concerned. He's always been at loggerheads with dear Aunt Anna, so he's hardly likely to start baling her out now.'

A good opening. 'What did he and Mike fall out about?'

'Who knows?' Peter shrugged. 'I never did. It did me a good turn anyway, or so it seemed at the time. I became flavour of the month which is what got me the job here – till Jess turned up and I was booted out.'

I refrained from doing some booting myself as Jessica retorted, 'Hardly. Mike had to boot you out because you merely stood by and watched while profits vanished into losses. Not my fault.'

'Nor mine. Brother Mike was hardly businessman of the year, as I'm sure you've discovered. I wish Glenn joy of the place. *And* Fenella. Now there *is* someone to spread joy.'

'I wish you well there,' Jessica said wryly.

'Thanks. I see her as an angel of mercy.'

Aspiring to commercial golden wings, I thought. For all his

jokey words, however, Peter seemed serious where Fenella was concerned, although whether out of true love for her or her connections I wouldn't like to bet. 'Do you live at High House too?' I asked him.

'No way. I'd be stark staring mad after a week. The only thing that keeps Ray going is his feud with Auntie Anna,' he said with scorn. 'And now that she'll be dependent on him, he's on a winning ticket. 'I've a flat, Rochester way – I'm an IT consultant. I run the business with a partner.'

Since Peter was lounging on a sofa at eleven thirty on a working day the partner must be very generous minded. 'Might there be a role for you back here at Old Herne's?' I asked casually, and saw Jessica freeze.

Peter raised an eyebrow. 'Now it's under new management, who knows? Could be some scope there, don't you think, Jess?'

He was exactly the sort to exploit any scope at all. This lazy debonair mask would slip at a moment's notice if it suited him. I saw the future of Old Herne's under his or Glenn's rule in my mind's eye. Gone would be the Tims at its core. In would come the neat display boxes, the uniform little café tables, and the layers of management. For Peter, Mike's death could be an ill wind that blew considerable silver linings. The question was whether these silver linings had been as a result of the ill wind or whether the ill winds had been planned with them in mind. Where was he at the time of Mike's death? I wondered. Jason, Arthur and Tim were at the track, Boadicea had been hunting for Ray who turned up at the bar. Glenn and Fenella were trying to find Arthur. But Peter? There had been almost an hour between the time Mike closed the doors to Thunderbolts Hangar for visitors and the time the concert had begun. Long enough for any of them to have entered Thunderbolts through the double doors, donned that greatcoat, picked up the axe – and dealt with the disposal of the blood-soaked greatcoat.

I went on thinking about this after Jessica and Peter had gone their separate ways and I was left alone at the table, contemplating my empty coffee cup and my next move.

'Boring old place, isn't it?' Hedda called across to me.

'It shouldn't be,' I replied, getting up to return the cup. 'This place will be humming with life when the public starts pouring in again.'

'Don't know about that,' Hedda said, leaning over the counter to stare dreamily into my eyes. 'What say we take off to see the world, sugar daddy?'

'I've a better idea. How about we start our own band?'

She giggled. 'I'll have to look for a new job of some sort, if that Glenn gets his hooks into this place.'

'If he replaces you with a machine, you mean? He won't – he'll need staff.'

'He and Dad don't get on.'

'That shouldn't affect you.'

'Grow up,' young Hedda suggested to me.

'I'm very grown up. Even the newest brooms don't sweep everything clean, and anyway, he might want his own personal line to Jason through you.'

She looked thoughtful. 'Right. But not after my spat with Flouncy Fan.'

'Who?'

'Miss Fenella. Peter fancies her you know – well, her or her money.'

'Still doesn't affect you.'

'It does,' she said dolefully. 'He don't fancy me. Wish he did, though. I could make something of him, but he sees himself and Flouncy Fan as an upwardly mobile couple. Hope they didn't knock old Mike off between them.' She threw this out as a challenge, as if hoping I'd deny it.

'Someone did,' I pointed out after I got my breath back.

A pause. 'Time to see my dad, Jack.'

'You're going to see him now?'

She sighed. 'Not me. *You.* Talk to him.'

'What about?' I asked patiently.

'You work it out.'

'I heard Arthur Howell was moving in.'

'Right. Room to swing a few billionaire cats in Dad's house. They get on OK. Talk to him too.'

Good plan, I thought. I opted for Arthur first, as he was employing me.

'How about tomorrow?' he suggested, when I rang his mobile, and then gave me directions to Jason's home.

Friars Leas lay several miles away in a maze of lanes that were unfamiliar to me and were further towards Canterbury on high flat land. It wasn't entirely in the wilds, but near a hamlet called Chartham Dene. It was along such narrow lanes, however, that burglars would be hard put to it to escape notice by night or by day. I had decided to bring the Lagonda on a rare outing, with the hazy idea that Arthur might like it, as it had been a favourite vehicle with World War II pilots.

Friars Leas was set in large grounds and I took the Lagonda up the long drive at a leisurely pace, savouring the experience of approaching this house for the first time. It was a staggering sight; from the bridge in front of me it looked as though there was a moat or at least a stretch of water in front of the house, and cars were obviously meant to be parked this side of it. On the far side of the moat the house reared up like a Wizard of Oz castle. What a place! Huge, part medieval-beamed, part Tudor brick, gables, turrets, a Georgian style wing, enough Victorian crenellations to make Dracula feel at home and sufficient chimneys to keep a sweep happy for life.

I walked over the bridge cautiously, but at least it wasn't a drawbridge and there was no sign of a portcullis with boiling oil ready prepared to drop on unwelcome visitors. I could see why this rambling concoction might appeal to Arthur as a temporary safe haven.

It wasn't Arthur who opened the door however. Nor a butler or footman. It was Jason Pryde.

He gave me one of his crooked smiles. 'Welcome to Nightmare Abbey.'

NINE

I was aware that Jason was waiting for me to say, 'I thought this house was called Friars Leas?' Tough. He was going to be disappointed. In a trice I was back in my father's study of long, long ago, where amongst other forgotten treasures was a copy of Peacock's early nineteenth novel of gentle mockery, *Nightmare Abbey*. I grinned at Jason, grasping for anything I could remember of this neglected classic which my father – mysteriously to me at the time – thought so screamingly funny. My memory – or Dad – obliged.

I then replied with some confidence as the book reared up in my mind more clearly, 'Mr Flosky, I presume. Mystery is your mental element. You see ghosts at noontide.'

Jason's eyes narrowed. 'Who doesn't? Scythrop Glowry in fact,' he added. 'The son and heir. Come in, do. Arthur's waiting for you.'

That was just as well. I'd reached the limits of my knowledge of Peacock's classic, although I had a vague memory that Scythrop, disappointed in love, had a passion for reforming the world. I'd bear that in mind in case it gave me an understanding of what made Jason tick.

As he led me through the hall and up a dark mahogany staircase – dark because little natural light percolated to this point – I began to feel I was indeed in Nightmare Abbey, although Peacock's idea of it could not have included a huge oil painting of Miranda Pryde belting out one of her famous songs. Nor would his Abbey have included paintings and posters of motor cars driven by a young Mike Nelson and whizzing round a track. My friend the Italian artist Giovanni would have been proud to acknowledge one of the paintings, so surreal was it. Then I looked closer and realized it *was* a Giovanni, with Mike's Porsche portrayed in it.

Nightmare Abbey, however, might well have accommodated, had the technology existed in Peacock's time, the dancing skeleton grinning at me from an alcove, or the ghastly apparitions looming over the staircase in a way I had not been loomed over since I last went on a haunted house trip at a local fair.

'Do they attack at will?' I asked Jason mildly as one of these dangled perilously near the top of my head.

'Only if you want them to do so. That's the secret of life. There's a dark lantern of the spirit,' he told me conversationally, 'that brings them out, but none see by it but those who bear it.'

I suspected we were back to Peacock's novel again, but I struggled to keep up. 'Do you see it?'

He considered this and stopped his progress along a corridor on the first floor as dark as the stairs. 'Oh yes. We all do at times.'

'This must be one of those times for you. A bad one, and I'm sorry.' It was a risky step for I judged this was a man who would only let me approach on his own terms.

'Yes,' he agreed, and indicated that we should sit down in an alcove halfway along, which was provided with two velvet upholstered chairs, a table and a huge carved angel looking down benignly upon us.

Although his brief reply was hardly encouraging, I continued, 'It seems to be general knowledge that you weren't on good terms with your father, and that must have made his death worse.'

He looked interested. 'Do the police think I killed him?'

'I don't know,' I replied truthfully. 'That depends on forensic evidence or lack of it.' I'd heard no more from Brandon on that front. 'On the timescale they might, or if they decide there's a link between the Porsche theft and his death.'

His sharp intelligent eyes flickered. 'Yes, I see that.' A moment's pause and then he added, 'But consider. Would I do such a thing to my father, to Miranda Pryde's son? It seems unlikely.'

I agreed, but capricious minds such as Jason Pryde's can jump enormous gaps at will – or worse without knowing it. I was wary of him and even warier now that Arthur was under his roof. How had that come about, and what was Arthur making of Nightmare Abbey?

'It does,' I replied. 'And the aftermath of your father's death can't be helping. You must feel strongly about Old Herne's passing out of your hands with Glenn running it. It's been part of the Nelson family story ever since it was founded.' I sensed I'd put a foot wrong – and so did Jason, but he let me off the hook.

'You're floundering, Jack,' he told me kindly. 'Do you need a lifebelt?'

I laughed. 'Yes please.'

'Then let me show you my tower.'

'You said Arthur was waiting—'

He brushed this aside. 'He'll understand.'

I hoped he would, as for all his slightly elfish appearance Jason Pryde was a man of steel. He set off along the corridor, we turned a corner, he opened a door – and I saw the tower. The room was circular and light streamed in from the huge bow window, although the door faced not that but the wall opposite.

At first glance the room looked like another tribute to Miranda Pryde and to his father. There were pictures and photos of her, of Mike, and even a ghost or two, I noticed. There was a repro-duction (perhaps an original?) of a Victorian painting, in which I recognized the ghost of Hamlet's father. Next to it was another painting with a similar ghostly figure, this time female. As for the photos, these differed from those of Miranda and Mike that I had glimpsed elsewhere in the house. The majority of them had Old Herne's as a background, although there was also one of Miranda surrounded by RAF personnel. Another striking adornment to the room was the huge number of model aeroplanes and cars. They peeped out between photos and files, adorned work surfaces, some were displayed on the floor, some in a showcase, and their quality varied. I could see a tinplate Schuco sitting next to a plastic London Routemaster.

I assumed at first that this was Jason's office or study, but I could see no computer, not even an old typewriter. At the far side of the room a twisting spiral staircase obviously led to the ground floor level and to another floor above. There was a small desk, a chair and armchair, a large china cat, some books, a Kindle lying on the desk. I took all this in first – and only then turned belatedly to the window itself. Here stood a huge telescope trained out on the Downs, and from the way that Jason was staring at me, I could see he wanted to see my reactions.

'This is your thinking room?' I asked carefully, feeling my way.

'It's where I think.'

'Music?'

'No. There's a recording studio downstairs and the routine music stuff I do all over the place.'

'So what then?'

'Look through this.' He trained the telescope and motioned to me to take his place.

Once the view had settled down from its usual blur of blues and greens, I could see to my amazement an unmistakable shape. 'Isn't that—?'

He nodded. 'Old Herne's control tower.'

I could see it so clearly that I could even focus on the empty garage. No Porsche, no Morgan. Then I managed to train the telescope on to the track, where a solitary car was whizzing around. No doubt about that stylish sports car. It was the Morgan of course, with, I presumed, Tim at the wheel, although I couldn't see the driver clearly enough.

'Fun, isn't it?' Jason said behind me.

'Yes, but why is it here?' What was it that he wanted me to understand?

'Castles in the air. It's the Scythrop in me.'

So we were back to *Nightmare Abbey*. I hoped we weren't going much further with this or I would be a sad disappointment to him. 'Can you explain?' I asked.

'Scythrop kept a stool to be melancholy on. This room is *my* stool,' Jason told me matter-of-factly.

He was looking so unmelancholy that this was a shock. 'Do you use it often?'

'Yes,' he replied. 'Roots. Mine. No one can sing without roots, even if one doesn't sing *about* them. Mine are Old Herne's. In the recording room I keep just one picture of Old Herne's to keep me going, but usually I come in here, get my dose of roots and then go and sing. Do you think that's why my marriage broke up?' he concluded disconcertingly.

'Possibly,' I said cautiously. 'Perhaps you spent too much time here?' I began to see how Old Herne's might be his Scythrop passion for reforming the world.

'No. I didn't own this place then. My wife walked out during my detox period, taking Hedda with her. She had got used to being on her own, she claimed, and I was too wrapped up in my grandmother Miranda.'

'Was your wife right?'

'Who knows? Hedda's my root now. Have you met her?'

'Yes. She's a great girl.'

'She can't sing a note, but that's good. Two singers in one family are enough. I went wrong in the nineties after Miranda died, so I don't blame my wife for giving up on me. Couldn't see my way through, so I went to dry out and detox, and landed back at Old Herne's to get back on track. I'm still on it, I hope – aren't I, Arthur?'

Arthur? I swung round to see that he had joined us. He had come in so silently that I hadn't heard him. It was the first time I'd seen Arthur standing and thought how incredibly upright and spry he was for a man of ninety or more. 'You are, Jason. The Pride of Old Herne's.' Then he turned to me. 'What do you think of Friars Leas?'

'Impressive,' I said. 'I can see why you wanted to move in here for a while.' I wasn't sure I did understand it, in fact, but my endorsement seemed to please both of them.

'I always look in on young Jason when I cross the Pond. First Old Herne's and the Cricketers and then Friars Leas. It looks kind of weird, but you know, Jack, it feels like a home.'

'Young' Jason put his arm round Arthur in affection. 'This is Miranda's home, too, Arthur. Always will be. And yours.'

Miranda's home? I wondered just why Hedda had wanted me to talk to Arthur *and* Jason. She must have been fond of Mike and as outraged as we all were by his murder. What more could they tell me, either together or singly, that was going to help find his killer?

The Porsche had been returned and so I had put that provisionally to one side as a factor in Mike's death. Nevertheless, it was odd that it didn't seem to figure much in Jason's mind. Was this because it had nothing to do with Mike's death or could it be that the car had only been one incident in a far wider scenario that placed Jason centre stage? And with Jason came Arthur, Nightmare Abbey – and Miranda Pryde.

I couldn't see where this line of thought was taking me, but I sensed it was taking me *somewhere* . . . in fact, quite a way, perhaps, given how they were both looking at me, with their long thin faces and their mild kindly eyes. Looking at me *expectantly*.

And then I was there. At last, I'd got the steering wheel gripped in my hands. How could I have been so blind? Was I the only person who didn't know? I could not believe that and yet it was so obvious. And it threw a die into the ring that changed everything. *If* I was right. So I took a deep breath. It was time to throw the die myself.

'Miranda's place,' I repeated. '*She* was the heart of Old Herne's and still is.'

Neither of them spoke. They were waiting for me to spell it out. So spell it out I did.

'Mike was your biological son, wasn't he, Arthur? Jason's your grandson.'

'I could do with a ride, Jack,' Arthur said almost apologetically, 'and seeing this Lagonda of yours outside, well, I guess that clinched it. After the Morgan, Miranda and I had a real liking for Lagondas. Anyway, we can talk better away from Jason. He's a weird one at times.'

And how, I thought. I'd expected denials, but instead they had both looked pleased at my deduction. So now that the truth was established, it was time to get answers. This discovery could well change the direction of the case, both for me and for Brandon.

Arthur had strapped himself into the Lagonda with great pleasure. No prizes for guessing where we were heading, he and I, on this jaunt of ours. Old Herne's. Arthur wanted a spin round the track in the Morgan, didn't feel up to taking the wheel himself and had asked me if I would. I'd been longing to have a go at driving it for years. I love Morgans. I love their history, I love their independence – and I love the cars.

Jason had said he would train the telescope on us as we went round the track, and I didn't discourage him in case he came with us instead. I didn't want him perched in the Lagonda's rear seat, while I tried to have a one to one with Arthur.

Arthur opted for tea in Hedda's bar before we took to the track, and we caught her just as she was about to close up for the day. There was great delight when she saw Arthur. 'Hi,

Grandpops!' she shrieked, rushing over to kiss him, and much excited chatter followed.

'Is Mike's parentage generally known?' I asked Arthur when we were alone again.

'No. Hedda keeps her mouth shut.'

'I presume Anna Nelson is in the picture.'

He managed a chuckle. 'She is now. I told her after Mike's death and she didn't know whether to be furious or pleased as she counted the cash she might get from me. She reckoned I'd chip in because Jason got the car and she seemed to think she was entitled either to that or the insurance for it. I put her right on that score and that made her mighty mad. And before you ask, Ray does know about Mike but grandson Peter does not.'

'And your family?'

He wasn't pleased at that. 'I'll tell Glenn in my own good time,' he snapped.

'I have to ask about Mike though. Did he know?'

I thought I'd get another flea in my ear, but I was wrong. Arthur sighed. 'Not until Miranda was dying in 1991. I agreed that with Ray – when I found out myself, that is. That wasn't until 1965 when Miranda and I met again. She told me while we were out in that Morgan we're about to drive. That's why it's kind of special to me. I bought the Porsche for Mike then and the Morgan for her. We'd driven in one of the thirties three-wheelers when we first knew each other, but we moved on to the Plus Four. Mike was twenty in 1965 and still hadn't the slightest idea I was his father. It went on that way till Miranda died.'

I whistled. 'Mike must have been getting on for fifty by the time he did find out – rather late to discover your parentage.'

'Thank Ray for that. He said it was better for Mike if he never knew. Like hell. He didn't care two cheroots for Mike. It was *me* Ray wanted to get off his patch, even though he owed his job to me.'

'He seems to have run Old Herne's well.'

'Miranda did,' Arthur said grimly. 'The moment she died, I told him he was off the books and Mike was automatically on under the trust agreement.'

I'd been right. Whole new scenarios were opening up, with this joker on the table. I wasn't pleased. 'You should have told me he was your son, Arthur. This could have affected Mike's death.'

'Why?' The tough billionaire emerged. 'If my own kid doesn't know, why the heck should you? I only told Jason when he started Pryde of the Past five years back and that was the reason he fell out with Mike – blamed him for not telling him immediately he knew himself. Jason couldn't get over it because he'd been so close to Miranda, yet never knew the half of it. So he's poured all his energy since into Pryde of the Past.'

'Which has opened up a new career for him.'

'Sure. He had turned himself around, but still couldn't get over the fact that Mike had kept him in the dark. I reckon that was because Anna didn't want Jason thinking of himself as Mike's successor at Old Herne's, in case Jason booted Mike out of the place. If she'd known he was my son she'd have been even more forceful on the subject. Odd lad, Jason. He didn't mind my not telling him earlier, only Mike.'

I was still confused. 'But now you have appointed Glenn, not Jason, to run Old Herne's. Is that because you don't see Jason as a good manager?'

'He'd be a darn good manager if he chose, especially if Jessica stays on.'

'So it's because he prefers to keep his own career?'

He didn't reply, and I saw he was beginning to tire. When he did speak, he still didn't answer my question. 'Let's get out in the air, Jack. Down to the track and the Morgan. Tim's got the car down there ready, and then I'll tell you about Miranda Pryde and me. I told you some but you don't know the half of it yet.'

I could see he'd had enough for the moment. My questions would have to wait awhile, so I found him a wheelchair to save his energy and off we went, me with a sense of guilty pleasure at this diversion, he – well, I couldn't speak for him but he was clearly set on it.

And there, as we reached the track, was the Morgan. There was no sign of Tim, but the Morgan was enough. A sight for jaded spirits. A 1965 Morgan Series IV, with true quality shining out of every inch. I took a moment or two to admire it before we took off. And 'took off' would be right for a Morgan, as Arthur pointed out.

'You heard of the Aero, Jack?' he said. 'Not that new one Morgans just brought out, the earlier one.'

'Yes. Around 1920, wasn't it? And a Super Aero a few years later.'

'Right. So called because of that flying ace of yours, Albert Ball, killed in 1917. He had an earlier specially bodied Grand Prix model, and said that to drive it was the nearest thing to flying without leaving the ground. That's what my Morgan does for me.'

And so we flew along the ground, Arthur and I. It seemed right for this track with its RAF provenance, and I could imagine myself in Ball's Sopwith Pup as the landscape whizzed by. It was an exhilarating experience, and when at last he'd had enough, he thanked me. Then we sat in the Morgan and he told me the story. *His* story, Miranda's story.

'My Miranda,' he began. 'You must have heard her recordings, Jack. Everyone has. What you can't know is what she was like. Take the phrase the love of my life. That was Miranda for me, and me for her. We were all set until Ray Nelson took a hand.

'I first met him,' he went on, 'after the Thunderbolt crash in 'forty-three, though I barely remember him then. Miranda put him in the shade, and I tend to forget that skunk was even then in the background. Miranda's partner he calls himself. He didn't play much part at all. He was OK as a crooner but he didn't have the X factor that Miranda did. She knew that, he knew that, so it was her show with back-up from him on occasion. The day of the crash in 'forty-three – well, I thought I was a goner as I came down. Got ready to meet my Maker. I told you Thunderbolts were sturdy beasts but the engine was failing. One strike too many. Then I blacked out as we hit the ground – don't know how long but I opened my eyes and there was this chap in overalls dragging me – and the heat was quite something. I had some idea it might have been St Peter so it seemed a good idea to go with the flow. The whole thing went up as he pulled me clear – he must have known it was about to blow but he came for me, and he saved my life. Just like my father, whose life was saved by that pal in World War I.

'War's a strange time, Jack. It stays with you, the few good times, the countless bad. The horror and the personal heroism you come across. That's why we remember it, all of it, and not only on Armistice Day. As I told you, next evening I met Miranda at the Twitch club. Just her, not Ray, who reckoned he was too high and mighty to sing to such small audiences.'

'Did they have a personal relationship at that time?'

'According to him yes, according to Miranda no. Strictly business. By the time I left West Malling a few days later I was hooked on her. I guess those fellows that first set their eyes on your Florence Nightingale at Scutari must have been the same way. The Lady with the Lamp you call her. Well, Miranda Pryde shed a light into my life that hasn't been extinguished since.'

'Was it instantaneous for both of you?'

'No. To her I was just some dumb Yankee pilot at first, but she was interested enough to come to Debden, where I was stationed. She could tell I was homesick for Ohio. She'd been to the States so we talked about that and about her growing up in Kent. After Debden she was due to do a tour of East Anglian bases with Ray, and by then she and I were well on our way. Ray could see that. He was – and is – a sly piece of work. No English gentleman, that guy.

'For the next year,' he continued, 'we saw each other when we could, which wasn't often. She had a 'thirties Morgan then, and because of her job she could fix the petrol situation OK. Petrol rationing would have put paid to it otherwise. Then came D-Day and the summer of 1944. West Malling base made an arrangement with the USAF that they could use the Malling base as an advance landing for refuelling and as an emergency landing ground, so they were well used to Yankee pilots. Same went for Old Herne's. We were mostly flying Mustangs by then. That was the time when the VI doodlebugs were getting active, and the USAF needed a liaison officer at West Malling – I put myself forward and I was all set. Miranda lived locally and for those six weeks it was hell by day in the air and heaven at night. We knew this was the real thing and had plans to marry just as soon as possible. Mike was conceived – and then Ray found out. Somehow he got through to my CO and my request for speedy marriage was turned down flat. I don't know what tale he concocted, but then my squadron got posted, so there was no chance of seeing Miranda for a while. I was in Europe, she was in the north of England.'

Arthur cleared his throat before continuing, 'When we met again in the sixties that jerk Nelson proudly told us he'd intercepted my letters and informed her I'd been posted back to the States. In those days she was a famous lady, she thought I didn't want her and there she was with a kid on the way. So she married Ray late in 1944. I thought that our love affair was over as she'd never replied to my letters and I'd no idea she was pregnant. So I got stuck into business life and making my millions. Got married, sired Glenn and tried to forget her. You have to get on with life.

'Then in 1965 I had to fly to London on business and heard that Miranda and Ray were retiring from their singing career, and that their son Mike was a racing driver. I did a bit of investigation and went down to Kent to find them. So I met Miranda again. Twenty years is a long time, but we took one look at each other and knew we felt the same. Nothing to be done about it; you didn't leave your marriage post so easily in those days.'

'And she told you about Mike?'

'Yes. One look at him and I knew he was mine, for all he took after Miranda. I couldn't tell him that though. We agreed that with Ray. So I bought Mike the Porsche and the Morgan for Miranda and Ray hated me for it. Can't say I blame him, but I never told Mike the truth. Ray was glad enough to take the job at Old Herne's with Miranda, for all he can't stand me.'

'And now?'

'That flame's still burning, Jack. Miranda has gone but I see her in Jason every time I look at him. And, dear God, his voice. And that's why I can't let Old Herne's die, Jack. I thought I could, but I can't.'

TEN

Arthur Howell, much as I liked and respected him, was one big powerhouse, I reflected as I drove him back to Friars Leas. Nevertheless, so far as Old Herne's and the trust were concerned he was focused on Miranda Pryde and through her on Mike and Jason. Miranda was 'back story' and yet seemed to control Old Herne's future. That wasn't necessarily a bad thing, however. A great many charities and other projects draw their inspiration from personal emotions, whether of grief, pleasure or conviction, and which of us is not affected by back story in one form or another? In Arthur's case, it had already had repercussions, though, in the form of the current financial straits of Old Herne's.

I didn't want to take that further and consider how that might have taken on a much darker perspective and led to Mike's death, but I knew I would have to before we parted, and it wasn't going to be easy. All I could do was tackle it head on.

'Arthur, I have to decide whether what you've told me affects the job I'm doing for you too much to continue.'

'Go on.' His voice was very clipped.

'Your reprieve for Old Herne's opens up the possibility that his killer didn't want the club to continue.'

'Why would that be?' Even more clipped.

Here goes, I thought. 'Either because Mike would still be at the helm which would mean the end of the club or because his death could open up opportunities. Mike being your son complicates either motive.'

I waited for the storm to break and by the look on Arthur's face it was imminent. But it passed to my relief.

'When we talked this job over, Jack, I told you there were no holds barred and I meant it, however close to home.'

I risked a step further. 'Now Mike is dead, there are already changes afoot—'

'Off limits, Jack.'

It was a mild reproof but technically he was right, or near enough for me not to fight it. 'So might this be, then. If the end of Old Herne's was the plan behind his death the threat to you also increases. We talked about that earlier. Does that conversation still hold good?'

'It does – or would if I were at risk. But I'm not. So that being settled, are you going on or not?'

I wrestled with this. The mortgage hovered above my head, my conscience pushed it away. Back it came, and this time I gave it a good kick. 'I will,' I told him, 'but you don't pay me. I'll do it for Mike's sake. That way I'm on a level playing field.'

A short laugh. 'You English. Always "Play up, play up and play the game" with you. OK, I'll go with that.'

'No game,' I said soberly. And then I braced myself. 'The Porsche,' I began. 'If I'm going on, I have to cover *every* possibility, so is it conceivable that Mike would have arranged for the Porsche to be stolen in order to get the compensation?'

That did it. He exploded. '*Are you crazy?*'

'I have to rule it out, Arthur. You paid the insurance premiums but Mike would have got the insurance if the car wasn't found. It could be one explanation for his death.'

'How does that go?' he whipped back at me.

'Suppose somebody – Anna, for instance – pushed him into it?'

This time the explosion was different. It was a laugh – of relief? 'Nothing, certainly not Anna, could have pushed Mike into parting with that car.'

'Not even if he desperately needed cash to put into Old Herne's as he offered to do? He couldn't have sold the car because it was Old Herne's icon – and yours.'

Arthur stopped laughing and weighed this up. Then he came back at me with a decisive: 'He wouldn't do it. Period. Full stop. Never.' With that, he courteously thanked me for the afternoon and went straight into Nightmare Abbey without a backward look.

Families. Was it the truth or only the truth as seen through a mental block because Mike was his son? Maybe family relationships have always controlled history right from Adam and Eve down through the ages. Look at Queen Victoria's offspring, spreading their influence all over Europe and beyond. Look at the Bushes, the Kennedys . . . Why should the Howells be different?

My perspective on Arthur was changing. With age, his emotions towards his family and his business instincts might have fused to a point where he could not see that putting Glenn in charge was dangerous – especially with Mike's death unsolved.

As far as Old Herne's was concerned, the reasons for the murder had now expanded from the impersonal business angle to the personal. The family trust and the rest of the family fortune could, from Glenn and Fenella's viewpoint, be at risk. And then there was Ray Nelson, who had clearly loathed Mike, not to mention the sleeping dog, Peter, who, whether he knew about Mike's parentage or not, could be sitting pretty for the biggest bone of his life if Old Herne's continued and Glenn returned to the States. He could be planning to cut Jessica out by teeming up with Fenella. The various angles spun around in my head, but in their midst sat Arthur.

Eventually, I abandoned the game of happy or unhappy families and cooked myself some spaghetti. This began with an uninspiring tomato sauce but, once it had captured my attention, I managed with the addition of a tin of anchovies, a half used jar of black olives, a few capers and some tinned tuna to make a passable puttanesca (Italian for slut – and that's being polite).

It wasn't until late in the evening that I thought of Jessica. Arthur might be in the centre of the web but she could be trapped within it. I thought of the weekend just past, I thought of the next date we had arranged and I glowed. Unfortunately, one can't glow for ever on a pleasant thought. Between now and the fulfilment of the glow Old Herne's still loomed, and with Arthur in the firing line (and it seemed to me he almost certainly was) I couldn't waste time. I could not question Brandon's witnesses or lines of enquiry but I could try Dave Jennings, especially if I could persuade him that the Porsche might still be a part of the picture, however minor.

On Wednesday morning I put this plan into practice and rang Dave. He wasn't encouraging and only surrendered when I pointed out that the Porsche was still on his books because the thief hadn't been tracked down. He said he *might* get back to me and, yes, Brandon was following up a family line. I'd reported the gist of my conversation with Arthur to him, but the news about Mike's parentage had not overexcited him. That was natural enough, I supposed, as he works from forensic evidence not emotional.

I had noticed yesterday that the Lagonda had a tyre that was looking past its prime, so I took her round from her barn-cum-garage and asked Len to check it.

'Not looking good,' he said, having scrutinized the whole car. Then he added, 'Could be the end of it.'

'What do you mean?' I yelped, terrified at this verdict on my beloved classic. 'It's survived over seventy years so it can go on for ever.'

Len straightened up. 'I meant Old Herne's. Not with a lightweight running it,' he said dismissively.

I struggled to restrain my wrath. 'Lightweight? Not when you know her.'

Silence. Then: 'I meant this Glenn fellow.'

I wondered uneasily why I had jumped so quickly to the conclusion that he was thinking of Jessica and why I felt the need to defend her.

'Probably he is,' I said, 'but it's early days.'

'Moving too fast, Tim says. Wants to throw out all the Mike's Track Day prizes and all the back issues of *The Automobile*. They're gold dust. And that's only the start.'

I was appalled. 'He can't do that.'

But we both knew he could. 'Take everything for the Glory Boot?' Len ventured.

Such a simple thing to say, but again we both knew what that would involve. So far the Glory Boot had remained as my father had created it. Nothing added, nothing disposed of. I regarded myself only as custodian, but now Len was suggesting that I turn curator by adding to it. That meant commitment, and however minor a matter it might *seem* both Len and I knew it wasn't minor at all.

'I'll think about it,' I told him.

Len said no more, but I sensed I had failed him. The subject passed, but I knew I should at least check into it. I swayed this way and that. Should I talk Glenn out of it? Talk to Arthur? No, that one wouldn't work. Accept these glories of the past myself? The Glory Boot was stuffed full at present which meant I would have to convert another outbuilding, and I hadn't the cash. Did I want to take everything? No, but I couldn't stand by and see all those glorious objects put on the scrap heap. Julian Carter's museum was a possibility but he had more than enough of his own unsorted automobilia.*

At the moment, a chat with Jessica seemed the most enjoyable next step, but when I called her she didn't answer. Before I could decide on the next most enjoyable step the phone rang, but it wasn't Jessica. It was Jenny Ansty.

'How's the Porsche?' she asked in a voice heavy with meaning.

'I'm sorry to say it's doing well under its new owner.'

'And he is?'

'Confidential information.'

'No it's not,' she assured me. 'I was just testing. Everyone knows it's Jason Pryde. Tell him I'll be along to see him shortly.'

'He'll be terrified.'

'Justifiably, but that's not why I rang. I've seen Simon Marsh.'

That was a step forward. 'To chat to?'

'No, and he didn't see me. I recognized his car in Sevenoaks, and there he was at the wheel. Before I could blink, he'd gone.'

Hopes raised were immediately dampened. 'So you still don't know where he lives or works?' Of course she didn't. Alex Shaw would be too careful for that.

'No.' She sounded irritatingly cheerful about it.

'Thanks, Jenny.'

'But before I blinked, I wrote down the number.'

Dave decided to follow this one up himself as the Sussex Police were involved, so I would attack the problem from the other end by trying to contact Doubler. The Porsche theft might or might not be tied into Mike's murder, but I don't like loose ends. Dave kindly tied up a few of them for me, courtesy of Brandon I presumed. I didn't ask as sometimes curiosity can kill of the best of relationships, let alone the wobbly ones.

---

* See *Classic in the Clouds*

'Still nothing on the prints side,' Dave told me, as I had expected, given that the Crossley was on public display.

'Not even the axe?' I asked.

'No. Too many. DNA but no match.'

More helpful. 'Anything else?'

'Yes. Clothing fibres on the greatcoat. Only one match so far. Tim Jarvis's overalls.'

Bad news, but then Tim could well have worn that quite innocently. 'And alibis?'

'Not leading anywhere so far.'

It was turning out to be an unproductive morning all round. I couldn't face Old Herne's, so I concentrated on Doubler and Alex Shaw. All I had to go on was Harry Prince and the Huptons connection. I would avoid Harry like the plague, especially as with my noble gesture to Arthur my mortgage payments were again under threat. Not that I regretted what I'd done. The trouble with barging into family problems other than with your own is that you can never tell which side anyone's on because the goalposts move too quickly.

Huptons is a souped-up garage as plump and gloating as Harry himself. I'd never had much to do with it since Huptons' glossy image precludes them from cultivating the likes of me in my private capacity. In my professional one with the Kent Police Car Crime Unit they hold up their metaphorical hands in horror at the idea that they could possibly have any connection with whatever monstrous crime I was investigating. They are probably right, because they had never been proved wrong, although my natural inclination is to think that its sweet scent hides a stink beneath. Especially as the mere mention of Doubler's name had produced him on my doorstep. Somewhere under this golden gloss there must be a touch of rust.

An elegantly dressed young man swanned up to me to enquire my business when I arrived at Huptons on Thursday morning, so I explained courteously that I wished to meet Doubler.

His expression did not change. 'Who is this gentleman?' he enquired equally politely.

'Just give him my name.'

'But we know no Mr Doubler.' He looked hurt.

'Can I take it Mr Prince won't know him either?'

His eyes flickered. 'One moment, I'll call Mr Harris.'

Another excellently cut suit glided up to me in due course, inside which was a somewhat older gentleman who also informed me that Mr Doubler was unknown to him, though it was true that every so often various ladies and gentlemen mistakenly thought he was. 'If this Mr Doubler should pass by, shall I give him your card?'

'Please do and speedily.' I handed over my personal rather than my Kent Police card.

'And what should I say your business is about?'

I took a random shot. 'He left some of his property at my house. I'd like to return it.'

'Shall I say of what this consists?'

'A Remembrance Day poppy.'

I noticed that the poppy made no impression on Mr Harris, but that didn't mean it would not do so on Doubler. Although that poppy could simply have been stuffed into a coat pocket and emerged by accident, I didn't associate Doubler with carelessness. I had stopped trying to interpret a possibly meaningless emblem, however, as I had more to think about. Such as if Doubler obliged me with a repeat visit, what exactly was I going to ask him? Plead with him to know more about the Porsche story? That would get me nowhere. Ask him about Alex Shaw? Same result. So what *would* get through to him?

Nothing came to me, but as I drove home it occurred to me that Liz might have some ideas. Time for a coffee, anyway. The garden centre she runs at Piper's Green is not gigantic but she knows what she is doing and the centre reflects it. This was evident from the number of people there even though it was midweek and Piper's Green is hardly on the beaten track. I could see no sign of her in her office, but spotted her outside standing thoughtfully with a potted patio rose in her hands.

'Bunch of lavender for the pretty lady?' I called out.

Taken by surprise, she dropped the rose. 'Thanks, Jack,' she said crossly.

I scrabbled to pick up the remains while she watched.

'Now you can buy me a coffee,' she commanded after I had performed this task.

Fine, just what I had in mind, and she led the way to the excellent cafe she and her devoted staff members run, and once settled at a table with refreshment, it was easy going. 'What would you do with a poppy?' I asked, too intent on my problem to make sense.

'Stop it spreading its seeds around.'

'An artificial one,' I amended. 'For a buttonhole,' I added.

'After Remembrance Sunday? Ours usually hang around the house until Colin throws them out.'

'You don't carry it around with you?'

'Good grief, no. Jack, do you have anything more important to talk about?'

'It may be important. Why would someone leave one in my house for me to find?'

She sighed. 'To irritate me. Cough it up, Jack. Tell me everything or get lost.'

So I told her the story, excluding Doubler's name which I deemed would be bad for her health.

Liz is a good listener. 'Perhaps this chap wanted to remind you of someone you have in common.'

'We haven't anyone in common except a crook, who's very much alive, and a car.'

Liz is quick on the uptake. 'Ah. The Porsche. Is this about Jason?'

'No.'

'In that case the poppy's probably something this mysterious visitor of yours wants you to follow up.'

'I could have worked that out for myself. What kind of thing?'

'No idea. Perhaps he thinks you're such a smart ass you'll work that out too.'

'Too kind, Liz. Always such a flatterer.' Change subject. 'Are you still standing in as Jason's singing partner? Or are all concerts off at present?'

'Ongoing. I was meant to be at a rehearsal today, but he's cancelled.'

'Arthur not well?'

'No. Urgent meeting at Old Herne's.'

I'd have thought little of this, if I hadn't checked my iPhone before I left Liz. A text from Jessica awaited me. 'Need U. Come OH asap.'

And then a voice message from Arthur Howell. 'Get up to Old Herne's, Jack. Stand in for me, if you please. And hurry.'

Old Herne's was still standing. I half expected to find it on fire when I arrived with Len. Behind my Alfa Zoe's old Fiesta was coughing and spluttering its way up the hill. Len has refused to drive in her car until she upgrades for a newer model, but her reply is that you could say that of him too, so it's stand-off at present. I had briefly touched base at Frogs Hill before I set off and Len and Zoe had promptly downed tools and declared they were coming too. I assumed they must know what it was about, but it turned out that Len was on edge because Tim had been full of dire forebodings and might need support.

'He said there'd be trouble,' Len grunted.

He must have meant big trouble to get Len and Zoe to leave the Pits with their Lea-Francis 1932 Ace of Spades to work on. It had been a long job, but then their jobs are always long. They love them so much.

The large notice board at Old Herne's gates proclaimed: 'Closed for renovations', but we took no notice as we sailed in, parked and then made our way to the sharp end of operations.

'There's Tim,' Zoe exclaimed as we reached the clubhouse. We could see him standing outside Morgans, the nearer of the two hangars. Len and I were a step or so behind Zoe as we hurried over to him, but Zoe stopped abruptly when we got closer. Then we could see why Tim had taken no notice of our arrival. He was sobbing his heart out. In unspoken agreement it was Len who went to join Tim while Zoe and I hung back. We were near enough by that time to hear his choked voice though.

'I'm going to be fired.'

Len stepped up beside him, no need to say anything. These old friends did not need words, but after a moment or two Zoe and I joined them. We were both appalled.

'They can't do that, Tim,' I said. 'You're an unpaid volunteer.'

'Told me I wasn't wanted. Keep away. Just because I protested when they said they'd be throwing out a lot of the junk in the hangars.'

A long silence. Then Len asked, 'Just you, Tim?'

'Dunno. But the writing's on the wall, Len. Anyone who knew Mike will be out, you mark my words.'

Not, I decided, if I could do anything about it. I was going to insist on talking to Arthur over this to make him see sense. He'd told me he didn't want Old Herne's to close, but under this management the Old Herne's he loved *would* in effect close. It was unlikely anything could yet have been signed over the trust, and the agreement would undoubtedly need redrafting if Glenn were to be trustee as well as manager. I had to make Arthur see what was being sacrificed: the Old Herne's he loved, and Tim too. Surely Arthur wouldn't agree to that? Not Tim of all people. Unwillingly, I remembered his DNA on the greatcoat and that he hadn't been present at the discovery of Mike's body, but there were other fibres on the coat and other people whose movements had to be accounted for. A terrible thought then came to me. Could Arthur possibly have sanctioned Tim's removal because he thought he might have been Mike's killer? I forced myself to examine this thesis objectively, but to my relief came up with the answer no – until a niggle reminded me I could be prejudiced.

I left Zoe and Len with Tim while I went back to the clubhouse. However much I felt for Tim my priority today had to be the meeting. All seemed quiet from the outside, but directly I walked in the main door I could hear voices. Lots of them, angry ones. There was already a slanging match in progress, and I thought it might be wise to take a quick intelligence recce before I entered it. Hedda would be ideal, so I nipped into the bar.

'What's going on up there?' I asked her.

'Merry hell,' she replied cheerfully. 'My dad's up there too.'

'He's not a shouter.'

'No, but the rest are. Ray, Glenn, Fenella, Boadicea, Peter, the lot. Jess too.'

'What are they arguing about?'

She shot me a look. 'Better find out yourself, boyo.'

The door was open and no one noticed me enter. The assembly was too intent on what was going on. I could see Ray Nelson's back, Peter next to Fenella on an uncomfortable looking sofa, Jason standing by the window with a slight smile on his face, Jessica and Boadicea both looking flushed and angry and Glenn sitting by himself on a managerial-type chair. Knives were obviously not only out but being flourished (metaphorically, at least).

Then Ray's voice rang out loud and clear over the general uproar. 'I've had enough of this. He wasn't even my bloody son, Arthur spawned him.'

The noise stopped dead and I tried to gather my wits. This beggared belief. Surely Arthur could not have been expecting this? Mike's parentage would be the last subject he would want discussed publicly. And worse, what if Glenn and Fenella still did not know the truth? There was nothing I could to help, however, and I awaited the repercussions with foreboding. When the silence was broken, it was by Glenn showing a chilling calmness.

'You telling me that jerk was my brother, Ray?'

Fenella's face had abandoned inscrutability for sheer horror, and Peter put his arm round her. She didn't seem even to notice. Looking at Peter, I wondered whether this revelation was news to him or not, as his face remained impassive.

Glenn spotted me, but swept on after a dismissive glance. 'That kind of explains the drain on the family fortunes. Blackmail, was it, Ray? A touch of your saying you got my wife in the family way, Arthur Howell, so how about you give me an easy ride for the rest of my life?'

I was here as Arthur's representative but I couldn't speak for him. How on earth could Arthur not have told Glenn before this? All I could do now was play observer.

Ray was purple in the face with fury, as though the pent up emotions of years were spilling out – spitting out would be a more accurate description. 'A drain on family fortunes, that's rich. What have you ever added to them? I brought up his son.'

'By my grandmother,' Peter smoothly observed. He must be between a rock and a hard place: should he support his family or keep in with the Howells? Either way, Miranda Pryde was his best card.

'Keep out of this, Peter,' Ray snapped.

'It seems to me,' Fenella said coolly, 'that he and I are very much part of this. We're the inheritors of this mess.'

Glenn came right back at her. 'No Nelsons are going to get in my path.'

'Not yours,' Fenella retorted. '*Ours*, Dad, and incidentally Peter's included in that. I've hired him as a consultant.'

Had she indeed? Peter's waiting game must be over.

'Then I'll fire him again,' Glenn shot back.

I caught Jessica's eye and prepared to weigh in on her side if she needed it but that didn't seem to be necessary. She was well below the parapet in this battle.

I was wrong, though, because she bravely intervened. 'Aren't we getting away from the future of Old Herne's and how it can be saved?'

It was a good try, but it failed.

'I'll decide what its future is,' Glenn said in his quiet I've-won-thousands-of-boardroom-battles-and-not-lost-one voice.

Boadicea then entered the ring, and with some dignity. 'In the light of my husband's death, it's up to Arthur to decide what happens next. He could surprise you all, when he has had time to reflect on *my* legal position with regard to Old Herne's.'

She seemed quite confident, and I wondered whether she was playing her own version of castles in the air or whether she did indeed have some firm basis for this?

'Meanwhile, Anna, I'll manage this place as long as I choose,' Glenn shot back.

Then Jason at last stirred lazily into life. 'Actually, Glenn, for as long as my grandfather and I choose.' He was no longer smiling.

ELEVEN

I returned to the car park a frustrated man. The number of things I didn't know about this case was shooting up rapidly, and the number I did know was definitely under query. On my list for the 'Don't Knows' was what Jason meant by Old Herne's not only being under Arthur's control but his too. Next came the question of what Arthur thought he was playing at over Old Herne's future. Top of the list of 'Do Knows', however, had been my belief that the Porsche had at least some minor connection with Mike's murder, but now I wasn't even sure about that.

Apart from Boadicea, who might still be asserting claims on it, the bone of contention currently being torn apart by the family was not the Porsche but a power struggle. The meeting had abruptly broken up (or rather down) at Jason's declaration. Glenn had duly asked me to leave, and as Arthur's representative I had duly refused while they were still gathered there, whereupon Glenn declared it at an end. No one had moved – certainly not me – until at last they admitted defeat leaving Jessica and myself gazing at each other with glazed eyes.

Instead of the heart to heart I wanted she simply said: 'I must go.' And to my surprise she did.

I had hoped to find Zoe and Len waiting in the bar but neither of them was there, which made me – unfairly – even more frustrated. When I reached the Alfa, however, I could see that someone at least wanted my company. Despite the fact that the car had been securely locked, Doubler was waiting for me in the passenger seat. The old raincoat he wore added the general air of insignificance that he seemed to favour.

I slid in beside him with resignation. True, I had wanted to see him, but not now, not here. 'Can I stand you a cup of tea?' I asked politely.

'That's most kind of you, Jack. I appreciate that. But I left my car at the Cricketers. Perhaps you'd run me back? We can chat there.'

'A pleasure,' I told him, less than sincerely.

'Run back, not over,' he said reflectively as we drove off. 'Not like our poor friend Mike. Who committed that deed, Jack? Do you know?'

'Not yet.' I wasn't crossing him off the list, not while the Porsche theft still held mysteries – although even if Doubler was still on my list, I didn't want to be on his.

It seemed strange to be walking into the hotel with Doubler, but he was clearly unperturbed. Another double for him, I supposed. The man who hid himself so carefully from prying eyes could walk with supreme confidence into public places. The raincoat only added to his aplomb. He reminded me of an acquaintance of my father's, who used to work for the intelligence services in the 1930s. No James Bond Martinis and flair for him. He had been another Doubler, small, slight, unremarkable and therefore unnoticeable. His sole effort at camouflage, so Dad had told me, had been to tip his Trilby hat over his eyes to avoid attention.

'Business first, I think,' Doubler said as we reached the Cricketers bar lounge. 'Then we can relax and enjoy our beverages. You wanted to see me?'

'I did. As my message said, I'd like to return your property, but I don't have it with me.'

'Remind me. What property is that?'

'An artificial poppy.'

'Dear me, is that all?' He looked quite disappointed. 'It seems a trivial matter. It must have fallen from my pocket during our last pleasant meeting. I'm a sentimental person, Jack. Poppies for remembrance and so on. I'll pick it up some time.'

'Excellent,' I murmured. 'Remembering whom?' I had been about to add 'Doubler' but stopped in time. He wouldn't appreciate that.

'Shall we stick to more material matters, Jack?' A note of steel now. 'For instance, I mentioned Mike Nelson. Are your police friends following up every line?'

'I was employed by them to find the Porsche, not his murderer.'

'But if the two cases are one?' he asked gently.

I froze. Was he probing for information or warning me to keep off? 'I still wouldn't be in the loop. The Porsche case is over.'

'But Nelson's murder is not. And that's a dangerous situation, Jack.'

'Only for his killer.'

'I disagree. When killers are frightened, they lash out, Jack. Had that occurred to you?'

I faced this one head on. 'Are you hinting someone else might be attacked, or are you threatening me?'

'Warning you, Jack. A friendly act. For my sake, keep a careful eye on the good guys. *Remember.*'

What on earth did he mean by that? And what good guys? 'Who—'

'Enough, I think. What else do you require of me?'

'Alex Shaw,' I told him. 'And the Porsche.'

'As for this Alex Shaw, I confess I'm bewildered. I heard a Simon Marsh was involved, and as you say the Porsche has now been restored to the owner's family.'

'Restoration isn't your line, Doubler, however beautiful the object.'

'What do you consider is my line?'

'Power.'

He pondered this. 'You may be right. Power, yes. I take exception to being double crossed, however. Remember that too.'

The pleasant smile that accompanied this failed to fool me. I would most certainly remember. 'Were you double-crossed over the Porsche? The police files are still open.'

A long pause. 'As to Simon Marsh – are you asking me for free passage if you find him?' Doubler asked.

'Yes. I'll go carefully with him.'

'In your shoes, Jack, I wouldn't go at all. I really wouldn't.'

When I arrived back at the Pits, albeit still in one piece, I was considerably shaken and wondering how I could best pull myself together. One solution might be to give the Alfa a good clean outside and in. It felt slimy from Doubler's presence even if the slime was only in my head.

As I drove through the gates, however, I saw I had visitors. Two cars. My spirits rose because one of them was Jessica's. There was no sign of her or of the other visitor so I made for the Pits. No one there, yet the doors were open and the Fiesta was back from Old Herne's so they were around somewhere. On a sunny day it seemed likely they would be outside, so I toddled off round the side of the farmhouse in case they were admiring the Lagonda and Gordon-Keeble.

No sign of them there either, but I could hear the sound of voices from the terrace so I opened the garden gate. There, sitting round the table outside the farmhouse windows, were Len, Zoe, Jessica – and Tim. They were engaged in such earnest discussion that they didn't even notice my arrival on the scene. Jessica was the first to spot me.

'War strategy being worked out,' she explained as I sat down to join the conference.

'Which enemy?' I asked cautiously. 'The entire Howell family?' It was great to see her, especially as her presence indicated she was taking Tim's side.

'No,' she replied. 'It's Glenn's plans. The balloon's gone up with a vengeance. Tim is going to be fired and the place is to be given a blitzkrieg makeover. We can put up with makeovers but we can't do without Tim. We have to do something to stop this madness.'

'What about Jason?' I asked. 'He implied he stood above Glenn in the pecking order.'

'I've no idea. He must just be trading on his good relationship with Arthur. Do you know what he meant, Tim?' she asked.

'It's Mr Arthur pulls the strings,' he replied gloomily, 'whatever young Jason says. You mark my words, I'm only the first to go. All of us old school will follow, you'll see.'

'I'm here as umpire, Jack,' Jessica explained. 'I'm taking Tim's case to Arthur.'

That was good news, but I wasn't sure she was going to get anywhere after this morning's showdown. 'Are you going with her, Tim?'

'Don't need to,' Tim replied with confidence. 'Arthur and I see eye to eye, always have. I look after that Morgan of his, don't I? He won't want me to go, but I can't stay on to see the heart and soul ripped out of the place. That's why Miss Hart can speak better for me than I can.'

'Not necessarily, Tim,' Zoe said – bravely, I thought. I suspected she was trying to hint that even Jessica had to consider her position.

'Tim's the last reserve,' Jessica said. 'If I get nowhere on common sense grounds then he can make a personal appeal.'

That sounded a good tactic. 'Whose side are Fenella and Peter on?' I asked.

'Their own,' Jessica replied promptly.

'On a united front?'

'Peter will make it look that way. He's hell-bent on trying to get rid of Glenn, whereas Fenella has her own agenda.'

'Also to get rid of Glenn?'

'No. To get rid of me,' Jessica said bluntly.

She could be right. 'Don't move too quickly,' I warned her. 'They can play a waiting game and drive you to crisis point in the meantime. You might try encouraging Glenn to make a mess of it and then pounce – before Old Herne's is wrecked.'

'He's moving too quickly, Jack, and only Arthur can decide to pull the plug.'

'Does Arthur know Tim's been fired?' I asked her.

Jessica looked embarrassed. 'I'm afraid he does.'

I could see the shock written all over Tim's face.

'Did you tell him or Glenn?' I asked Jessica steadily. This was looking very bad.

'I did. I rang him before that disastrous meeting. Glenn called that, and I knew there'd be trouble of some sort.'

Which explained my urgent orders from Arthur to attend it. I was puzzled by the fact that Jessica had pre-empted Glenn over Tim and why Arthur hadn't stepped in. 'What did he say?'

'That Glenn was in charge and would be making his report to him in due course.'

Not the Arthur I thought I knew. The one I knew was decisive, clear-minded and believed in action. Had Miranda Pryde thrown more of a spell over his judgement in the last day or two than I had realized? With Mike's death that was entirely possible. It might also explain his reluctance to tell Glenn and Fenella about Mike. He and Miranda were currently together in a separate compartment of his life. Even so, Arthur liked being in control, and I wondered uneasily whether his reaction to Jessica's call had been a move on his chessboard? If I was right, what other moves might he have up his sleeve and did they relate to Mike's murder?

That took me back to Doubler and his warning (or threat) that murder might not stop with Mike. And that was a very unpleasant thought. Now another one occurred to me. If it had been a warning then – as Doubler was not going to be concerned over the Howell family, only Mike's – that meant, as I'd feared, that Jason or, much more likely in the circumstances, Arthur could be the target.

Jessica looked exhausted, so we called a halt on Old Herne's, and when Tim, Len and Zoe had departed we turned to more private matters. The late afternoon seemed to call for a walk over the fields to a country pub where we could feed the ducks on the village duck-pond and then ourselves. Idyllic. And so, as Samuel Pepys so famously said, to bed.

I rang Nightmare Abbey early on Friday morning in some trepidation, and was glad that Jason answered not Arthur. I shot questions at him. 'Is Arthur OK? When can I come over? I take it you've told him what happened at the meeting?'

Jason didn't sound surprised at the question. 'Some of it, and yes, he's here. Visitors. Dust needs to settle. Lots. Come tomorrow.' A pause. 'Should I be there?'

'I'd like to see you, but I need a chat with Arthur alone.'

'Up the airy mountain, down the rushy Glenn,' Jason misquoted cheerfully. 'Glenn's *very* rushy, isn't he? We daren't go a-hunting, for fear of Great Big Men. Such as you, Jack.'

'I don't terrify people.'

'Perhaps you should. Don't you want to know the truth about my father's murder?'

I was getting used to this jack-in-a-box style. 'Jason,' I said patiently, 'what time should I come?'

'Nightmare Abbey looks its best in the late afternoon sun. Not too many ghosts walk then.'

There was no point asking whose ghosts these might be, so I said I'd be along about four o'clock, and Jason informed me he'd have the cucumber sandwiches ready.

'You took your time,' Arthur observed as soon as I arrived. As it was exactly four o'clock I presumed he was referring to the gap since the Old Herne's meeting. The two-day gap must have been Jason's choice, perhaps to give Glenn and Fenella first shot at protest or perhaps Jessica. Arthur was in his own rooms, which were on the first floor overlooking the gardens at the rear of the house. No moat though; just a trickle of a stream wound its way through the gardens into the distance.

'I was giving you dust-settling time,' I replied.

'One thing I've found in life, Jack. Dust seldom settles, it merely rests before the next swirl.' Arthur looked buoyed up rather than flattened by the storm that must have erupted around him in the last couple of days. 'Jason's bringing tea in later. We'll get the talking done first.'

'Old Herne's,' I began. 'You asked me to go to that meeting, but that wasn't why you employed me or why I'm still involved. You wanted me to investigate Mike's death.'

'And that is what it's about, Jack,' he replied. 'Old Herne's, the people who run it, whether it should be run at all – that's all nothing beside the loss of my son. Not for one moment is that not in the foreground. All this crazy stuff that's going on at the club – it's a way to find out whether what happened to Mike had anything to do with Old Herne's itself. Even I can't foresee everything though. I didn't see Ray Nelson's coup coming. I've heard about it now from Glenn, Peter, Ray himself, Jason and Jessica. Now I want to hear from you, the outsider, about every blow, every move, every word that you can remember from that meeting.'

I was prepared for this, having made notes when I returned to Frogs Hill, so I made a good job of reconstructing what had gone on. When I finished, Arthur nodded slowly. 'That more or less fits in with the other accounts, all of which unsurprisingly had different slants. You've put it together well. Now tell me what's bothering you, Jack. I can see something is.'

I chose the easier of the two issues. 'First, Jason. He said he was in control of Old Herne's as well as you. What did he mean by that?'

'I'll explain but tell me the next problem before I do.'

'Why hadn't you told Glenn about Mike? It would have avoided all that uproar on Thursday.'

'Because I reckoned – and still do – that he already knew.'

'*What*?' I was exasperated. 'Then why not tell me that?'

He'd had time to prepare his answer of course. 'Because it

was me Glenn was mad at. It had nothing to do with Mike's murder.'

Surely he could see it had everything to do with it. Removing a trustee-cum-manager from control was one thing, removing the trust founder's son was in a different league.

I tried to keep calm. 'And Fenella? Did she guess too?'

'Probably. Glenn couldn't keep his own bank password a secret if someone pressed him hard enough.'

My face must have betrayed my reaction.

'Surprises you, eh?' Arthur continued. 'I'm a billionaire, Jack, and I didn't get that way by putting my heart instead of my head first. I love Glenn, don't think I don't, but a businessman he'll never be.'

'But –' I struggled for reason, wondering if Arthur had taken leave of his senses – 'you've just put him in charge of Old Herne's.'

'Correct – or nearly. That's what I need to explain. I don't believe some passing maniac killed Mike – which means it was someone close to Old Herne's, including the Nelsons and Howells. You think I'd go back to the US with my family with Mike's murderer not yet found? No way. I've appointed Glenn manager, not trustee, for three months or so to keep him quiet until Mike's murderer is behind bars. It will keep them busy. Glenn assumes he'll be staying on but all I want is to find out who murdered my son, which won't happen if I scatter the players. I'm not leaving until it's sorted out, and nor is my family. This is the way to do it. Understood?'

'Loud and clear.' This was no time for all the 'buts' rushing through my mind, chief of which was Jason.

'Right. Next. This matter of Tim and the other volunteers that Jessica's told me about. That's off centre. Tim's staying on at Old Herne's. Paid, this time.'

'Working for Glenn?'

'No. Answerable to Jason.'

Back to the joker in the pack. The cards in my hand seemed far fewer than I had realized. It was Arthur who held all the kings, queens and aces – and now it appeared the joker too.

'Jason has a watching brief on my behalf,' Arthur continued, 'on what's going on with Old Herne's. As for Tim, his official role will be Curator and Track Manager.'

Excellent. 'Paid by Jason privately?'

'No, by Old Herne's.'

Arthur was playing a dangerous game. 'Isn't that awkward if Glenn's CEO for three months?' I asked. 'At this rate there'll be no Old Herne's left to save. You know Glenn's planning to chuck out a lot of the automobilia from the hangars? Can you and Jason stop that?'

'I have. I guess even I can get old, and thinking about Mike I took my eye off the ball and let it get away from me. But I'm back on top now. I've told Glenn that from now on he's only in charge of the clubhouse, including bookings, reunions, renovations – it needs that. Fenella can do her makeover.'

He saw my expression. 'It's crying out for it, Jack. The hangars won't be touched without Tim's agreement.'

'Good.' I tried not to sound too clipped. I felt I'd been working on this case as an assistant junior rather than an independent sleuth, and if it wasn't for Mike and Jessica I'd throw in my hand completely.

Arthur came near to an apology. 'Too used to keeping things to myself, Jack. I like working on a need to know basis, but I got it wrong. Here's how it works. Glenn is temporary CEO but Jason is effectively in overall control until we get a new trust agreement signed. He'll be in it. Jason feels as strongly about the place as I do – and, incidentally, as strongly about Mike's murder. Trust agreements have to cover what happens in emergencies if the trustee is incapacitated or dies as Mike has. So as well as the trustee, a successor trustee had to be named. Mike was the successor trustee to Miranda. Only Mike, myself and more recently Jason knew what was in the existing trust agreement which was drawn up when Miranda died.

'As you know,' he continued, 'I came over here with the intention of closing Old Herne's down, but when the family and the Nelsons came to the Cricketers for drinks the evening before Swoosh I was still in two minds. There were questions about what would happen when Mike retired so I told them how the agreement worked, with the successor being his wife and, after her, Jason. With Mike's death, and Lily no longer being in the picture, Jason will be the trustee under a new agreement. Unless, of course, I change the terms or revoke the trust completely.'

And therein, I thought, could lie a threat to Arthur. 'Does Glenn know about this?'

'Only what I said at the lunch. In view of Mike's death, he knows only that he's acting manager and that Jason's representing me in overall control.'

I had to ask. 'And Jessica?'

Arthur smiled. 'Miss Hart will forge her own way.'

A polite rebuff. 'Does she know the situation?'

'Only as much as Glenn does.'

'What about Anna Nelson's position?'

Arthur sighed. 'Leave her to me. I'll see she's all right. She's out to please at present. She insisted we had a family gathering at High House last evening to decide about Mike's funeral. Not that we've any idea when that will be yet. Ray was not pleased, but he had to be present, of course.'

At that moment Jason arrived with the tea and cucumber sandwiches as promised and the ensuing conversation centred on the hangars, on Tim, and on possible fund-raising events for Old Herne's – for which they both claimed my input would be invaluable. The Porsche was not even mentioned, so I asked whether the registration had gone smoothly.

'Thank you, yes,' Jason told me.

'And it's running well?

'Perfectly.'

Another stone wall. 'Will you take it back to Old Herne's?'

'Not yet.' Jason picked up a sandwich. 'I grow the cucumbers myself. Did you know that?'

It all sounded great, but whether it would work out in practice was another matter. I decided to let the dogs of Old Herne's lie for a day or two in the hope they were sleeping off the effects of the rows, and Frogs Hill seemed a comparative haven for the next few days – I say comparative because Len and Zoe had the Lea-Francis to finish and it was clear from the set look on their faces that it wasn't going well. For me, it represented a stretch of clear road, however, after the recent gridlock at Old Herne's. There's something about looking out at the rolling hills beyond and the peaceful fields that does wonders for putting matters into perspective. Common sense might tell you that these peaceful fields are hiding a mountain of woes and centuries of crime and that even chalk downs have their sinkholes, but for me the sight was blissfully reassuring.

I had my doubts over Arthur's plan, partly because it seemed too full of possible pitfalls. I had to choose between thinking of him as a great brain now bowed down with grief and age and trying to figure out if something else lay behind his plan. Glenn manager for three months, Arthur wanting everyone under his eye while Mike's killer was hunted down . . . did the two mesh? Was Arthur pinning his hopes on me by keeping the group closest to Mike together? Hopes were surely too vague a basis for Arthur to work on, unless he was indeed too tired and sad to cope. Did he *expect* a result? I couldn't see any grounds for it so far. I realized it was much more likely he had his own ideas on who killed Mike. Was he guessing, though, did he know, or did he *fear*? What if the result he feared was that his own son Glenn was the culprit? That would fit the plan. Glenn had motivation if he'd been counting on the club closing down. To me that translated into a need to eliminate all other possible factors in Mike's death – including any remaining doubt over the Porsche's involvement.

Accordingly, on Friday I drove the Alfa to Lewes, with Brandon and Dave's reluctant permission. Alex Shaw had been traced, arrested, charged and released on police bail. I'd come alone which made me feel as though I were leading a Charge of the Light Brigade, every man jack of which had turned round and gone home except for me. I figured that it would not be in Alex Shaw's interests to tell Doubler of my visit on the grounds that Shaw had little hope of proving his innocence in the case, which meant that the further he kept from Doubler the better for his health.

My plan today was to behave as though Shaw was not aware that the car had been stolen, thereby hoping for an indication of whose idea it had been to steal it in the first place. I had rung him on this basis, telling him I'd come from the Kent Police Car Crime Unit and angling it that it was in his interests to see me if he was an innocent party.

Shaw lived in a village near Lewes in Sussex, which is a civilized and gracious town, not instantly associated with crime. Its international claim to fame is that in the eighteenth century it had hosted Tom Paine as an exciseman. Paine later went to the States where he helped draft the Declaration of Independence and wrote his best-seller, *The Rights of Man.* Alex Shaw, enterprising though he might be, was hardly in the same league.

His house was in a highly respectable close in a highly respectable hamlet called Dunsley. It looked so respectable that no criminal would dare to live there, which is probably why Shaw chose it. Such was my cynical thought as I stood on the doorstep awaiting the pleasure of Shaw's company. He proved to be tall, anxious-looking – a handy talent in his job – and good-looking, although not so outstandingly as to draw instant attraction on that account.

'Do come in, Mr Colby,' he murmured, peering round to see if the neighbours were watching. Then he led me through his highly respectable household to his living room where there were signs of a highly respectable wife and children, although none was visible at present.

And then we began the game.

'The Nelson family,' I kicked off, 'are delighted to have the car back, but it's hard on the innocent – Mrs Ansty and yourself.'

He pulled a face. 'You could say that. I'm sure you know I've been charged.'

'I do.' I waited to see if this led further.

It did. 'It's quite ridiculous,' he said. 'I was duped, just as Mrs Ansty was. I bought it from a dealer who it now appears doesn't exist.'

I decided to avoid the subject of dealers. 'You did buy it under a false name, Simon Marsh,' I pointed out.

A shy smile flashed in my direction. Good heavens, he had a dimple too. 'It's difficult, Mr Colby. It wasn't only myself involved.'

Ah, so that was the escape route.

'I suppose it will come out at the trial,' he continued, 'so I might as well tell you. I'm forced to have two names. I have a girlfriend.'

Nice one, Alex. 'How difficult for you,' I sympathized.

'It is. The car was for her.'

Naturally. One always buys a car worth well over a quarter of a million pounds for a girlfriend. Shaw was good, but he had all the hallmarks of the fraudster. The charm button had been pressed, but sooner or later he would relax his guard. There's a lack of what one might call aura around fraudsters or at least those that I've met. You can't tell that the charm is switched *on* because it appears to be so natural, but you *can* tell when it flicks off, even for a moment or two. The fraudster has retreated into an invisible icebox cut off from contact with you and only cold remote eyes look out at you through it.

I decided to slide over the topic of Jennifer Ansty. 'As I told you on the phone, I'm scouting around for the Car Crime Unit to find out just how the car came to be stolen in the first place. This dealer of yours – any idea how he came by the car? Could he have had a commission to steal it?'

He looked puzzled. 'A commission? You mean a customer asking him to steal it for him? No, he sold it to me.'

'Perhaps something went wrong, or perhaps the theft was the result of an insurance scam.'

I thought I'd gone too far, but he merely looked thoughtful. 'I see what you mean. Mike Nelson arranged for it to be stolen and then he was murdered. That's a terrible thought, poor chap. What a loss to Old Herne's – that's a great place. It says in the press that the owner is over here with his family. Isn't that singer Jason Pryde involved somehow? But I can't see a scam working – they must have plenty of money, so it seems unlikely.'

'What is unlikely,' I said chattily, 'is that a professional car thief would choose that particular car to pinch and hope to escape notice.'

The charm vanished as Alex Shaw closed his icebox around him. 'If you say so, Mr Colby. I'm not a car person – I'm in business. Frogs Hill, isn't it, where you live? Near Pluckley? A car restoration business?'

Now how would he know that if he wasn't a car person or didn't know Doubler? But the mere fact that I had got under Shaw's skin convinced me that I was on the right track about the Porsche theft being an inside job. What I didn't like, however, was his knowledge of Arthur and Jason. I couldn't yet see how they fitted into the Porsche story, but coupled with Doubler's threat to me about Arthur's safety it was ominous.

On my return I rang Nightmare Abbey in some trepidation to speak to Jason. 'Could you lay on extra security?' I asked him.

'Why?'

'I like to sleep easy and be sure that Arthur's OK *and* you.'

'We're both in the pink, Jack, thanks, but I'll do it.'

'Tell him I'll be along to see him.'

A pause. 'Always welcome,' Jason said.

I slept badly that night. I had nothing tangible to suggest that Arthur could be a target, but the thought had been well and truly planted. If Arthur died, to whose advantage would that be, as Cicero asked. *Cui bono?* Not the Nelsons', not Jason's, Tim's or Jessica's, but it would be to Glenn's and Fenella's. One way or another, there could well be a fuse laid where Arthur was concerned – and sooner or later it would be lit.

It was sooner, but I was wrong in one respect. On Tuesday morning came a call from Jessica who had just reached Old Herne's for the day. We'd spent a pleasant Sunday together and talked of meeting during the week so I wasn't surprised at the call – but then I realized her voice wasn't normal. She sounded frightened. 'The whole place is buzzing with police, Jack.'

'Friars Leas? Arthur? Jason?' That was my first fear.

'No. Old Herne's and High House. There's been another attack.'

I was so stunned I couldn't take it in at first. 'On Ray?'

'Boadicea. She's not dead, but near to it.'

TWELVE

I remembered Boadicea's hints that she might yet have a stake in Old Herne's future. Perhaps I had been reading too many Agatha Christies, but could this be the reason for the attack on her? Arthur had made it clear that so far as he was concerned, she had no stake at all, but that did not rule out the fact that someone might have believed her. It was possible that Arthur was misleading me, but I doubted that, and yet she, not Arthur, had been the next victim after Mike. I should have paid more attention to her. Dubbing someone with a mocking nickname can take them outside one's radar, and having been pigeon-holed they tend to remain there. Now Boadicea had stepped outside her pigeon-hole and left me temporarily floundering.

I drove straight to Old Herne's. No time today to admire scenery. I scarcely noticed it anyway as I cursed the number of vans thundering towards me on the single lane roads of the Downs. Vans can be arrogant vehicles, so this involved my stopping, reversing and hoisting my car up on to any handy verge or gap to allow them past. This sent my tension levels rocketing and I felt sick by the time I reached Old Herne's. I had calculated that there would be so many police cars and vans at High House that it would be better to park at Old Herne's and walk the rest of the way. Besides, I hoped to find Jessica here.

I mentally cursed again as there was no sign of her in her office and no one else around, so I took the footpath to High House, half of me wanting to run at the double to get there, the other half wanting to stay right where I was. The first half seemed to be controlling my legs, however, and the path brought me up to the side of the house, from where I could see plenty of activity in the forecourt where I gathered Boadicea had been found. I braced myself to join it and saw that Jessica had not been exaggerating. It was a major crime scene. I saw Brandon with several scene suited forensic personnel standing by the cordon, which sealed off the whole of the forecourt and some of the front garden, and more scene suited figures were working within it. I could see Jessica and Peter watching from the garden, and as soon as she spotted me Jessica came over.

'What happened?' I asked. All she had told me on the phone was that Boadicea had been found outside the house badly injured but still alive, not long after midnight.

'The police say she was hit from behind, probably as she parked her car last night. Ray had gone to bed at about nine, knowing that Anna was still out, as she always goes to choir practice on Monday evenings, getting home about ten. Ray sleeps downstairs but he's fairly deaf so he heard nothing. He woke up in the night, wondered why the house lights were still on, and got up to switch them off. He can walk a little bit and he found the front door still unlocked, peered out, saw the car and realized something was wrong.'

'How badly hurt is she?' I asked.

'I don't know. What's happening around here, Jack?' Jessica looked distraught. 'First Mike, now Boadicea. I don't think I can take any more. There are other jobs.'

'Don't make any snap decisions,' I told her. 'Old Herne's needs saving, and so it needs *you*.'

'I suppose you're right.'

I gave her a quick hug, just as Peter joined us. 'Any news on Ray?' I asked them.

Jessica answered. 'Suffering from shock, so he's been taken for a check-up.'

'A gory sight for the old chap, judging by the dried blood on the ground,' Peter commented. 'I've been here most of the night, and believe me, there's plenty of it around.'

'A word, Jack?' Brandon came out of the crime scene to talk to me. He's not a tall man, nor particularly prepossessing, but he does have an uncanny way of exuding authority without saying a word, so Jessica and Peter retreated. The cordon area was even larger than I'd thought, as the house was included in it, which bemused me until I realized that theoretically it was possible that Ray was the assailant or that someone else had come from the house or through it to attack Boadicea.

'No random attack then,' I said.

The answer was obvious and Brandon didn't bother to comment.

'No sign of a weapon yet, but it's a large blunt instrument of some sort. Luckily for her she had a heavy rain hat on, which gave some protection and threw off the assailant's aim.'

'Someone waiting for her?'

'Probably. That means someone who knew her movements. This was no random attack by someone hanging around in the hope of pinching a mobile phone.'

'Any car tracks?' I asked. The forecourt was paved which didn't help but there were verges, and the gravelled drive to High House might show something, especially with the recent rain.

'Vans and cars calling here all the time, but we're working on it. I'm treating this as connected to Mike Nelson's death. You agree?'

I was being *asked* my opinion? Glory be. 'High probability, I'd say. It looks as if the Grim Reaper's still hanging around Old Herne's. If I were in Arthur Howell's position, I'd be locking every door twice.'

Brandon frowned. 'You think he's at risk?'

'I did – but this has thrown me.'

'The forensics on Mike Nelson aren't throwing up a clear line yet, but I'm concentrating closely on the families involved, especially the Howells. That might fit in with the attack on Anna Nelson but not with a threat to Arthur Howell.' A pause. 'Could the staff, paid or unpaid, be involved?'

'I can't believe—' I stopped. What I believed was immaterial. Those who didn't know Old Herne's had been reprieved with no change of management, and who desperately wanted it to be saved, had just as much reason to want Mike out of the way as those that didn't want it to go on, if they saw Mike as the root problem. A new manager might achieve wonders.

Did Boadicea fit in with that scenario? If she knew who the killer was, yes, or – it occurred to me – if she herself had a genuine claim to Old Herne's.

I shivered although the day was already a warm one. There was a chilliness about High House for all its red-brick solidity and sheltered position. Houses reflect those who live in them, and this one had fared badly with Ray and Boadicea, at least since Mike's death. Perhaps it, too, was in mourning.

'Does Ray Nelson get on well with the victim?' Brandon asked.

'Far from it, but they're dependent on each other so it's unlikely that either of them would go too far, even if Ray were physically capable of such a blow, which I doubt.'

'And the rest of the families? I have the impression the victim wasn't universally loved.'

'She wasn't. There was enough family ill will around to stoke a lot of fires.'

'There was more than ill will here last night,' Brandon observed.

'She'd been hinting openly that she might have a stake in Old Herne's future, but Arthur Howell doesn't seem to agree and he should know.'

'I'll talk to him again. This attack looks planned. Someone either knew her regular evenings out or went out of their way to discover them.'

'Ray Nelson had been complaining about people traipsing in and out of High House so that could have been one way her movements became known.'

Brandon's gimlet eyes stared thoughtfully into mine. 'If she dies who would it materially affect?'

'No one as far as I can see, unless this claim of hers was significant. Arthur keeps all his cards close to his chest to say the least, but he told me the trust doesn't include Anna Nelson.' I gave him a run down on its provisions.

'So why this claim of hers?'

'I don't know. Arthur says he told them all on the evening before Swoosh what the situation was. When he died, the person who would take over would be Mike's wife—'

'You just said no one would gain by Anna Nelson's death,' Brandon broke in.

'No, his first wife, Lily.' Then I groaned. '*That's it*! Arthur told them the successor was Mike's wife under the trust agreement. That was drawn up in 1991, but Boadicea didn't know its provisions and assumed the wife he referred to that evening was herself. It wasn't – it was the first wife.'

'Careless of Howell not to redo the agreement when they were divorced.'

'Maybe Mike didn't want to change it. But even if Anna Nelson insisted it was her, she must have realized that Arthur could revoke the trust at any moment, so it wouldn't take her far.'

'She didn't strike me as the brightest of individuals,' Brandon said, and he was right. Boadicea could easily have convinced herself she was taking over Old Herne's, and if Arthur died she might think . . .

But that didn't make sense. Arthur might be at risk, but it was Boadicea who had been attacked. Nevertheless, if I were in Arthur's shoes I'd forget about staying on here for three months and get right on the next plane back to the US, before his Someone Up There was forestalled by someone a lot closer to home.

I spent the rest of the day with Jessica at Old Herne's, mainly because – understandably – she was jittery. There were few people around, and no one in the clubhouse except for Hedda indefatigably serving at the bar. She had brought in some life-saving pizzas which, coupled with a drink, served to occupy our minds for a while.

By the end of the day, however, the news was good. Ray was back home with a carer and Boadicea was off the danger list. Jessica and I decided to walk over to High House to check how Ray was, but security seemed likely to thwart us. There was a guard at the door, and when it opened a firm looking nurse informed us that there were to be no visitors.

Ray thought otherwise, because his voice rang out: 'Let them in.'

We were conducted frostily to Ray's bedroom where he was propped up on pillows looking remarkably good humoured.

'How's the old biddy then? Not this one –' he pointed at the nurse – 'the other one. In hospital. They won't tell me.'

'She's doing well,' Jessica told him.

'Not safe in your own home nowadays,' he grumbled.

'That's why I'm here,' the nurse said grimly, but she was ignored.

'Are you worried about being here on your own while Anna's in hospital?' I asked him.

'Won't be on my own. Security. Courtesy of bloody Arthur Howell.'

'That's nice of him,' Jessica said weakly.

'Not if it was him who tried to do Anna in.'

'That seems unlikely at his age.'

'Sent someone. You probably.' He glared at the nurse. 'After me now, are you?'

Did he really believe that? Possibly, I suspected. On a dark night, I reminded myself, a bush holds bears for most of us. The trouble with dismissing one's fears is that sometimes the bush really does harbour a bear – and some bears might hunt at night.

By unspoken assent, Jessica and I went our separate ways home to our separate homes, agreeing to 'start again' in the morning. When I reached Frogs Hill I realized I'd forgotten to check my mobile for some hours, and that and my landline has been busy. There were missed calls from, among others, Dave Jennings, but it was too late to call him back. This was briefly done on Wednesday morning, however.

'Alex Shaw,' he told me. 'Broke his bail conditions and might have done a runner. Thought you should know.'

'Why?' I asked cautiously.

'Might be after you.' Dave didn't sound bothered over this.

'Me?' That was a chilling thought, but then I struggled to reason it out. I couldn't see that my visit presented any worse threat to him than HM's justice system had. Then I remembered his oblique threat to me and mine, and thought the matter over more carefully. It didn't look good, even though I couldn't see what he would achieve by carrying it out.

'You and Mrs Ansty both,' he added.

This was getting serious. 'I didn't think Shaw was vicious?'

'He's a cornered rat. On the books he's violence free, but there's always a first time.'

'Very cheering.' I knew Dave was right, and anyone as involved with Doubler's affairs as Shaw wasn't going to be squeamish at the sight of blood – nor at spilling it. Still, this seemed out of proportion. Vengeance in the form of violence isn't a normal retaliation to being nicked for possession of stolen property. I'd put Shaw down as the front man doing the delicate jobs by day rather than the tough stuff at night. In Doubler's world, however, nothing is certain. I met a hardened killer once and he was a real wimp to look at. Only his eyes were those of a murderer. What were Shaw's eyes like? I stopped myself right there.

I then tried to ring Arthur, who had also tried to reach me, but he was on voicemail, so I left for Old Herne's where I waved at Hedda and bounded up the stairs straight to Jessica's office as arranged.

I stopped short on the threshold. Someone was sitting at her desk, but it wasn't Jessica. It was Fenella, looking as though she was making herself at home and enjoying it. Ominous.

'Well, hi,' she greeted me. 'Come in, Jack.'

'Isn't Jessica around?'

'Can't see her, but it's a nice office. Better get used to seeing me here.'

'Are you sharing it with her?'

'No. Let's say it's a temporary rearrangement. I'm here to superintend the refurbishment.'

'Does Jessica know about this?'

She smiled (inscrutably). 'Yeah. Not too pleased.'

'Does Arthur know?' I asked her.

'Is that your business?'

'Indirectly yes.'

'Because you two are an item?'

'Because the Porsche is an ongoing case and Jessica is involved.'

'Her office arrangements don't figure in that.'

'Everything and everyone here figures in it, since the Porsche case is linked to murder and now attempted murder.'

'Surely over-dramatic as regards my office affecting the issue. Is dear Jason number one suspect?'

I wasn't getting drawn in on that. 'Aren't you jumping the gun on refurbishment? I understood Glenn, and therefore you, is only in charge for three months.'

A flicker of emotion on the immaculate mask of her face. 'Three months to prove we can make it work, then my grandfather will firm the arrangement up.'

'With Jason in overall charge.'

'Jason's no problem.'

I tried another tack. 'You're a beautiful woman, Fenella, and intelligent and clever. Why knowingly bother to get on someone's wick?'

She came back just as smoothly. 'Because nothing will be

achieved by sitting back and doing nothing. That's why Old Herne's is where it is today – gasping for proper management.'

'Why not win Jessica over to your side then? She wants to save Old Herne's and she isn't exactly a dinosaur.'

'No,' Fenella agreed. 'If she was, I wouldn't have to play offices.' She looked as smug as though she had won game, set and match, but I was only pausing for the next game, guessing that Jessica had little to do with the root cause of Fenella's ploys.

'Why the need to play? Because you now know Mike was your father's brother?'

'Family business,' she snapped. 'Out of bounds.'

'Well within them considering there's been one death and another attempted killing.'

'Why do reckon my grandfather put us, his own family, in charge?' she flashed back. 'Because he knows the Nelsons were behind Mike's death.'

'A ninety-year-old man, a woman who has just been nearly killed herself and Peter, your friend and admirer.'

'How quaint,' she whipped back at me. 'Admirer indeed. Do you *admire* Jessica in bed, Jack?'

Before I could answer with the words that came immediately to mind, Jessica herself arrived on the battlefield, quivering with rage.

'I hope so,' she said coolly. 'Time to go, Jack.'

No way. I'd unfinished business here. 'You go, Jessica. I'll catch you in the bar.'

She must have seen the look in my eye because she went like a lamb. I then turned to Fenella and explained, so that she was in no doubt, that I was not going to fight on a personal level but when her three months was over I was *personally* going to have a discussion with her that would speed her on her way back to the States.

She didn't say a word.

'Skinned alive, are you?' Hedda asked cheerfully when I reached the bar, where Jessica looked pleased to see me.

'I'm by way of being an amateur tanner myself,' I replied, glancing at Jessica who gave a slight shake of the head. So she hadn't been having a girls' own discussion with Hedda. Good for her, she was keeping personalities out of it too.

'Don't worry, Jack,' she said, when I joined her. 'Humpty's put together again.'

'Good.' I kissed her, then added, 'I don't hold much brief for the lady, but she doesn't seem to me a natural biter.'

'What other sort is there?'

'A tight corner biter. Fighting to protect her own.' Just like Alex Shaw? Now that was an unpleasant thought.

'You mean the family name?'

'Plus interests.'

Jessica frowned. 'Peter's giving out signals that he'd like a quiet takeover in conjunction with me if they don't make good in these three months. He'll even help them not to make good.'

'That doesn't fit with the fact that Fenella was and still is his main chance. Perhaps he's aiming to be a compromise candidate by knowing the ropes but not being part of the inner management.'

'Like me, Jack?'

Damn. Foot put right in it. 'Is that what you want?'

'Not to the extent of exterminating the opposition,' she said drily. 'But I told you I wouldn't be number two for ever, and I do have the advantage of knowing the ropes.'

'So does Tim,' I joked to lighten the atmosphere.

She didn't laugh. 'Yes, and Arthur has told him his job is secure. And told me the same.' A pause. 'Even if I have been turned out of my office.'

I thought I'd find Tim in the little cubbyhole with the Information sign above it when I went to Morgans Hangar to congratulate him. I once went to a car museum where the information guy kept me captive for three hours while he lectured me on the forerunners to the motor car from the Stone Age to Nicolas-Joseph Cugnot and Richard Trevithick. I couldn't see Tim doing that – not yet, anyway.

Tim wasn't there, however, although a new sign, clearly painted in haste, read: *Curator*. Underneath was a printed notice that if he wasn't here try Thunderbolts.

I duly did so, and had better luck. Tim was there, although as the information sign had not yet been changed, I wondered if this was the first time he had been here on his own since Mike's death.

He could still be plucking up the courage to make any change at all to a place that held such happy and tragic memories.

'Good for you, Tim,' I greeted him. 'Glad to know you're staying on.'

'Just a misunderstanding,' he told me complacently, forgetting that I knew all too well that it hadn't been. 'So as for that stuff I told Len you could have for the Glory Boot, no problems now. I'm keeping it.'

'That's good. I take it there's been a change of heart over the refurbishing of the hangars at least.'

'Another misunderstanding,' he said firmly. 'Now I'm curator I'll have more say in things. No more misunderstandings, eh?'

'Great.' Then I switched topics. 'You've heard about Anna Nelson?'

'Couldn't miss it. Bad thing after all that happened . . .'

His voice trailed off, so I hastily asked, 'Can you work with Glenn Howell at least temporarily?'

'Sure, provided he keeps out of my way. I'm worried about young Hedda though.'

'Jason told me she wouldn't be affected.'

'I wouldn't be too sure of that. Cunning, that pair.'

He was right, so I returned to the bar before leaving. I could not believe Jason and Arthur would sanction hostile action against her, but anything was possible at present. I found father and daughter both in the bar, Jason sprawled in the window seat and Hedda sitting with him.

She grinned at me. 'You've had your last cup of coffee from me, Jack.'

I was horrified. 'You've been sacked?'

Jason raised an eyebrow. 'Glenn wouldn't dare. His own great-niece – how would that look in the management stakes?'

'I've resigned before he could do it,' Hedda said, straight-faced.

I was still at sea. 'What will you do now?'

'Well . . .' Hedda considered this. 'I could apply to be Ray's carer, I could ruin Dad's band by singing in it – or I could be a Bond girl.'

Still at sea. 'A film extra?'

'Not exactly.'

Jason had that laid-back look of amusement that I was beginning to know well. It meant I was expected to use my brain. Which I did, and made an educated guess.

'Assistant Curator under Tim?'

'Got it in two, Jack. He doesn't actually know yet, so I'm off to tell him. See you.' She swanned off with her shoulder bag swinging jauntily, leaving me with Jason.

'You play a cool hand, Jason,' I said with admiration.

'Mostly,' he agreed, then grew serious. 'I have to. This attack on Anna has brought it home to me. I can't play cool any more. There's Arthur to think of.'

'You agree there's a risk to him?'

'In a jungle you don't know where the enemy's hiding. Of course there's a risk.'

THIRTEEN

The Downs, the villages lying at their feet, the chalk cross carved into the grassy hillside – I'd reached my haven. I sat on the grass taking deep breaths of air in the hope of relaxing. Even though Arthur seemed to be exercising some sort of control, I had driven away feeling that I was escaping from a net so closely woven around Old Herne's and its politics that it was all too easy to be blind to what lay outside it. Such as that a murderer was on the loose.

Old Herne's itself seemed a mental fortress for those within it, while outside the barbarians hammered at Rome's gates. Come off it, I told myself impatiently, we're not in ancient Rome but twenty-first century Kent, a county that was accustomed to surviving against great odds. Surely I could manage this challenge measured against that yardstick. Hence my parking the car and walking along the Pilgrims Way track to the white cross carved into the hillside above the village of Lenham. The cross, a memorial to those who had died in the First World War, defined the village it guarded, a symbol of its history.

As was the red poppy.

A poppy like Doubler's. Who was far too young to have been in the Second World War let alone in the First. His family perhaps? But family was not a word I associated with Doubler.

Outside the core of Old Herne's stretched tentacles that had led to Mike's murder, the attempt on Boadicea's life and the shadow that still threatened it. The first tentacle I should follow up, I decided, was Boadicea.

I'd sought permission from Brandon to visit her and been given an ID pass as there was still a watch on her. She was well enough to talk, he told me, but so far had given little of value.

Hospitals can be scary places even for the visitor. Step inside, they seem to say, and prepare to leave the everyday world behind. This is *our* world. I couldn't have been properly prepared as, the next day, I entered the huge hospital in Ashford to which Boadicea had been brought, and I was taken aback at the sheer scale of it. Taking a deep breath, I plunged in and found my way easily enough through the maze of corridors, everyone intent on his or her own destinations. Boadicea was in a room to herself, of course, but I was alarmed to see no sign of a uniformed guard on any of the doors. Had she died after all?

I hurried back to the reception desk where I found that I was not the only enquirer. Peter was there.

'After the same bird, are we?' he greeted me. 'I gather she's flown to another hospital.'

'Which one?'

'Classified information. Even I can't be told and I'm family. Aunt Anna is an orphan, poor lady, so we Nelsons are all she has, apart from darling Jason. But here I am, turned from the door, so why don't we enjoy a coffee and you can tell me what's going on?'

If only I knew. Personally, I had no inclination to enjoy a coffee or otherwise with Peter Nelson but in Arthur's interests I had to take the suggestion up, so I prepared to be companionable as we walked to the café.

'Have you heard how she is, Jack, or are the police keeping mum about that too?' he asked me. 'All Ray and I are told is that she's doing well. I even rang dear Half-Cousin Jason but he claimed to know no more than we do. Any clues, Mr Detective?'

'*Car* detective. I only hear what's relevant to the Porsche. That's my limit.'

'Rather more than a car detective, I'm sure of that.' Peter gave his attention to his coffee as though it were the finest claret.

A sigh seemed in order. 'Only in that I'm a known face to DCI Brandon. We don't go drinking together.'

'You're close to Arthur too,' he said dispassionately.

'Over the Porsche.' I tried being wearily patient. 'He asked me to keep an eye on it and the Morgan.'

'And do you?'

It was time I threw this yapping little terrier off my track, albeit carefully. 'I don't sleep outside the control tower at nights, or outside Friars Leas, if that's what you mean.'

He grinned. 'Perhaps you should. The horse seems to have bolted from its stable. I saw the Morgan on the A20 this morning.'

I had a momentary alarm, but dispelled it. 'Must be some other Morgan. Great car, isn't it?' I added in the spirit of chumminess.

'Sure.' A pause – a calculated one, I thought. 'Who,' Peter continued, 'do you reckon attacked Aunt Anna? One of us, or a thwarted burglar?'

I parried this one. 'The jury's out, especially as she seems to make a policy of upsetting people, including Ray, although he's hardly likely to have nipped outside to attack her.' I had meant this as an attempt to lighten the atmosphere, but it failed.

A raised eyebrow. 'Why not?'

'Age, infirmity, and the energy it would require to bat someone from behind with a heavy implement from a wheelchair.'

He regarded me pityingly. 'Wheelchair? He can get out of it when he wants to. He plays the sympathy card.'

'Then I feel even more sorry for your aunt.' Could he be right? I wondered uneasily. I'd seen Ray only when he *was* in a wheelchair so I'd no means of knowing.

'Aunt Anna can hold her own, believe me. Probably held it too strongly with the wrong person. She was going around dropping mysterious hints about being in a difficult position and needing money.'

'She does seem to believe that she has a claim on being the next trustee of Old Herne's.'

'She hasn't,' Peter said shortly. 'She just thought she was going to blackmail Arthur into forking out a fortune for her.'

'It could be a genuine mistake, a misinterpretation of what Arthur told you all about Mike's wife being the successor trustee. She thought it was her, not the first wife.'

This was instantly dismissed. 'Don't you believe it, Mr Car Detective. Dear Half-Cousin Jason would make sure nothing and nobody comes between himself and Arthur.'

I could see why he might eye Jason with great suspicion, but of what? Of being Boadicea's attacker or of his having a major say in what Peter might see as his own rightful role at Old Herne's? Peter didn't strike me as a chap who paid hospital visits out of sheer good-heartedness, especially to half-aunts by marriage, which raised the question of whether

his interest in her recovery had altruistic or sinister motivation
behind it.

I reached Frogs Hill, to find the Pits humming. On the forecourt
was a Vauxhall estate car I didn't recognize – and then I spotted
Tim having an earnest discussion with Len and Zoe in the Pits.
It didn't take a lot of little grey cells to work out what about.
They were grouped around a car that looked like Arthur's Morgan.
So Peter really had seen it on the A20.

Len looked almost happy and Zoe was beaming. 'Tim brought
the Morgan in this morning, Jack,' Len explained. 'Wanted us
to take a look at it and he's returned for the verdict. Reckons
she's not firing on all four.'

'And that's all?' I asked.

Tim looked surprised. 'All? It's a serious matter. Jack.'

Of course it was – in terms of the Pits. 'Does Arthur know
where it is?'

'Yes. He's no problem with it.'

Then it wasn't with me, save for the responsibility of putting
this glorious classic to rights. With Len and Zoe cooing over it like
turtle doves, who was I to gainsay their pleasure by pointing out
there was an Armstrong Siddeley awaiting their urgent attention?

I was still meditating on Morgan Plus Fours long after the Pits
closed at six and Tim, Zoe and Len had departed. Until my mobile
rang, that is. It was Jason and he sounded upset. I was so used to
the laid-back Jason that his voice had sounded unfamiliar at first.
It was only when he mentioned Arthur that I clicked into gear.

'It's fine,' I said soothingly. 'Tell him we've got it safely in
the Pits.'

'What?'

'The Morgan.'

'It's not about that,' Jason said impatiently. 'Can you come to
Friars Leas this evening? Quickly. *Now?*'

The last thing I wanted. Frogs Hill had never seemed more
attractive, and a return to the Downs and their problems was less
than appealing.

'I don't call it Nightmare Abbey for nothing, Jack,' he
continued. 'I've had an anonymous call.'

Not unusual nowadays, but even so I didn't like the sound of this.

'He said to tell Jack Colby that if he wanted to be in at the end of the game he'd have to come to Friars Leas this evening.'

'Did you tell the police?' My first thought was that this was a mere frightener, but my second was that it might not be just that – and indeed almost certainly wasn't.

'Yes, they said they'd keep an eye on the place. But that's not the point, Jack. I've got my own security guards here, plus extra ones I've laid on – enough to challenge every shadow they see or sense.'

Security sounded very much the point to me. 'Outside and inside?' I asked.

'The place has been searched from top to bottom and then the extra guards moved in. I want you to come, Jack.'

It was a clichéd situation: 'Come unarmed into the dark lonely wood at midnight. Signed: a friend.' But clichés come from overuse not under. I had to treat it as a serious threat, especially as I had been specifically summoned.

'Could you get Arthur and yourself to safety elsewhere – the hotel?'

'No. He won't budge. Says if it's serious they will have thought of that and get at us on the way. So I won't go either.'

They will have thought of that . . . The indefinable enemy is always 'they'. The incalculable, the shadowy menace that might be there, that might be illusion. Which was it in this case? Hit men stationed on the roads around Nightmare Abbey? Over-dramatic, but taking care never killed the cat, so Arthur could be right to remain at Friars Leas. Talking of care – what about me? No one could have my murder as their prime objective, only as an additional extra. Arthur must surely be target number one with Jason number two and me either as witness – or third victim.

I seemed to be back to the Charge of the Light Brigade, whose ethics had seemed the epitome of gallantry to me when I was a youngster: 'Cannon to right of them . . . Cannon to left . . . Forward the Light Brigade . . . Was there a man dismayed?' Answer in my current case: Yes, me.

But even so I charged.

'I'm on my way,' I told Jason.

*   *   *

I took the Gordon-Keeble. If the Light Brigade was to be massa-
cred, it seemed right to go out in style. The Alfa was for every
day, the Lagonda for summer picnics, but the Gordon-Keeble
was my rock. A fragile one, I admitted, after having been used
literally as a rock once.* I only hoped Jason's security guards
weren't so jittery that they'd shoot on sight – and that they didn't
have the caller or his best mate amongst them.

It was almost an anticlimax when I was stopped at the gates
to Nightmare Abbey at about eight o'clock, gave my name,
showed my ID and was allowed to drive on with both the Gordon-
Keeble and myself unharmed.

Perhaps this was a storm in a teacup, I thought hopefully.
Jason had said that the Abbey looked its best in the fading
light, but how would one define 'best'? In a lowering storm
or heavy snow, those gables and towers might look even more
effective. When the Abbey door had closed behind me,
however, all seemed normal save that it had been opened by
a guard.

Jason, however, did not look normal. He was even paler than
usual and distinctly jittery. He couldn't be feigning this degree of
tension.

'Thanks for coming, Jack.'

'Part of the service,' I murmured. 'How's Arthur?'

Jason managed a grin. 'He's Arthur. It's me who's hitting the
panic button.'

'On his account?'

'On all our accounts.' He glanced at the portrait of Miranda
Pryde. 'Arthur's worried for you and for me, not himself. Usually,
when I'm wound up, I go into the studio, play or record and lose
myself. It's like stepping into the world of Oz. All tornadoes left
outside. It's not like that today.'

'Any idea at all who made that call?' The police would trace
it, but it would be handy to know now.

'No.'

He said it rather too quickly, I thought, but perhaps I was
mistaken. 'A man's voice?'

'Yes. Mobile. No answer when I rang back.'

---

* See *Classic in the Barn*

'Did he use your name?'

'I don't think so. No.'

'Then he knew you. He had to be sure of his target to ask you to pass on a message to me.'

Jason didn't comment, a useful way to avoid the subject being taken further. I comforted myself that if someone was planning my death, why bother to summon me to Nightmare Abbey where there would be witnesses? He could accomplish the same thing most evenings at Frogs Hill with just the stars watching. Unless, of course, Jason himself had plans to wipe me out? Or the caller wanted to down three in one go? I put these notions firmly behind me.

'Can I check the house again?' I asked.

'Go ahead.'

I opted for having a word with Arthur first. He was already in his bedroom, dressed for the occasion in a magnificent royal-blue dressing gown and the most comfortable furry slippers I'd ever seen. Nothing suggested he was expecting an armed killer. It was a large room and included two armchairs, a table, a TV, a pile of books and several newspapers. Then I froze. Lying on top of one of them was a red poppy. Coincidence? No way. Doubler was definitely back in town, and all my alarm bells were working overtime.

No one had mentioned a poppy. I'd got the message though, even if these two had not.

'Caught any spies yet, Jack?' Arthur asked, laying aside his glasses.

'Not yet. Preparing my Bond armoury. C's been describing the mission.'

Arthur laughed, but Jason looked at us both severely. 'You're not taking this seriously.'

'Wrong,' I told him. '*Very* seriously. What's your choice, Jason? Guard Arthur outside the room and let him go to bed, or all of us sit up together?' There was already a guard at the door.

'I'm going to bed,' Arthur declared before Jason could reply. 'You two can decide what you want to do.'

'Is this room vulnerable from outside?' The curtains were already drawn, but I moved across to check it myself.

'It's not,' Arthur told me firmly. 'No trees close enough to fire arrows or guns at me. Furthermore, as you two Sherlock Holmeses will observe, my bed's in the centre of the room, and there are no holes above, below or anywhere else from where snakes can slither down bellropes. It's just a perfectly ordinary room with windows over a sheer drop.'

I was peering out into the dusk both through his window and the adjoining bathroom. No handy trees or drainpipes and no chimney stacks, and the ground was sufficiently far beneath Arthur's window to deter the most intrepid cat burglar. Even Doubler's men.

'*And* the door locks,' Arthur added.

'*And* there's a guard on it,' Jason pointed out.

'Who will guard the guard?' I enquired.

Jason went pale. 'I'll pick another at random to join him. You and I can sit in the room opposite this one, Jack. We'll keep the door open, and there's an alarm bell to bring the whole army of them running.'

Basic stuff but valuable, even if Doubler's plan would take this into account. As we left Arthur to establish our temporary domain I realized I was here for the night. I only hoped I'd live through it. Harry Prince might not have to wait that much longer before he could put in his bid for Frogs Hill. Had I been a fool to come here? No way, I told myself. After all, I was leading the Light Brigade.

And then the lights went out.

I rushed to Arthur's room, which fortunately was not yet locked, colliding with the guard and with Jason cannoning into me from behind.

Jason's voice came out of the dark. 'Give it a few seconds, Jack. The emergency generator should kick in. One of the guards is down there.'

I fervently hoped that he wasn't lying unconscious or dead. Whoever planned this macabre evening would have reckoned on auxiliary power. He'd given Jason full warning after all, and now the show was beginning.

To my relief, Jason was right. The lights came on again, dimmer and flickering, but they held.

'Where *is* the generator?' I asked.

'In the cellars.'

'Door to the outside?'

'Yes, locked and bolted. No way, Jack, without heavy artillery.'

'I'll check there isn't any.'

'Maybe that's what they want you to do.'

I tried not to think that way. 'You and the guards stay with Arthur.' The second one had appeared by now.

Somehow the enemy – I decided that the less I thought of him as Doubler the better – had to reach Arthur if his plan was to work, so either he was hidden inside the house so cunningly that he had eluded discovery or he had an even longer range weapon trained on Arthur's window than I'd estimated and was waiting for an opportune moment. The other option was that he was one of the guards.

'How many guards inside the house altogether, Jason?'

'Two here, one on the main door, two at the rear doors, two at vulnerable windows, one in the cellars.'

'Chimneys blocked?'

'Covered by the outside guards.'

'I'll check the cellars again, then the rest of the house. Could you warn the guards?'

Even though the lights were dimmer now, searching the house wouldn't be as bad as crawling around in the dark or by candle-light. I reflected, however, that it was all very well to say I'd search the whole house but I was one man, Nightmare Abbey was huge and I didn't want to risk being harpooned by an overzealous guard who saw a dark shape creeping along a corridor or coming round a corner and had temporarily forgotten I was on the loose. It was agreed I would yell out 'Colby' when turning out of or into a corridor and the guard would yell back 'Jack'. A simple but I hoped effective plan, stupid though I would feel.

It was a strange ritual. I was straining for the least noise that was out of the ordinary. I duly yelled out 'Colby' at every turn, aware that if one of the guards was the assailant he wouldn't be yelling back and that I'd be walking straight into a bullet. Start at the bottom or the top of the house? Top, I decided. That way I could chase the enemy down rather than up. Or, of course, be chased. I didn't want to find myself jumping from a parapet into a moat that didn't exist.

In this antiquated building it was hard enough even with all the lights on, not to imagine a masked enemy round every corner. Turrets, corridors, bedrooms, bathrooms, storage rooms – each one sent a thrill of fear through me. Suppose I found myself looking directly into the enemy's eyes? The only weapon I had was a torch. The corridors were lined with prints and paintings, few of which I recognized, save for some eighteenth-century cartoons of Nightmare Abbey – Dr Syntax leapt out at me from one such print gloating over my predicament, it seemed. Impassive gentlemen and ladies from the past stared down at me in contempt as I crept by. I checked each room, leaving the door open in case of movement outside. No one came. The atmosphere was heavy but it told me I was alone, save for the guards whose voices dutifully rang out as arranged. Slowly, I worked my way down to the first floor and back to base with Jason.

'Nothing up there,' I said, 'except for the guards.'

He nodded but I could see he wasn't reassured.

Down to the ground floor. The lights seemed to be growing dimmer all the time, or perhaps that was my imagination. I went into the dark recording room, with the dimmest of lights. Nothing here but knobs to be turned, buttons to be pressed, instruments to be played. No music tonight.

And then I came to the cellars. No wine of ages here, just another workmanlike studio, storage and a generator. Plus its guard, who looked edgy as I called and then approached him. Every one of my muscles tensed up, in case he plunged us into darkness again or, worse, plunged something into me.

'Evening, sir,' was all he said, and sat down again, looking as relieved as I felt.

So the threat had to come from outside, and there was little I could do there, so I went to rejoin Jason on the first floor where a tray of sandwiches and drinks had appeared in our chosen base.

'Arthur okay?' I asked.

'He's snoring, so yes. What now?'

'Just you and me, Jason, and the long night ahead. If we're allowed it.'

We drank the hot chocolate, he and I. Jason was a teetotaller after his 'bad patch', as he termed it, but in any case I wouldn't have touched alcohol tonight. We ate the sandwiches, we talked of cars, we talked of music, of Miranda Pryde, of women in general (a little). We talked of daughters too, he of Hedda, and I of Cara, my daughter in Suffolk. After surviving her own bad patch – in her case with her partner – she had settled down to a rural life, and seemed happy enough to do so.

And so the long night passed until, at three thirty, the first bird began to sing. He had perceived first light, and never had his song been more welcome. We left it another half hour until Jason said at last: 'Go home, Jack. This has been a wild goose chase.'

'Unless we were deliberately kept together in this room.'

'You don't believe that, and nor do I. Arthur is safe and the guards are still at their posts. The night's over and dawn is coming.'

I wanted to believe him right and I did. No one would attack in the light. In summer people rise early. There are cows to milk, fields to plough, harvests to reap. It took the darkness for black clad figures to roam through it with guns.

I drove home in the Gordon-Keeble, past tiredness now, just wondering about life, about Jason and about tomorrow – or rather the day that now lay ahead of me. A day I had been by no means certain I would have when I set off yesterday evening. Time with Jessica? Just the two of us away from Old Herne's? Perhaps.

I reached the lane to Frogs Hill under a silent sky, with dawn barely yet here. The spirits are low just before dawn and I no longer felt elated that nothing had happened. I felt nothing but a great numbness. As I drove through the gates, I decided to leave the Gordon-Keeble on the forecourt. There were no car thieves prowling and the milkman was hardly likely to take a fancy to it so I clambered out of the car and headed for my front door.

And then I saw it.

A rounded long bundle on the gravel not far from the farmhouse door, as though a delivery van had called and merely dropped the merchandise where its courier stood, annoyed at the lack of reply. *Someone* had called . . . and left something. Even though the security lights were blazing it felt dark and I had a terrible foreboding as to what I was looking at.

The words of Jason's caller came back to me. *Tell Jack Colby if he wants to see the end of the game come to Friars Leas this evening.* He hadn't said that was where the game would be played. The game was with me and it was here.

This was the game.

A hand was poking out of the carpet wrapping. The delivery was a body.

FOURTEEN

had to force myself to go closer. I had to check in case there was still life extant. After all, I could be wrong. It might not be a human body – although I knew it was.

The food I had eaten earlier was on the brink of rejoining me, and I fought to keep it down as I struggled with fingers that wouldn't obey me. A rope needed cutting and I remembered the knife in the boot of the Gordon-Keeble. And then I had to do the cutting. I tried not to think of anything as I did so, but terrible images kept flashing through my mind. Was it Len – Zoe? Was it Jessica?

It was none of them.

It was a face I had only seen once before, but I recognized it immediately despite the staring eyes and gaping mouth. It was Alex Shaw's.

I rocked back on my heels, aware that my face was wet not with sweat but tears, perhaps for Shaw and his family, perhaps out of relief, perhaps because of the bloody senselessness of the way fate has of intervening in what we each see as our own privately arranged destiny. I was punching 999 into my mobile even as I struggled to regain control. Once that was done I felt reasonably back on course and stood up waiting for it all to begin. Brandon, Dave, the endless parade of scene-suited experts going painstakingly about their gruesome tasks. I tried not to think further than that. After the nightmarish night with Jason, I now had to face an equally daunting day ahead. I'd take it step by step – if I could – and not let this tsunami overwhelm me.

I watched as the first police car arrived, then the rest of the vans and cars. I answered questions, I dealt with issues, in the way one can after a night completely without sleep, seeing everything with a detachment and unemotional involvement as if standing behind some invisible screen in one's mind.

Even so, eventually my brain broke through sufficiently to wonder why the farce of the detour to Nightmare Abbey had been necessary. I sleep (usually) during the night, so why couldn't the body have been left here during the small hours without the trip to Friars Leas? The security lights and noise of the car on the gravel would not have presented a problem, as the body could have been deposited and the car be away before I was even downstairs, so why had Jason and Arthur been brought into the picture? A jolt of fear made me realize that perhaps by now they had been. Perhaps they had relaxed their guard with the night past and me gone.

A phone call fixed that worry. A guard answered and told me that Jason and Arthur were asleep. I hardened my heart. I had to *know*, so I insisted on speaking to Jason. I needed to be sure that mayhem had not broken out as soon as I left. It hadn't, and Jason promised to keep the guard going *and* stay up himself.

I supposed the diversion tactic might have been a strike against me personally because of my interest in the Porsche. Frogs Hill was my castle, my fortress, my home and it had been attacked. I couldn't see that scenario working either though – again, why bring Jason and Arthur into it? The name Alex Shaw inevitably resurrected the name of Doubler. There could well be an issue between the two of them, but why me too? And – a sickening memory – why had that red poppy been lying on Arthur's table?

The whole of the forecourt and part of the lane had been speedily cordoned as soon as Brandon arrived, leaving me marooned in the farmhouse, contemplating the peaceful green fields and garden to the rear of my home which contrasted so sharply with the disaster zone in front. It was still only five thirty in the morning, but as soon as was decently possible I would have to ring Zoe and Len, as the Pits was clearly not going to be operating today. A vastly different operation was in progress under the Forensic Management Unit.

I duly gave the police my DNA, my fingerprints online and my shoes, then I rang Len who grunted and said he'd ring Zoe for me. I wasn't entirely surprised when she called me back. 'We're coming in, both of us. I'm picking Len up.'

My sympathies to Len for his second ride in the old Fiesta. I reminded her of the cordon but she cut me off with a brief: 'Footpath.'

I realized how sleep deprived I was. There was indeed a

footpath passing the end of my garden which led through the fields to access points on the lanes where she could park the car. I watched through the kitchen window until I saw their familiar figures stomping up to my garden gate, both with a backpack, and went out to meet them. Zoe took one look at me and ordered me to bed.

So I obeyed, leaving them in charge of coffee and biscuits for the troops outside. I only slept for an hour and a half but it restored me to a working machine at least temporarily. The working machine then did its best. The first thing I saw when I came downstairs was Doubler's red poppy, not yet returned to him, which focused my mind wonderfully on the subject of Doubler. He must surely be involved in the execution of Alex Shaw – for execution is what it must have been. Somehow Shaw had disobeyed orders. I remembered Doubler's statement that he didn't like being double-crossed. But how did red poppies fit with that?

The second item I saw was Dave Jennings awaiting my arrival. Brandon was outside somewhere, he told me.

'Payback for the Porsche, Jack?' Dave looked quite perturbed.

'Why me though? Your team got there as quickly as I did, and I didn't give Shaw any aggro when I went to see him.'

'Brandon's set on the car theft being connected to Mike's death and your midnight dash to the new owner's place makes that possible.'

'Nothing happened to the Porsche last night though,' I pointed out.

'Can't be our Mrs Ansty going on the spree, can it?'

I didn't even smile. Too much effort. 'Whether it's connected to the Nelson murder or not, Doubler's involved in this, Dave.'

He groaned. 'I was hoping you wouldn't tell me that.'

'No choice. He was. He masterminded the nicking job with Shaw or someone else, then Shaw could have disobeyed orders. I can't see how, but the fact that the body has been dumped on my doorstep must indicate something.'

'That Doubler's planning to nick the Porsche again?'

That hadn't occurred to me, but I couldn't see much mileage in it. I wondered whether to mention red poppies but as I couldn't see how they fitted in there wasn't much point in attracting Dave's standard withering silence when presented with apparent irrelevancies.

'Unlikely,' I replied.

At which point Brandon came into the kitchen to join us. 'Then why go dashing up to Friars Leas last night, Jack?'

'Not because of the Porsche. I'd been told to go if I wanted to see the end of the game, the nature of which was not specified. With Shaw dead, the game seems to have been the Porsche.'

'Let's get after Doubler then,' Brandon said. 'Who's your contact, Jack?'

'Via Huptons garage.'

'But the chap Jack spoke to has left their employment, surprise, surprise,' Dave said.

'Have you talked to Harry Prince?' I asked.

'Yes. He's never been so horrified in his life. Fancy employing someone by mistake with forged references and forged identity, what was the car world coming to? And to think that had apparently happened at a Harry Prince garage. He would be *taking steps.*'

I wasn't surprised. Harry is good at turning blind eyes, but the minute a situation gets lukewarm, let alone hot, they are mighty good at becoming crystal clear, especially when his own safety is involved. So was Doubler, of course, but in a different way. Harry is genuinely nervous of tripping over the wrong side of the borderline he walks so carefully. He wouldn't knowingly have sanctioned Huptons having a *direct* line to Doubler. Indirect maybe – at a safe distance and hidden in a labyrinth.

'Is Arthur Howell still at risk, Jack?' Brandon asked. 'What's your feeling?'

I thought this through. 'If there's only one game on the go then, as I said, it could be finished with Shaw's death. But if there's two, linked or not, then there may be more to come.'

The silence that greeted my statement confirmed my own fears. Mike's murder was carried out by someone who knew Old Herne's and the Swoosh programme. The theft of the Porsche also indicated a knowledge of Old Herne's. Boadicea's attack and Shaw's death could be linked to Mike's or the Porsche – or neither.

I went out with them to the crime scene where the team were popping endless tiny items into evidence bags with infinite care and inching to and fro on their painstaking search. Never had I felt so frustrated. I couldn't help physically nor, it seemed, mentally.

'He'd been shot, Jack. But not here,' Brandon told me. 'The car was parked and the body dragged over the gravel. That could be why you were called away. It takes some time to manoeuvre a dead body out of a car.'

'If Doubler wanted Alex Shaw out of the way,' I said savagely, 'he had a thousand places he could have chosen to leave it. Instead he makes it visible by dumping me right in it. Why?'

'You tell us, Jack,' Brandon said blandly.

It was mid afternoon when I woke up after my second attempt at sleep – a more successful one than the first. Len and Zoe told me that I'd been asleep for three hours, by which time they were firmly established in the farmhouse organizing their own work schedules – including Arthur's Morgan – and fielding umpteen calls from the rest of the world, including Jessica, Glenn and Peter. News travels quickly. Most calls were quickly disposed of, but not Jessica's. I wanted to talk to her.

After I had finished my brief survey of events, she said simply: 'That's terrible for you, Jack.' She had picked up immediately how I felt about the desecration of Frogs Hill. 'Come and spend the night with me,' she urged.

I was tempted to accept so that I could forget the past twenty-four hours for a while. But I knew I couldn't leave Frogs Hill. 'I need to face it, sweetheart, not make for a bolt-hole.'

She brushed this aside. 'Do you want me to come to you?'

For a moment I hesitated, fool that I was, then thought of the long, lonely night ahead with so many unanswered questions out there in the dark. 'Yes, please.'

'Then I will. Len told me there was a footpath. I'll be with you by six thirty bearing dinner.'

I didn't protest. It sounded a great idea.

And then there was Jason, who had rung several times. I only hoped that didn't mean there'd been trouble at Nightmare Abbey too, but I needed to have a word with Brandon before I returned his call. I rang Jason ten minutes later and he answered the phone immediately it rang.

'Trouble?' I asked him.

'Not here. The police have been, though. You knew this man, Jack? The police wouldn't give us any info on him.'

'He was involved in your Porsche theft.'

'Not the famous Alex Shaw?'

'Yes. Simon Marsh was an assumed name. I doubt if he organized the theft though.'

A silence, then Jason said: 'I don't like this, Jack. I take it that phone message was merely to get you out of the house, but why here?'

'I don't know.'

'And why dump the body on you? You'd think it would be me since I'm the owner.'

'*I don't know.*' I was getting fed up with everyone assuming I knew the answer to everything. 'I'm a car detective, not a supernatural all-seeing god.'

But Jason was remorseless. What was wrong with the man? 'You thought Arthur was at risk.'

'He still could be.'

I was gritting my teeth in earnest now. Jason was a grown man for all his elfin looks and fragile appearance. He was Mike's son, Arthur's grandson and he was tough. So far I only had his word for it that there had been a call at all. I'd asked Brandon if he had checked that and of course he had, but the answer had not been conclusive. There had been a call from a mobile at the time Jason claimed, but the phone was not traceable. The nearest they had got was that the call had been made in the Friars Leas area. It could therefore, as Brandon pointed out, have been Jason himself who called. And incidentally, he had thrown in for free, the power line feeding Friars Leas had been cut.

For all my irritation with Jason, I couldn't see how he could be connected with Alex Shaw, despite that red poppy. On a scale of ten, the probability was less than one. Besides, I respected Liz Potter's view that Jason was a good guy. I then reminded myself that that wasn't something to rely on in a murder case.

'How did Arthur take the police visit?' I persevered, as Jason didn't comment.

He did this time though. 'He insisted on seeing them, but it upset him.'

'Because of the Porsche?'

'No, because of Old Herne's. Glenn, Fenella and Peter were remarkably quick off the mark with visiting him today.'

'Routine visit or because of last night?'

'The latter, but they regularly check in to ensure I'm not diverting the family fortunes away from them – even Peter. I didn't tell them about Shaw, but a police sergeant has been doing the rounds up at Old Herne's.'

The net seemed to be drawing closer around the club, so perhaps the police were trying to link Doubler both to Shaw's murder and Mike's. If so, Old Herne's was central – and at its heart was Glenn.

I decided to take a risk. 'I noticed a red poppy on Arthur's table last night.'

Jason's surprise seemed genuine. 'What about it? It came in the post to Arthur a week or two ago. Don't know why and he didn't tell me.'

'It might be linked to the car theft.'

'It isn't,' he said flatly.

Jessica was a lady of her word. At six thirty precisely she appeared at the gate to my garden laden just like Len and Zoe with a backpack, but she was also carrying a large basket in one hand. She was sturdily dressed in trousers, anorak and trainers, which surprised me – although I don't know why it should. Jessica would dress to meet every occasion suitably clad. I ran down the path towards her with a lift of the heart. The garden on this late June evening was looking its best and murder seemed a long way away. I kissed her and took the bag from her.

'Careful,' she warned.

'It's a soufflé?' I joked.

'You should be so lucky. I've brought soup, bread, cheese, smoked salmon, strawberries and various bits and bobs.'

'That'll do, I suppose.'

She aimed a mock blow at me. 'Shall we eat out here?'

Another great idea. The evening was warm enough and it seemed further away from the horror of the forecourt than did the house itself. It was pleasant to be dining here, I thought as I scurried to and fro bringing all the necessary paraphernalia and clutching a bottle of Chardonnay. Dad had built a sort of arbour to display his beloved roses, and we dined underneath its canopy of fragrance. I'm no gardener but I make sure that his roses are happy for his sake. My lost love Louise had loved this arbour, but there would be no thinking of her tonight, I resolved.

'Tell me about it, Jack,' Jessica said at last when the wine bottle was empty, our stomachs full and some of the evening still stretched ahead. I took her at her word, leaving out Shaw's name, and she listened intently.

'It doesn't make sense,' she observed.

'My thoughts entirely. What line was the Old Bill taking with you today?'

'He had a photo of this man and questions, questions, questions. Did we know him? Had we seen him around Old Herne's? Could he have had access to the keys?'

'He was concentrating on the car theft then.'

'Yes, not much about Mike.'

'Did he talk to Tim?'

'He did. Tim's so besotted with his new role that he'd have been furious if he'd been omitted. He's getting one over Glenn, as he sees it. He said he thought he'd seen the man in the photo before, but he wasn't certain where. The only person who thought he recognised him was Ray Nelson.'

'Really? Where?'

'High House.'

'Is that possible?'

'Not really. The chap he saw was delivering logs.'

Let-down, so I switched topics. 'How's the Glenn arrangement working?'

'Early days. He and Fenella are being careful not to upset me, and vice versa. We're all trying not to upset Arthur. I still have to button my lip every time Fenella shows me some of her crappy designs for the clubhouse, even though she pretends to take in what I'm saying. Glenn actually does listen to me about bookings and catering.'

'Has Hedda departed from the bar?'

'Yes. She and Tim are getting on like a house on fire. He orders her around, she takes no notice, and he loves the results.

So it works a treat. The bar has two staff now as well as a couple looking after special events.'

'How about Peter? Still waiting in the wings?'

'I think he's bored with it. Fenella is repelling all advances, so he's decided to be a knight in shining armour; he's keeping Arthur informed of every step, even about Ray and Boadicea. She seems to be progressing.'

The rest of the evening swam by in a romantic haze. The time was ripe for romance. We ceased talking about murder, we even ceased talking about Old Herne's, and as the last of the light faded we retreated into Frogs Hill. I took Jessica's hand and led her upstairs. My bedroom is at the rear of the house and so fortunately we didn't have to overlook the crime scene, which was deserted save for a guard.

As I took Jessica in my arms, however, my eyes fell on the bed – but for the wrong reasons. My head began to swim, and by the time we both reached the bed, romance had vanished. I must have fallen asleep instantly because when I woke up it was long past dawn. Someone was shaking my shoulder, who in my dream I thought was Brandon castigating me for attacking Jason with a tyre iron. It wasn't Brandon, it was Jessica to tell me that breakfast was ready.

I groaned as my humiliation came back to me. 'Sorry.' It wasn't much of an apology for the night now past.

She laughed. 'Don't be. There's always next time.'

I pulled myself together and as soon as Jessica had set off along the footpath I remembered the outside world and what aspect of it lay closest to me – the crime scene. Before I could get any further, the phone rang. Not Dave, not Jason, not Len or Zoe.

It was Jennifer Ansty.

It wasn't hard to guess why she was ringing. 'You've heard about Simon Marsh?' I asked. In the back of my mind a faint bell was ringing.

'Yes, Jack. They want me to formally identify him as the man who sold me the car. Would you come with me? It's today.'

Her voice sounded strained and I could see this was going to be an ordeal for her. No problem. Of course I would go with her – especially as it meant I could get away from the crime scene.

Soon, very soon, I hoped, it would be lifted and I could return to the Frogs Hill I loved, although that wouldn't be easy.

I drove to the police mortuary at Charing, where I had arranged to meet Jenny, as she wanted to get the ordeal over first before having the lunch I'd suggested. She arrived only a few minutes after me, and Dave joined us right away. 'I won't come in,' I told her, 'but Dave will look after you and I'll be here when you come out.' I didn't think I could face seeing Shaw again, and Dave was an excellent substitute. We were honoured. He didn't often work at weekends.

Jenny seemed happy with this, though she was definitely not the merry widow I remembered from Burwash. Dave, a solid family man, clearly saw her as Mum from his protective body language with her. They weren't gone long, and when they emerged, I had a discreet thumbs-up from Dave and a nod from Jenny

Dave left us rather regretfully and I took her to lunch at the Plough Inn at Stalisfield Green on the Downs. The pub and village are a long way from anywhere, but the food is so good that it feels like the centre of the universe. I hated to spoil their welcome and brilliant fare with work but I had no option. Something wasn't adding up.

'You're sure it was Marsh, Jenny?'

'Positive. One hundred per cent,' she snapped. 'OK?'

'Understood. So why do you still look so tense?'

She looked taken aback. 'There's the paperwork, I suppose, and – well, it takes time, doesn't it?'

'*What* does?' I asked flatly. She'd accepted my offer for a purpose, I suspected.

'Let's finish lunch, then I'll tell you.'

'Why not now? Has the merry widow found a merry man?'

'No,' she said shortly.

So I took the hint. Simon Marsh, Alex Shaw, Jason, the Porsche – and Jenny. The mix of ingredients was beginning to cook. Nevertheless, I wouldn't gain anything by pushing too hard, so all talk of murder, car theft, and fraud was suspended while we chatted about the glories of Burwash and Piper's Green. She insisted on a large dessert and cheese, and I suspected that these were delaying tactics as she left half the dessert and only had a minuscule slice of cheese.

'So what are you here to tell me, Jenny?' I said firmly as tea and coffee arrived.

She toyed with the teaspoon, avoiding my eyes. 'It's difficult.'

'So let me help.' My turn to get exasperated.

'You'll have to, that's the problem.'

I didn't like the word problem. 'I've got enough of my own,' I said unchivalrously.

I don't think she even heard me. 'I said I'd be coming to see the family about the Porsche,' she continued. 'I meant it, and I'm here.'

I stared at her. '*Now*? Now is not the time to talk compensation. You must have heard that Mike Nelson's widow is in hospital, victim of a vicious attack, and the new owner of the Porsche is Mike's son Jason, also grieving.'

'I know that, Jack. It's Jason I've come to visit.'

'But he—'

'My name isn't just Jennifer Ansty,' she interrupted. 'It's *Lily* Jennifer Ansty.'

Lily? Where had I heard that name – and then I remembered.

She nodded. 'Jason's my son. I was Mike's first wife.'

FIFTEEN

Caught off-guard, it took me a moment or two to adjust, but then many things began to click into shape. And an unpleasant shape it was. Jenny gave me a faint smile. 'Sorry to do this to you, Jack.'

'Was Jason behind the theft of the Porsche?' I shot at her, but answered my own question before she could reply. 'Of course he was. It was a set-up up job, wasn't it, because he was afraid Boadicea might inherit the car. Was Mike threatening to rewrite his will?'

She looked appalled. 'Absolutely not. It was nothing like that.'

'Then what was it like?' I felt a rare anger. I'd been used in a game I wasn't aware was being played – although perhaps I should have been. I remembered what had triggered that faint bell in my mind. Jason had mentioned Alex Shaw at a time when he should not have known the name. So he had undoubtedly been involved in the theft. 'What was so important that you had to string along not just me but the police too?'

Her turn to get angry. 'If you'd taken time to think before you spoke, you would have remembered that the car was stolen *before* Mike's murder.'

I calmed down, but only slightly. 'True, but you've both had time enough to put the record straight without having half the Kent and Sussex police on its trail.' At the back of my mind, reassessments were flashing through at Formula I speed. Boadicea attacked, future health not yet known; Arthur, ignorant of what his family was doing behind his back; Glenn, set on vengeance on his brother who'd held Arthur's heart; and Fenella, intent on feathering a swansdown nest for herself. 'Mind telling me why we've not been honoured with this information before?'

She winced. 'Yes, I do mind. It's not my story. It's Jason's. He's expecting us, *if* you can spare the time. I told him I intended to break the news to you.'

'Hold the horses, Jenny. If this story of yours has anything to do with Mike's death I'll have to call the case officer right now. Has it?'

'Not directly – but maybe indirectly. I don't know, Jack. That's why I had to tell you who I am.'

I weighed this up, and on balance decided not to call Brandon yet, although with the proviso that whatever she and Jason now graciously proposed to reveal they should be aware that I'd have to pass it on if relevant. And how, I thought angrily, could it not be?

And so we set off, she in her Astra and I in my Alfa still seething with fury that I – we – had been led round and round the mulberry bush by Jason Pryde and his mother. A tiny question mark popped up in the shape of a red poppy, but that was a detail.

Jenny had taken a different route to Friars Leas than I did, and so when I drew up at Nightmare Abbey and saw no sign of her I thought she'd done a runner. At least I was wrong there, for up came the Astra and we presented a united front at the door.

Jason looked not a whit perturbed as he greeted us. I seemed to be his best buddy – I suppose that was thanks to the vigil we had kept on Thursday night.

'Jack's not pleased, darling,' Jenny told him ruefully.

'No,' Jason said, still unperturbed. 'I can see that. Have you told him why it happened?' he asked as he led the way up the stairs.

'Your job,' Jenny said briefly. 'Is Arthur around?'

'No. He hit the roof when I told him the full story. Said he wasn't going to sit through it all again, and he'd join us for tea.'

'Very civilized,' Jenny said brightly.

'Neither of you,' I said through gritted teeth, 'seems to be aware you're conspiring in a police murder case.'

'Believe me,' Jason replied, 'I do. I merely did part of your job for you.'

On this infuriating note we reached the turret room where the telescope provided an evocative reminder of what this was all about – or so I presumed.

Jason followed my gaze and thoughts. 'Mum and I are successor trustees, remember.'

'I do. Do you?'

Jason flushed. 'Point taken.'

I hadn't finished. 'Why steal the Porsche, Jason?'

He looked completely thrown. 'I didn't.'

'Then what the blazes is this all about?' I asked in exasperation.

'I knew who *had* nicked it. Would you have stood by and seen that Porsche destroyed, Jack?'

'No, but who would be insane enough to do that? Not even Doubler – and I take it that he comes into the story?'

'I don't know, but that's beside the point. That's what would have happened to the Porsche if I hadn't stepped in with Mum's help.'

'But in whose interests would that have been? The car was worth its insurance value and would have been sellable at the slightest hint it was on the market whether sold by Mike or Doubler. Who was behind the theft, Jason?'

He *still* hesitated and Jenny answered for him. 'Anna Nelson.'

'Boadicea?' I blinked. 'She alone arranged it?'

'Paid for it to be pinched with instructions for it be destroyed. Crazy that she believed anyone would do that, but she *is* crazy.'

'She did it because Mike asked her to?' Even now I couldn't believe that.

'No. For her own sake. Dad never knew, of course – he'd have gone ballistic. She did it for the insurance money they would have received. They were in debt and my father was putting the majority of his salary into Old Herne's, which was going downhill so fast that it didn't help. He had refused to sell the car, which was the only major asset they had.'

I saw it now. It fitted. 'But then Mike died and the insurance money would have gone to you if we hadn't found the Porsche.' I'd discounted Boadicea's involvement because Mike's death was the last thing that she would have wanted in her position.

'She's a very stupid woman, Jack,' Jason said. 'My father was alive when I discovered what she'd done, but I couldn't stand by and let the car be destroyed or let her get her hands on the insurance. Nor could I tell my father.'

'Question,' I threw at him. 'How did you find out Anna had been behind it?'

'Not easily,' Jason told me, 'although I guessed it was her right from the beginning. We've never got on, Anna and I. But I couldn't prove it, so I talked it over with Tim, who feels as strongly as I do about the Porsche. He reckoned Anna, not being too bright, would have gone straight to their regular garage, Huptons, so I went to them on a fishing trip. She – and later me – were passed down the line until we ended up with the same man.'

'Doubler,' I said.

'If you say so. He called himself Guy Blunt when he strolled up here to see me one day.'

'Undoubtedly Doubler,' I said wryly. 'Two Cold War double agents, Guy Burgess and Anthony Blunt.' The man who didn't like to be double-crossed didn't seem above a spot of double-crossing on his own behalf – or rather the Porsche's.

'Blunt came a week or so after the car disappeared and told me he'd been asked to destroy it, so we worked out this plan. I paid him not to destroy it as ordered, but to return it here the day before the insurance was due to be paid out in order to cause the maximum annoyance to my stepmother. Petty, but justified. I knew this would be tough on my father, but things weren't great between us, so that didn't worry me – until he died.'

Jason stopped for a moment, and Jenny put her arm round him. 'Then you turned up at Swoosh, Jack,' he continued steadily. 'So I had to move things along much more speedily than Blunt would have liked. Blunt had fixed fake paperwork and had the engine and chassis numbers slightly altered, then arranged though this man Alex Shaw to sell the car on and register it for Mum at the DVLA in Swansea, but we were going to leave it a week or two before its whereabouts became officially known. Then Dad died and you were nosing around so I knew we had to get our skates on. I told Mum to register it with the Porsche Club 356 Register, knowing they would smell a rat right away, so that you'd get things moving. Clever, eh?'

'Very,' I said sourly. 'Thanks for crediting me with the wit to track it down.'

'I wasn't exactly thrilled to have the car landed on me,' Jenny said, also sourly, 'especially after Mike died. I was still fond of him, and we'd had great times during the good years.'

'Were you still in touch with him?'

'On the quiet, yes. Anna raised hell at the mere mention of my name. Mike did want me to continue as successor trustee, whatever Anna claims. He knew I understood Old Herne's, and she didn't. Arthur knows that too.'

'Arthur does indeed.' The man himself came in to join us. 'I thought this is where you might be. Lily, my sweet.' He gave her a bear hug. 'I heard you've been involved in this iniquitous conspiracy.'

'It seemed a good idea at the time, Arthur,' Lily replied ruefully.

'Understood. There are more important thing to fret over, pet.' Then he turned to me. 'Good to see you, Jack. You've had a rough time, and yet you're an outsider. That was, and still is, your value, if you stick around. My son's death comes first, not his Porsche though.' He walked stiffly over to sit in an armchair, looking tired, but in view of what he'd said, I had to go on.

'Did you meet this Guy Blunt, Arthur?'

'Nope.'

'Not under his nickname, Doubler?'

'Nope.'

I leapt the gap, desperately hoping I was right. 'But he sent you a red poppy.'

'*He* did?' Arthur looked incredulous. 'That was nearly three weeks ago, and it had nothing to do with the Porsche or Jason's visitor *or* Mike's death.'

'What *did* it have to do with, Arthur?' I hated to press him, but I had to know. 'Jason's visitor Blunt is known in the car underworld as Doubler, and we have to know.'

Arthur still looked in two minds, and was clearly upset, but he gave way. 'If it's who I think it is, my family owed his. In the First World War my father was in the same infantry company as his great-grandfather, Tom Barney, in Forty-Seventh London Division on the seventh of June 1917 at the Battle for Messines Ridge. It was Tom who saved my father's life. They became pals, and when my father later emigrated to the States, every year he'd send Tom a small thank you and Tom would send him back a poppy on the anniversary day. His son Robert carried on the tradition, so did Robert's son Christopher, and I guess this man you call Blunt or Doubler could be his son. He'd be around forty now. One poppy still comes every year, no name no address, so I've no means of continuing the tradition from my side. When this year's poppy arrived on the eighth of June – it had been sent to the Cricketers and forwarded – I reckoned Tom's great-grandson must have read in the press that I was over here. I'm still by no means sure he's this Doubler or Blunt though.'

'If he is, he doesn't seem to have followed the family tradition of saving life,' I said drily. 'Doubler is a prime candidate for the death of Alex Shaw.'

'And the attack on Anna too?' Arthur looked even more upset. 'Do you reckon that's down to him?'

'It could well be. As for evidence that Doubler is your poppy man – and your mysterious caller of the night of Shaw's death, Jason – Doubler called to see me at Frogs Hill and left me a poppy too.'

'Why?' Arthur barked back at me. I could see he was still not convinced.

'It must have been his way of hinting that the Porsche story linked up with you and Jason. And,' I added, 'that you were both under his protection.'

Arthur stared at me for a moment, then chuckled. 'Pity you didn't think of that before calling in the Marines for Friars Leas.'

He wasn't going to get away with that. 'I hadn't seen your poppy then.'

He gave in gracefully. 'Right on target, Jack. Now, see here, we're going to have a coming home party for Anna when she's well enough. That will be a few weeks yet. You'll think we're crazy and perhaps we are, given that she'd planned to have the Porsche destroyed. But Jason and I are going to do it. Understand?'

No answer needed or given. 'But here's one for you, Jack,' he continued. 'Where are you on Mike's death? That can't be down to Tom Barney's great-grandson. Mike would have been protected from this guy as he was my son.'

'But Doubler didn't know that.'

He glared at me but his fighting spirit was gone. 'Have it your way, Jack. I want Mike's killer found, and if you can help do that, I'll send you poppies or Porsches every damn year.'

I had to tell Brandon about Doubler. I had to tell Dave too, and I would do both and in person, when I felt ready. But that wasn't yet. I needed to think first. Not at Frogs Hill, not in a pub, not at old Herne's but on the Downs in the open air. There is a point on the Pilgrims Way that passes a former chalk pit, now an open land area, which has been left for nature to make of it what it will. Nature had done a good job, I thought as I climbed the steep slopes and looked down on the pit, now overgrown with wild flowers, humming with bees, fluttering with butterflies and busy with birds. I had the place to myself and walked along the pit's edge to a point where I could look over the glorious valleys and flat Weald of Kent as far as the sea while the birds, bees and butterflies ignored my problems on their own serene quests for sustenance.

I sat down on the grass and emptied my mind, as if shaking out the floor mats in my car. They do their job day after day, collecting dust and other tiny fragments of rubbish, but every so often they require attention. I'd just had my own shake-up and opted not to let dust settle but to rid myself of it.

A few walkers passed me and I waved cheerily. Down in the valley I could see cars that seemed to crawl along the highways, and I felt blissfully divorced from everyday life. There was only one hitch in this cleansing process. The shake-up produced the interesting conclusion that maybe the only person who had been straight with me – up to a point at least – was the notorious killer Doubler, which was hardly something I could brag about to Brandon. Then the fresh air kicked in another angle. 'I take exception to being double-crossed, Jack,' Doubler had said, but how had Shaw double-crossed him seriously enough to warrant his death? It must be to do with the Porsche case or possibly Old Herne's because the body had been dumped at Frogs Hill – after I had been diverted to Friars Leas where the one man in the world whom Doubler would never harm was living.

Had Alex Shaw been playing his own game, not Doubler's? There'd been no sign of that when I met him, except his acquaintance with Old Herne's which he could well have had anyway. And yet Ray Nelson had known his face, I remembered. He'd thought Shaw was *the log man.* What if he was right and he had indeed seen Shaw at High House, ostensibly delivering logs but on another mission?

Step by step, I warned myself.

Why would he go to High House?

Possible answer: to arrange the theft in the first place. Likelihood: one out of ten. With Mike around, Boadicea would have chosen somewhere far more secluded than High House.

Second answer: on a mission of his own, over which he had the upper hand. Likelihood: eight out of ten. What mission though? Answer to that one: blackmail? Boadicea had been crying out for money – because she had to pay a blackmailer.

It was a line to work on, I decided, and would most certainly tie in with Doubler's notion of a double-cross. Furthermore, if Boadicea had refused to pay Shaw and threatened to notify Doubler – there could be the reason for Shaw's attack on her. That fitted, so the next port of call was to break the news to Brandon and then Dave.

The best of intentions can be foiled by Brandon, however. He was out when I reached Charing on Monday morning. Dave was not. He is usually the better bet when a case is going well, Brandon when it isn't. Today I had Dave. What Dave likes is a quiet chat over a problem in a pub or café. He's not fussy which, but he doesn't like being given bad news in his office – especially just before lunch. As now.

'Let me get this straight.' He leaned menacingly forward across his desk, after I'd told him the full story about the Porsche, including my theory about blackmail. 'This Anna Nelson paid for it to be pinched. Dear old Doubler has a change of heart – if he has one – and reprieves it from the knacker's yard. Doubler then arranges for it to be sold on and tracked down by *you* –' not us, I noted – 'and returned to its rightful owner. *What the hell for?*' he finished with a roar.

'To prevent it from being destroyed.'

'So once Pryde knew, why not mention it to us and return the car to his dad? Why keep us on a fool's errand?'

Trust Dave to leap on the weak point. 'I gather Jason wanted to teach his stepmother a lesson. A sort of joke.'

'*Joke?*' Dave snarled. 'I know a joke too, Jack. Forget your invoice.'

Sometimes I'd let this familiar gambit run its course, but not today. 'I was called in three weeks after the car was stolen. Any of you think to interview Jason or Mrs Nelson in that time?'

To do him justice, even in a rage Dave sees reason. 'Fair enough. Send in the bill. *This* time.'

That out of the way, I faced the other matter. 'Brandon's out,' I told Dave. 'I can ring him with this blackmail theory, but he needs to know about Lily Ansty pronto. Shall I wait?'

It was like offering a child sweeties. Dave's eyes lit up. 'Leave it with me. I'll tell him.' From rage to a chuckle. 'Mike Nelson's first wife as a player in his game, eh. How did he miss that one?'

I returned to Frogs Hill, feeling like Len's beloved oil rag, rung out and in dire need of renewal. Oddly enough, when I saw the crime scene cordon was no longer there and that Jessica's car was in the forecourt I didn't automatically think of her in terms of restoration. It wasn't her fault, I argued to myself, but she represented Old Herne's, and at the moment I wanted nothing more than my home, including the Pits, whose seductive aroma – at least to petrolheads – wafted out to me as I shut the Alfa's door behind me.

Jessica turned out also to be in need of restoration – so it wasn't a good pairing. She emerged from the Pits, still in smartish working clothes and her face looking set and grim. Had she heard the news? I wondered. Jason had indicated it was open house on his mother and the Porsche story, but neither of these subjects was necessarily bad news for her personally.

'Trouble?' I asked cautiously as we walked to the farmhouse together.

'It's pistols at dawn, Jack. Hope you don't mind my unloading myself.'

'Go ahead,' I said warily, 'provided the duel's not with me.'

She took that as a green light, naturally enough, and the dam burst. Words just poured out as I ushered her though to the living room. 'I see now what Fenella's game is. It's straightforward enough. She wants my job *now*.'

'I thought she'd been fobbed off with her design work.'

'No way. She's aiming for the number one job.'

'But that's Glenn's for three months.'

'Quite, but Fenella is making it quite clear she's here for keeps. Nothing obvious, she's too clever. Just little things like: "Of course it's not my job, but I reckon that if you do such and such . . ." That sort of thing. I can see through it, but her game is to ensure Glenn makes a mess of things in Arthur's eyes, so that she can get rid of two birds with one stone. Glenn *and* me.'

Interesting plan, if Jessica was right. 'Who's to be her number two, if she's alienating you? Peter?'

'Good grief no. He's history as far as she's concerned, with the result that he's busy buttering up Arthur and Jason on the grounds that he's Miranda's grandson and he knows all about Old Herne's and its customers.'

I offered her a drink and was glad when she opted for tea. I was tired and needed as clear a head as I could still manage if I was to distinguish between my private life and Old Herne's. All I longed for at that moment was that Jessica would go away. I knew this was unfair of me, especially as the physical Jack Colby was all too well aware that he didn't want her to go away and that the night lay ahead.

I made an effort. 'Where does that you leave you?'

'I get on well with Arthur and Jason. Someone needs to look after their welfare and their interests.'

'You don't fancy being a number two to Peter if he takes over or if Jason gives up the band and runs Old Herne's himself?'

I had put it too bluntly and she turned a blank face to me. Nor did she reply – which was all the answer I needed. In the midst of this game of politics, what, I wondered, had become of the Jessica who liked saving things, and in particular wanted to save Old Herne's? As an unpleasant result of Mike's death, Old Herne's seemed to be getting a raw deal by being manipulated this way and that.

'Any news of Boadicea?' I asked Jessica. 'Arthur seems to be planning for her return.'

She groaned. 'That's the last straw. A welcome home party. It was Jason's idea, whatever Arthur says. I ask you, Jack. I – *I*, mark you – have to organize it at Old Herne's, and everyone's leaping on the bandwagon with bright ideas for *me* to put into operation. It's too bad, Jack. If I agree, it'll be my fault if it's a disaster. If I refuse, I look like an uncooperative employee who can't cope. Either way, they win, I lose. Glenn is pretending to be all in favour, of course. No help there.'

'Too bad.' I was on automatic pilot by now, but quickly switched it off when I realized that this was somewhat ambiguous and tried my best to put it right. 'That's a challenge, Jessica. Why don't you make it a resounding success and then everyone will forget whose idea it was and praise your expertise?'

She brightened up. 'Do you know, that's a good idea. I'll visit Boadicea in the hospital and get her input. That'll win me brownie points.'

'So it will,' I murmured.

'I'll bring Glenn in on it, but not too far.'

'Why did Jason suggest this party?' I had been contemplating its oddity.

Jessica was taken aback. 'Goodness knows. Why?'

'He loathes Boadicea, and Arthur himself doesn't seem so keen on her, and I wouldn't have thought,' I added, 'that Old Herne's would be her first choice of venue.'

Focusing on that angle put an airlock in my fuel flow, which had only been flowing gently while Jessica had been recounting her woes. It was indeed a kind gesture to welcome home Boadicea, but a family dinner would normally suffice in these circumstances – especially as she had been the cause of so much trouble over the Porsche.

A grim thought came to me – would a public appearance by her attract her attacker to have another go and thereby bring this gruesome saga to a close? Her attacker was – we were assuming – Alex Shaw, but that didn't mean he hadn't been paid to do it. My blackmail theory fitted but it could still be wrong.

'I wish Old Herne's wasn't the venue,' she said fervently. 'It's Arthur and Jason who specifically want it there, although it's aimed to please her by its content. She told them about her orphaned childhood and how she missed out on childish pleasures, so the general idea is to give her a taste of them.'

Jessica was wandering around my living room aimlessly as she talked about it, and I noticed I hadn't put Louise's photo away. Her eyes fell on it, but she didn't comment.

Jessica elected to go home that evening to get an early start for the morning, and I didn't try to stop her. There was a distance between us that I was too despondent to bridge. However, the next day Old Herne's proved to be my own destination too, after Brandon rang me. He'd heard my theory about Alex Shaw and Boadicea from Dave and wanted to talk. Boadicea was indeed being discharged from hospital within the foreseeable future and although she would by then be more or less back to normal she still claimed to have no idea who had attacked or why. My theory fitted rather well with that. Brandon told me he was heading for High House and Ray Nelson; he would then tackle Boadicea, he said, and anything I picked up at Old Herne's would be helpful.

So I went to the Old Herne's fount of information: the curator. Tim was an independent voice and not involved in club politics. He was also the one closest to Mike – or so I assumed. However, I was soft pedalling every assumption at present. Old Herne's was Tim's passion, only equalled by his devotion to Mike, but they did not *necessarily* dovetail. I'd bet my last (almost) dollar that they did, but when the road sign speed limit reads five miles per hour it's wisest to obey. Go slow.

I found Tim in Morgans, not in his curator's office, but tenderly unwrapping a chequered flag from one of Mike's early races, which had been bequeathed to Old Herne's by a former track steward. Len had told me it was on its way, and Tim was so engrossed in his task that he didn't notice my arrival.

I cleared my throat meaningfully. 'I'm told you knew about Jason's hand in the Porsche story,' I remarked.

Tim jumped, then took in what I'd asked with some embarrassment. 'Part of the story,' he muttered. 'She was going to have it destroyed, Jack. I've never taken to Mrs Nelson and now I know why. All she can think about is money. Sad, really, when you think of Mike.'

'I hear there are plans for a welcome home party,' I said, trying to sound casual.

His face darkened. 'It won't be a car day, Jack. She's not one for wheels, but I don't hold with people being murdered, or as good as, so I'll go along with it. Mr Arthur had a word with me. Asked me to do my best for Mike's sake. So I will. After all, it's all for Old Herne's one way or another.'

'Don't you think it risky?'

'It's all money coming in, isn't it? The place'll go under without a boost.'

'I meant risky for Mrs Nelson,' I said drily.

A long silence. 'Maybe, but so's life, isn't it?'

Perhaps Tim had come to the same conclusion as I had: that if Mike's killer was still around, Boadicea would be put directly in the line of fire, but with the net drawn closer around her. There was another interpretation of the risk to her – that the excitement so soon after her release from hospital could be bad for her recovery, especially with the party being held at Old Herne's where her husband had been murdered.

'Having it here seems undiplomatic,' I told Tim, but surprisingly he disagreed.

'There's good reason to have it here. Protection. And besides, you've got to consider the soul of the place. That's why they want it here. Soul. To show Old Herne's is going on. That's what it needs.'

'Plus a good manager.'

'Yes.' Tim looked round his beloved hangar. 'Mike wasn't much of one, was he? If he'd gone on the way he was we'd have gone bust. Mr Arthur knew it, Mr Ray knew it, Mrs Anna, them Howells – and me too. It had to be saved one way or another.'

SIXTEEN

July passed in low gear, perhaps because I was impatient for that welcome home party to be over and done with and it was fixed for the last Saturday of the month. It still seemed to me the height of madness to gather the staff and family to welcome Boadicea home when one of them could have been responsible for her attempted murder and probably Mike's death too.

Brandon more or less admitted that the hunt for Mike's killer had stalled. The trace evidence on which he'd placed so much faith had produced no clear path and without new input was likely to remain that way. Alibis presented the same problem – no clear path. Those closest to Mike had known-whereabouts for most of the vital period but in view of the crowds milling around at Swoosh none of them could be pinned down to the *whole* period.

I, too, felt I'd stalled. I rarely saw Jessica – it always seemed to be: 'Sorry, Jack, far too much to do – next week, I promise you.' Zoe had taken a week or two off. Len was here (his idea of a week off is to come in on mornings only) but was so preoccupied with a new baby to admire – a Lancia Fulvia under attack from rust – that he was one hundred per cent in dreamcarland.

July hosts the beginning of the so-called dog days, the hottest days of the year (if we're lucky) when the sun beats strongly, the wind drops and everything is still, as there's no wind to drive one's sails.

I felt just like that now though there was precious little heat in the sun. But I was becalmed. No word from Dave – save that he declared he would pop in on the welcome home day, and Brandon had told me he would be there. Not, obviously, to cheer Boadicea back, but in her interests. Altogether the festive day was beginning to take on the air of Armageddon rather than a summer party.

I paid a couple of visits to Old Herne's but was no further forward. It was like a disturbed ants' nest – everyone rushing around and doubtless doing their own jobs but looking like chaos to an outsider like me. Glenn and Jessica seemed the best of friends, Fenella seemed to be doing her best not to take over Jessica's job, and Tim was in a perpetual sulk because cars and hangars were not going to be the feature of the day. I could persuade no one to stop and explain what this great day was going to involve.

At last, a week before the event, I managed to buttonhole Jason.

He grinned. 'Arthur told me Anna was to have whatever she *really* wanted.'

'Old Herne's?' I asked.

He answered me seriously. 'No. Anna doesn't care two hoots about the place. She wants a childhood.'

'So I gathered, but how do you give her that? A visit to the seaside?'

'What do kids like, apart from mobiles and computers? Playing with animals, fairgrounds, clowns, all of that stuff.'

'You're turning Old Herne's into a children's paradise?' If so, no wonder Tim was sulking. It seemed a crazy idea. Boadicea had had a tough time, and as Mike's widow a duty of care towards her was certainly in order, but to this extent? Billionaire or not, Arthur was pushing the boat out. And then it struck me that this could be one big throw of the dice in the hope of moving his main objective forward: finding out who had killed his son.

'That's the idea. Only for the day,' Jason added reassuringly. 'It'll be fun. It'll be fifties Dodgems, ghost trains, Punch and Judy – all the things she missed as a child. I can just see you riding a carousel horse, Jack. I'm looking forward to it. We're calling it Whoosh by the way.'

'Open to the public?'

'By invitation only. You'll come, of course.'

'Thanks.' I was torn. I had to be there. I loved fairs, but this one was going to be work too, as far as I could see. 'What about Anna herself, Jason? Somebody has tried to kill her once, and someone did kill your father. They could well strike again.'

'They could anywhere, anytime,' he replied seriously. 'And at Old Herne's she can be guarded.'

'Brandon said he'll be there.'

'That means one man, maybe two, Jack. I'll have more than that around on guard.'

Against who or what though? Can guards guard against the unexpected, which was what we would be dealing with in this case? Reason told me that no one would choose a public place like Whoosh; much better to leave the strike until Boadicea was at High House and vulnerable. Reason didn't have it all its own way, however. The 'what if' factor kept breaking in. What if someone was determined to make a point? Welcome Home Day would be ideal.

What point though? Old Herne's must come into the picture, either for its monetary value or its heritage. 'Vaulting ambition', as Shakespeare termed it, has led to many a murder in the past, and there were too many gloating eyes fixed on Old Herne's to ignore its possible importance in this case. I thought of President Kennedy's famous speech: 'Ask not what your country can do for you, ask what you can do for your country.' Substitute Old Herne's for country and how many of those at Whoosh would forget self? Was that even possible in today's world? I wondered. It comes down to choice for us all. I'd made a choice in turning my back on the oil trade in favour of Frogs Hill, classic cars and little money. Arthur, Jason and Tim would go to the battlefield for the coming Armageddon on Old Herne's behalf.

I consoled myself that Whoosh might have its lighter side, confirmed by a phone call from Liz asking what this crazy Whoosh day was all about.

'Jessica says she's hired me a dress,' she wailed, when I explained.

'What on earth for?'

'Jason's giving some kind of performance and wants me as a partner. Fine, but I've got to dance with him too. *Dance* and a *dress*, Jack. Me! Can you imagine?'

I couldn't. Liz and skirts were strangers. And as for dancing – forget it. 'What sort of dance and dress?' I enquired.

'Get this. In a pantomime. He's Harlequin and I'm *Columbine*. Ugh. I'll look like a tarted up fairy queen. Could I wear my jeans underneath?'

'No,' I said firmly. 'You can't dance in jeans.'

'I can't dance anyway. I'm a singer.'

'Is Colin going?'

A pause. 'I'm afraid Jason has cast him as Clown.'

I hadn't laughed out loud for some time, but did so now. It was only when I rang off that I remembered that pantomimes included villains.

Should I take the Lagonda? I was still dithering over this vital matter when Armageddon in the form of Whoosh arrived. No, the Lagonda was for sheer pleasure. The Alfa? No. Whoosh was no ordinary working day. I settled for the Gordon-Keeble again, the nearest in age to the fifties theme of the day and, as a grand tourer, more suitable to face Armageddon. I felt comfortable in it as I slid into the seat. The Gordon-Keeble and I knew adversity, and could face anything – or so it seemed as I set out. I was on my own because Len and Zoe were driving to Old Herne's with their respective partners again.

I'd seen nothing of Old Herne's since my conversation with Jason, so I was unprepared for the extent of the transformation when I reached it. For starters, the car park was presided over by human pixies and humans in jolly animal outfits. Jolly little squirrels and monkeys and owls peered down from the surrounding trees – stuffed ones, not human. The Gordon-Keeble and I had arrived just after Len, who gazed in severe disapproval at the jollification around him.

'Don't know what Tim's making of this lot,' he muttered.

I could guess, but 'this lot' proved nothing compared with what awaited us at Whoosh itself. It was like walking into the Land of Oz. It looked like Disneyland competing with an English fairground, and there were hordes of people here to enjoy it, despite its being by invitation only. The grand opening was to be at twelve noon, less than half an hour away, which just gave me the time for a speedy reconnaissance. Before my amazed eyes, I saw swings, carousel, coconut shy, Punch and Judy, a Haunted House, dodgems, tame animals roaming around through the crowd and plenty more. Looking towards the track, I could glimpse what just might be ponies. Tim must be apoplectic. Somewhere, however, I could hear one of those Laughing Sailor automata which to me had always struck a sinister note, and I had my first shiver of the day.

Had Jason had a hand in choosing all these attractions – for want of a better word – or were they Boadicea's choice? I suspected Jason, for Whoosh held the spirit of Nightmare Abbey, the fun with the dark carefully hidden behind. My imagination? Or perhaps it was intentional. I passed the Punch and Judy stand which looked, from the already attached gallows, as if it was going to present the traditional Punch rather than the modern softened down version. Of course it would be in its original form, I realized, because that's how it would have been when Boadicea was a child. Of course the Laughing Sailor would be cackling his head off. Of course there would be screams of fright and fear from the Haunted House. Fear was part of growing up, provided good triumphed. As I fervently hoped it would do today. But if Boadicea knew who had killed Mike and perhaps held a vital clue . . .

I stopped this train of thought. I had to remain alert, and detached observation was best for that.

A small stage had been erected for the opening ceremony just outside the clubhouse, and Arthur and Jason duly led Boadicea out at twelve o'clock with Peter wheeling Ray behind them. Boadicea looked pale; she was wearing cream which didn't help her looks but showed the ordeal she had come through. She looked round at us all, but did not seem to be taking much in during Arthur's short speech of welcome. Her gaze returned to the delights all around her, but she did manage a: 'Thank you,' in a low voice, before spotting something more interesting – a tame deer trotting past the stand.

'Bambi!' she cried out.

It caused a general sympathetic laugh, but Boadicea took no notice. She threw off Arthur's arm, stepped down from the dais, and went over to the deer, crooning to it, until Jason took her arm and led a procession round the treats in store for her. I followed, watching as she went from delight to delight, taking no notice of anyone.

Where, I wondered, could an attack take place? The carousel? The Haunted House? The latter was an obvious possibility, although it would be difficult for the assailant to set it up. He'd have to hide himself (or the bomb?) inside the house. I seized the chance to have a word with Jason, when Boadicea exchanged escorts.

'Is she up to this?' I asked.

'No, but she's insisted,' he replied. 'Wants to try everything, and why not?'

I couldn't think of any rational reason, but I was on edge. It was beginning to feel like a replay of the Nightmare Abbey false alarm, and I remembered how that night had ended. 'You do know the guards?'

'Yes.' He grinned reassuringly. 'It won't happen, Jack.'

I only hoped he was right, but couldn't believe that. Or were these just bogeys of my own? Whom should she trust? Whom should she fear?

Sure enough, Boadicea headed for the Haunted House, and I could see Jason and Peter arguing about who should go with her in the little train that ran on a track through the house. The train was divided into boxed compartments, and Jason won the argument by jumping into the leading box beside Boadicea. Peter promptly jumped into the second. I was relieved to see that, even though I was uneasy. With the two of them there, one could not act – but perhaps I was wrong. On tenterhooks, I listened from outside to the shrieks as unexpected skeletons must have loomed up or ghostly figures drifted by the passengers. I only hoped none of them held an unghostly knife. The tension level rose until at last it sank as the train appeared again with Boadicea in fine form, laughing in genuine pleasure. I noticed Peter wasn't laughing, however, as he grimly held on to Boadicea's arm after they'd disembarked from the train.

Jason came over to me. 'See, Jack? Nothing to worry about,' he said, with a touch of mockery.

Wrong. There was plenty to worry about, and the funfair had only just begun.

Jessica had told me there would be a longish break for a lunch to which she was invited. I was not, which was frustrating, even though I had no formal responsibility for Boadicea. It was hard to see how anyone could attack Boadicea at the lunch table, but nevertheless it was possible. Did she have a poison taster . . .? There was nothing I could do, so feeling like a spare wheel, I went to the outside café to get something to eat. Jenny Ansty was there, which was welcome.

'Ah. Just like me, excluded from the Top Table, I see,' she

greeted me cheerfully as I walked by her table with my tray of food. 'Come and join me.'

'I take it you're here to spare Anna's feelings? That's if she knows who you are,' I said, glad to accept the offer.

'I've never met her, but Arthur deemed it politic to omit me, successor trustee or not. She's OK, a bit strange, but it should improve, the hospital says. I told Arthur my absence was fine with me. And before you ask, the merry widow's doing well.'

'Found your merry man yet?'

'I have my eyes on one. Depends on how merry he is.'

'I hope it works.'

'So does Jason. He's tired of having an over-merry mum. Wants me to settle down and bake cakes for him. I told him to get married again. He told me to get lost, only he didn't use those words. I then pointed out that he owed me because of the Porsche. Talking of which, Jack, are the police going to charge us with wasting their time?'

'Not if you're lucky.'

'And what about Anna?'

I'd asked Dave what he intended to do about Boadicea and the Porsche, though I couldn't tell Jenny that. 'Nothing,' Dave had told me, 'much as I'd like to. No point wasting more police time as the car's back safely. When she's well we'll have a chat with her. The sort of chat I have when I'm not feeling happy.'

'I pity her,' I had said feelingly.

Boadicea, on her reappearance from lunch, gave every sign of enjoying her day of glory, and being back on self-imposed duty I followed her route. Her first port of call was the Punch and Judy show. She and most of the lunch party sat down to watch, and she stared at it entranced, clapping her hands in glee and shouting out at the appropriate moments. I couldn't share her delight. To me the gleam in Punch's eye as he lashed out at Judy had the same maniacal gleam in his eye as the Laughing Sailor. The rest of the party, however – Glenn, Fenella, Peter, Jason and Jessica – seemed as glued to the show as Boadicea, as though it were the height of theatrical experience. Perhaps it is, encapsulating murder, punishment, family life, marital relations and a few other aspects of life, yet we all cheered at the end because they were unreal puppets and Punch got his comeuppance.

I'd seen no sign of Doubler thankfully, but any relaxation I felt was promptly squashed when I realized his men could be around. Which brought the unwelcome question of where Jason's guards were, and – sudden fear – were they covering the ladies' toilets?

'Yes,' Jason reassured me when I tracked him down. 'Only just thought of it, Jack? And you a detective.'

'Car detective,' I reminded him. 'Car washes don't need guards.'

Whoosh was going to wind up with a grand parade round the track which included Jason's performance, and as the afternoon wore on, it became an increasingly peaceful day. A Teddy Bears' Picnic was laid out on the grass at four o'clock, at Boadicea's request. Cucumber sandwiches, jelly, trifles, scones and cream, and urns of tea and orange squash made their appearance, plus wine for the sturdier older folk, overseen by a small army of both stuffed and human teddy bears. Boadicea was sitting in one of a small group of chairs, appropriately looking as pleased as Punch, with her nearest (and I hoped dearest) grouped around her, and overlooked by the beady eyes of several guards. The rest of us sat on cushions on the grass. Nothing happened to disturb this peaceful scene, but the contrast between this and what still might lie ahead was something that still lodged uneasily in my mind. I pushed it away, telling myself this was time off. Until Boadicea suddenly rose to her feet.

'I want a bunfight,' she shouted. 'Let's all throw custard pies.'

A stunned silence followed, until Jessica gave a resigned nod. Luckily, she quickly improvised a plan that those who wished exemption from this treat should wave a white paper napkin. Even so the bunfight was not a huge success, as very few people joined in. Fenella was not one of them, but a blob of trifle arrived on the beautifully made-up face, courtesy I think of Jessica. I looked round hopefully for Colin as a target but there was no sign of him and Jason too had disappeared, so I took it that the Harlequinade was in preparation.

I felt myself relaxing but struggled to fight against it. The fat lady hadn't yet sung, I reminded myself. A row of seats had been set at the side of the track for Boadicea to watch the parade, and she sat down between Glenn and Arthur, with Peter, Fenella and Ray on the far side. Arthur was looking tired now and no wonder.

Then the parade began – and what a parade. Clowns doing somersaults, furry animals (with humans inside), and various assortments of witches, fairies, and wizards. The procession seemed endless, and the strain of constantly watching for a threat that never materialized began to get to me.

When at last I thought it was coming to an end, I remembered there was still Jason's performance to go. The stage had been set in the centre of the track opposite the line of chairs, and it was there that Jason as Harlequin and Liz as Columbine enacted a brief mime of stolen sausages and then danced, together with Colin the Clown. Only, in Colin's case it wasn't much of a dance, it was more of a lumber, whether intentionally or not. It served to contrast with Jason's elegant dance with Columbine (doing her best). It finished with Harlequin throwing a bouquet to Boadicea, which she rose to catch with a squeal of delight. A fairy tale ending for her fairy tale day. Now, surely, I could relax.

And then came the dark.

I don't know what alerted me – a cry or an instinct that something was wrong, a lack of action perhaps . . . Glancing over as the audience was dispersing I could see Glenn was still in his seat, slumped – and surely not sleeping? Terror gripped me as I pushed past the people in my path as I hurtled towards him. He'd been next to Boadicea. Had the knife or bullet been meant for her? As I reached him, I saw there was no knife, no blood – and no movement.

'Fainted,' one of the guards said uncertainly.

No ordinary sleep, this; there was no response. 'Get the first-aiders over here,' I yelled. 'I'll ring for an ambulance.'

The St John Ambulance first-aiders, a stalwart presence at such events as this, were there in a flash. My initial role was over while we waited for the ambulance and the police. Fenella and Arthur were at Glenn's side, but Arthur looked so shaken that, having reassured myself that Glenn was alive, I took him to sit down some yards away, just as Jason, now changed from his Harlequin outfit, came rushing up to us. I left Arthur to him while I remained with Glenn and Fenella.

With a lurch of my stomach I realized I had paid scant attention to Boadicea. What if Glenn were the diversion and Boadicea was the main target? Thankfully, I spotted her with Peter and

Ray. She didn't seem to have noticed that anything was wrong, even when the ambulance arrived.

'I'll go—' Arthur began.

'Stay there,' Jason ordered him. 'Fenella can go with him.'

Arthur sank back, and after the ambulance had left I found myself alone with him. Jessica was taking charge of the disrupted Whoosh, Peter was looking after Ray and Jason had taken Boadicea to the clubhouse.

Arthur began to speak, disjointedly and with difficulty. 'Glenn was mad at Mike,' he said. 'He could have done that murder, Jack. Did he?'

I decided on truth. 'There's some evidence but not more than there is for other possible suspects.' I paused. 'Is that why you asked me to step in? Because you were afraid Glenn was guilty?'

'I reckon so. Is this a suicide attempt?'

'No,' I said gently. 'I don't think Glenn would ever try to kill himself. And even if he wanted to, why here where it would distress you even more? It doesn't add up.'

Arthur took no notice. 'But if it was he who killed Mike and attacked Anna—'

'We don't know that, Arthur – and this wasn't a suicide attempt.'

He still took no notice. 'He could have been afraid of what I might give Mike, or that I might put every dollar I had into Old Herne's. I wouldn't do that, Jack, and Mike wouldn't have let me. He told us all at that lunch that if the Porsche wasn't found, he'd have the insurance money to put into the place.'

'So Glenn wouldn't have wanted to rush out and kill Mike,' I said firmly. Glenn, if driven into a corner, could murder someone, I thought, but not in the way Mike had been killed. Glenn was too fond of his own skin. I came round to the obvious. It was much more likely that whatever drug it was had been put into the wrong teacup. Glenn had been sitting next to Boadicea at the picnic as well as at the track.

Obvious? I did a double take. What *was* obvious was that I'd been a blithering idiot. Of course it hadn't been the wrong teacup! It was the intended one.

Boadicea had been as pleased as Punch at the afternoon's events. Punch, who had battered his wife – just as surely as she

had swung the axe at Mike, climbed into the Crossley and run
him down. Just as surely as she had probably dropped her strong
sleeping pills into Glenn's tea to further her own imagined claim
to run Old Herne's.

'I'll be back,' I told Arthur as, groggy with shock, I forced
myself into action.

Brandon – find Brandon. Where the hell was he? In the clubhouse? I tried his mobile. Voicemail. I'd not seen him since the
ambulance had left. But then I caught sight of Dave. Wonderful
Dave, who listened and acted.

'Get going, Jack,' he said. 'I'll find Brandon. Trust me.'

I did.

I found Jason and Boadicea sitting peacefully in the window
seat of the bar with Hedda temporarily back in her old job. I told
Hedda to go to the track to look after Arthur and then went over
to the window seat to join them. Jason was silent and Boadicea
was happily chatting about the events of the day. Then, when
she saw me, she broke off from her rhapsody about cuddly
animals. 'What are you doing here?' she snapped.

'I've been enjoying the Punch and Judy show,' I said in as
normal a voice as I could manage, and sat down in an armchair
that would block her exit if need be.

Jason must have caught the tone of my voice because he looked
up sharply.

'I'll be staying some time, Jason,' I continued.

His eyes went to Boadicea and then back to me. 'Is anyone
joining us?'

'Several people,' I told him.

He nodded. 'I'll stay too.'

Boadicea didn't seem to notice anything strange as she chatted
on about ghosts and animals. Even when Brandon arrived with
two female constables she didn't query their presence. Even when
they asked her to come with them for questioning and led her
to the waiting car.

Neither Jason nor I went with her, and afterwards I let out a
long sigh of relief. 'Did you realize she killed your father, Jason?'
I asked, when he still said nothing.

I had discounted Boadicea because I had reasoned she had
nothing to gain from murdering Mike, but she had. Oh yes. She

was, as Jason had said, not a clever woman. She'd planned the theft of the car and its destruction, banking on the fact that she and Mike would have the insurance money. But then on the eve of Swoosh Mike had announced that he would put that into Old Herne's. That, combined with the lunch at which Arthur had said Mike would go on running the club, clinched it.

So how did the attack on her fit in? I'd probably been right about the blackmail, but not about the reason for it. Shaw knew she was responsible for the theft of the Porsche, but if he'd also known or made a lucky guess over her guilt for Mike's death then how much more she would have had at stake? But she couldn't pay, and she knew who Shaw was. Which meant that his private enterprise could get back to Doubler. And Doubler didn't like being double-crossed . . .

'I suspected she'd killed my father,' Jason answered me at last. 'Eventually, Arthur did too, but like me he couldn't quite believe it. He was still afraid Glenn was guilty. Whoosh was a way of bringing it to a head.'

'A risky one,' I said.

'We had to play with the cards in our hand. I hoped and hoped it wasn't true because of Ray. He was the grandfather I grew up with, and although they fought like cats and dogs, he and Anna managed to get on in a weird way.'

'And now?' I asked.

'Arthur and I will look after him. And, I suppose, after Anna too. She's quite mad, you know.'

I was worried about the effects on Arthur, but Jason assured me he could cope. Boadicea was duly charged, and for once Brandon talked to me for quite a while about the case.

'I doubt if she's even fit to plead,' he said. 'Couldn't wait to tell me about her wonderful day with the animals. It took some time to get her on to whether she killed her husband. No problem then. She was amazed that we seemed shocked. Of course he had to go. First he wouldn't sell the car, which is why she had to arrange its theft. Second, he wouldn't listen to her advice on how to run the place properly. Didn't he realize they would be penniless? And then Arthur Howell had the cheek to say Mike could stay on, and after pouring his salary into the old place

Mike said he'd use the insurance money too. She'd seen the accounts; they'd be out on their ear in a few months or a few more after that if the insurance money went in. So she'd asked Mike to talk it over with Arthur Howell in the hope of his giving them more capital, but Mike wouldn't do it. Said he'd rather put all his salary in or take a cut, so he had to be stopped immediately.

'She went to talk it out with Mike one more time in the hangar, but Mike wasn't interested. Said the Crossley was playing up and he had to get it to the track, so could she start it while he opened the bonnet to check the engine. She saw the axe and the greatcoat in the Crossley when she climbed up and realized what she had to do. Put on the coat to take the blood, swung the axe as he closed the bonnet, then got back in to make doubly sure of the job. Then she shoved the coat in that storage cupboard and hurried back to High House to change clothes and shoes. Came back, went to the track to join Arthur. Just like that.'

'And Glenn?' I asked, sickened.

'She said she knew he had to go because that would mean Arthur having to put Old Herne's back into the hands of the Nelsons, preferably her. Sleeping pills, just like all the best detective stories. Glenn Howell has pulled, through by the way.'

That was good news. 'And how does she explain the attack on her?'

'She doesn't – though she admits there was someone trying to extort money from her. We're still after your chum Doubler. Dave says you might have some more ideas on tracking him down.'

'I haven't a clue now the Huptons line is closed. I gather the price is on his head for Shaw's murder?'

'There is. And other matters.'

I didn't expect to see Doubler again, though, and I didn't. About a week later, however, I had a phone call. When I picked up, no one spoke. There was only a whistled tune which I recognized all too well. It was 'John Brown's body'.

'You can't go on for ever, Doubler,' I said.

The tune promptly changed. This time I couldn't put a name to it. It was only when the caller rang off that it clicked with me. It was a First World War troop song:

The bells of hell go ting a ling a ling
For you but not for me.

Which left me with Arthur and the Old Herne's situation to consider. The latter was currently under Jason's control with Jessica's help, and Arthur asked me to go there to meet him – ostensibly to take the Morgan for a spin.

Not surprisingly I ran straight into Jessica before I even reached the garage. By unspoken assent we had not spoken since Whoosh. She looked neither pleased nor sorry to see me, merely busy. I think we were both surprised that it had been so long since we met. Two weeks. As the song says, smoke gets in your eyes. Mine had cleared now, and it seemed hers also.

'Lunch?' I suggested, for want of anything more romantic to say.

'Take a rain check?' she asked.

'Of course.'

She hesitated. 'I'm leaving Old Herne's, Jack.'

I said the right thing. 'That's bad news – except, I hope, for you.'

'You're right. It's good for me.'

'Who will run Old Herne's?'

'Arthur had a plan.'

'You've got another job?'

'Yes, one that's right up my street. Big hotel in West London. Jack,' she said, softening, 'it was great while it lasted.'

'It was,' I said gratefully. 'Have you something to save at the new job?'

'Could be. Maybe it's myself. You know, it wasn't really Old Herne's I was interested in saving. It was you, Jack.'

I froze. 'Me?'

'I couldn't break through. You're still lost somewhere.'

I watched her go, stunned. Some enchanted evening, I thought, one can easily make a mistake. Ah well. Everyone does once in a while. But lost somewhere? That was a conundrum. I pushed it aside in favour of the immediate, remembering with gratitude that it was time to meet Arthur and the Morgan.

Tim proudly drove up in the Morgan just as Arthur and I reached the track. 'Here she is, Arthur, good as the day she was born,' he announced.

'You too, Tim.' Arthur gave him a bear hug, and I could see tears in Curator Tim's eyes.

I took the wheel, and Arthur and I had our spin in the Morgan. The day was sunny, the canvas top was down, the breeze blew and the Morgan's familiar growl echoed in our ears. Arthur was silent, but I could imagine the conversation in his head. For him it was not Jack Colby at the wheel, it was himself, with Miranda Pryde beside him. Perhaps to him this was the 'thirties Morgan, the year was 1944, they were laughing and enjoying the taste of first love when all looked bright for their future. Or was it this very same Morgan, in 1965, when she told him of Mike? The Morgan, Miranda and Mike – all three went together.

Then Arthur did speak. 'Time for a quick talk, Jack?'

I didn't want to spoil this idyllic drive for him. 'Tea in the clubhouse first?'

'After,' he said firmly. 'It's grand out here in the fresh air.'

So we stopped at the far end of the track from where we could see the whole of Old Herne's spread out before us.

'You, me and Miranda,' he said. 'What would she have made of this nightmare, Jack?'

'She'd have been right with you, Arthur.'

'I reckon she has been. It was a shock about Anna, but I can tell you I'm mighty glad it wasn't Glenn. He needs roots and wanted them so bad. He'd set his heart on being here in England. I'd had Miranda, but Glenn's mother is no longer with us and he's divorced from his wife. I knew he was mad at Mike being left in charge of Old Herne's but I thought I could cope with that. Then I feared I was wrong.'

'He's recovering well, I heard.'

'Sure, he's as chipper as the day is long. Had some help though. From a lady.'

'Fenella?'

'No. My granddaughter is as mad as hell at my new plan. Glenn's real happy though. He's met a lady he fancies. She was at the hospital day after day and now the house.'

'Who is she?'

'We both know her, Jack. Lily Ansty.'

I laughed at the pleasant surprise. 'She told me she'd met a merry man. That's good. It may bring Jason and Glenn closer too.' I hesitated. It was time for the big question for us car lovers. 'And how about the future of Old Herne's? You're not closing it down, are you?'

'There really would be a threat to my life if I did that. Tim would be on the warpath. But I guess you've noticed he's got one big smile on his face.'

'So is it Glenn in charge or Fenella? Is that why Jessica's leaving?'

'That young lady sure is impatient. She's driven by an over-heated engine, Jack. No, not her, not Fenella and not Glenn. Lily and I are sorting something out for him. But Old Herne's is going to be in good hands, Jack.'

'Jason's?'

'As trustee, but he's not managing the place.'

'Who is then?'

'Hedda.'

I felt as though I'd been kicked off my feet. 'Hedda? But she's far too young.'

'That's what it needs, Jack. Youth. And she's got help. From Peter.'

I was poleaxed for a second time. 'Peter as number two? She won't stand a chance.'

'Won't she? I know Hedda, Jack. She'll be the making of Peter Nelson.'

'Does *he* realize that though?'

'I reckon he does. This business over Anna has shaken him up. He thought management was just politics. Now he sees it's more than that. It's a matter of caring. Caring for cars, caring for people.'

'Are you sure he's capable of doing the job?'

'He's sure about Hedda. Wait till it's your turn.'

I tried to laugh it off. 'Getting late for that. Tried it once and didn't like it.'

'Never too late,' Arthur said. 'I'm ninety, Jack. Miranda and I are still an item, and Mike's around somewhere. And I can tell you they're both whooping for joy about Old Herne's.'

The Pits was still open when I returned to Frogs Hill. I went in, ostensibly to give Len and Zoe a report on how the Morgan was running after its retune. I told them just fine, but I was aware that wasn't the real reason I'd come. I needed company. I needed to chat to them, to tell them that everything was fine at Old Herne's. That it was all settling down, that Tim was happy and therefore, it followed, that Old Herne's would be happy.

They made suitable noises of pleasure. Then Zoe said: 'And are you happy, Jack?'

'It's a great solution,' I parried.

'You, not Old Herne's.'

My weariness returned. Jessica had gone, but I didn't mind about that. I was back at Frogs Hill and that was all that mattered.

Or was it?

Zoe was looking at me uncertainly as though she wanted to say something more and didn't dare. Len was devoting as much care to cleaning the wheel of his Vauxhall, as if he were deliberately avoiding looking at me.

OK. I got the message. I'd get out of their hair and go and cook myself some supper. Have a beer perhaps. Even go to the pub. I walked out of the Pits as though I had a plan for life in mind. Which I didn't.

As I approached the farmhouse door, I saw a piece of paper lying on the step with a stone lying over it to weight it down. Doubler? Surely not. Who then? Without much interest, I picked it up and read it.

Twice.

Three times.

It read: 'Just passing, Jack.' It was signed: 'Louise, with love.'

Somewhere beyond the clouds a rainbow shone.

The Car's the Star
James Myers

Jack Colby's daily driver: Alfa Romeo 156 Sportwagon

The 156 Sportwagon is a 'lifestyle estate', which means that it's trendy, respectable to have on the drive, although it lacks the interior space of a traditional load-lugger. For those who value individuality, its subtle and pure styling gives it the edge over rivals such as the BMW 3-Series. It gives a lot of driving pleasure even with the smaller engines.

Jack Colby's 1965 Gordon-Keeble

One hundred of these fabulous supercars were built between 1963 and 1966 with over ninety units surviving around the globe, mostly in the UK. Designed by John Gordon and Jim Keeble using current racing car principles, with the bodyshell designed by twenty-one-year-old Giorgetto Giugiaro at Bertone, the cars were an instant success but the company was ruined by supply-side industrial action with ultimately only ninety-nine units completed even after the company was relaunched in May 1965, as Keeble Cars Ltd. Final closure came in February 1966 when the factory at Sholing closed and Jim Keeble moved to Keewest. The hundredth car was completed in 1971 with leftover components. The Gordon-Keeble's emblem is a yellow and green tortoise.

Jack Colby's 1938 Lagonda V-12 Drophead

The Lagonda company won its attractive name from a creek near the home of the American-born founder Wilbur Gunn in Springfield, Ohio. The name given to it by the American Indians was Ough Ohonda. The V-12 drophead was a car to compete with the very best in the world, with a sporting twelve-cylinder engine which would power the two 1939 Le Mans cars. Its designer was the famous W.O. Bentley. Sadly many fine pre-war saloons have been cut down to look like Le Mans replicas. The

V12 cars are very similar externally to the earlier six-cylinder versions; both types were available with open or closed bodywork in a number of different styles. The V-12 Drophead starred in Jack's earlier case, *Classic in the Barn.*

1965 Porsche 356 Carrera 2

The ultimate engine option for the Porsche 356 in the fifties and sixties was the Carrera engine, designed by Dr Ernst Fuhrmann. This remarkable engine featured four overhead cams, dual ignition and a complicated series of internal gears. Its prodigious power output ensured numerous race victories, but it was a complex engine to repair and keep tuned – not for the faint hearted!

Porsche offered the Carrera engine option for 356s for around ten years. The four-cam 1966cc Carrera 2 version produced 130-horsepower at 6200 rpm, and was red-lined at 7,000 rpm – powerful enough to propel the aerodynamic car to 130 mph.

1965 Morgan 4/4

For over a hundred years, the Morgan Motor Company has been noted for its traditional British sports and racing cars. Its famous three-wheeler was launched in 1910 and, including a short revival after the Second World War, was produced until 1950. In 1935 the four-wheeler, the 4/4, was introduced, and the Plus 4 added to the range in 1950. In 1968 the Plus 8 with the Rover V8 engine appeared and successfully continued until 2004 when it was replaced with the Roadster V6.

In 1920 the company had launched the Aero model, so-called in honour of the First World War flying ace Albert Ball, and the name has been revived in the twenty-first century with the Aero launched in 2000. Since then the Aero has been constantly updated by this remarkable company.

1940 Crossley FWD Airfield Fire Tender

The Crossley FWD (Four Wheel Drive) truck and tractor were manufactured from 1940 to 1945. The main customer was the RAF. The chassis was designed to meet the War Office's specifications for a five-ton payload truck. The tractor units were frequently used to tow the large 'Queen Mary' trailers.